JOHN FEINSTEIN

VANISHING
ACT

[SPORTS]
J
FIC
FEINSTEIN

ALFRED A. KNOPF

New York

Library of Congress Cataloging-in-Publication Data
Feinstein, John.
Vanishing act : mystery at the U.S. Open / John Feinstein. — 1st ed.
p. cm.
SUMMARY: Eighth-grade sports reporters Susan Carol and Stevie reunite at the U.S. Open tennis championships where they investigate the mysterious disappearance of a top Russian player.
ISBN-13: 978-0-375-83592-6 (trade) — ISBN-13: 978-0-375-93592-3 (lib. bdg.)
ISBN-10: 0-375-83592-X (trade) — ISBN-10: 0-375-93592-4 (lib. bdg.)
[1. Journalists—Fiction. 2. U.S. Open Championships, New York, N.Y.—Fiction.
3. Kidnapping—Fiction. 4. Tennis—Fiction. 5. Sports agents—Fiction. 6. Mystery and detective stories.] I. Title.
PZ7.F3343Van 2006
[Fic]—dc22   2005035823

Printed in the United States of America
August 2006
10 9 8 7 6 5 4 3 2 1
First Edition

This book is dedicated to the memory of my parents,
Martin and Bernice Feinstein,
who taught me that nothing matters more
than family—especially your kids . . .

ACKNOWLEDGMENTS

Once again I am grateful to the people who helped make this book possible: Nancy Siscoe, my ever-patient and understanding editor at Knopf, and Esther Newberg, my completely impatient agent, and her remarkable assistants, Chris Earle and Kari Stuart. Thanks also to Shanta Small in the publicity department at Knopf and everyone there who has helped along the way with this new endeavor.

Thanks also to my real-life friends who appear in the book, notably Bud Collins, Mary Carillo, and Tom Ross, who have all taught me so much about tennis through the years. I am also extremely indebted to all my friends and family who have been so supportive in this last year and these past few months. My wife, Mary, is blessed with one of my mother's best qualities: the ability to find the good that exists in all of us—enabling her to somehow find good in me through eighteen years of marriage. My kids, Danny and Brigid, challenge and inspire me every day. There is a good deal of each of them in Stevie and Susan Carol.

1: IM FROM SCDEVIL

STEVIE THOMAS knew he needed a shower but, as usual, he couldn't resist sitting down at his desk to see if any of his friends had e-mailed while he had been out playing golf with his dad. It was a hot, humid August day, and walking eighteen holes had worn him out.

"You aren't even fourteen yet," his dad had said as Stevie slowly climbed the last hill on the eighteenth hole at Bluebell Country Club. "You aren't supposed to get tired."

Stevie would be fourteen in September. But he *was* tired. He had played pretty well—breaking 90 always made him happy—but a hot shower and a nap before dinner was all he wanted right now.

First, though, he would check his e-mails. He signed on to his computer—his sign-on was "kidwriter"—and had begun trolling through the spam and notes from friends when he heard a ringing sound that told him he had an Instant Message coming in. When he saw who it was from, he smiled.

"Wht R U up to?" was the opening question from "SCDEVIL."

"Just played golf w/my dad," he answered. "2 hot."

The response came back almost before he had sent his reply. "It is a balmy 99 here—heat index much worse than that."

Stevie could imagine what it was like in Goldsboro, North Carolina, given how hot it was in Philadelphia. "Wht R U doing?" he asked.

Susan Carol Anderson—aka SCDEVIL, because she was a fanatic fan of Duke, a basketball team Stevie had only recently learned not to hate—was a month younger than Stevie but, at least the last time he had seen her in April, a good four inches taller and much older-looking too. Still, not long after they had met in New Orleans during the Final Four, Stevie had conceded to himself that he had a crush on her. He told no one, not even his dad, in part because she was too tall for him, in part because he wasn't going to admit a crush on *anyone* at this point in his life.

Stevie and Susan Carol had been the winners of a writing contest that had earned them each a trip to the Final Four, complete with press credentials. It was the most unbelievable thing that'd ever happened to Stevie. Literally. Soon after arriving, they had stumbled across a plot to blackmail Chip Graber, Minnesota State's star point guard, to throw the national championship game. They had managed to foil the plot, allowing Graber to dramatically hit the winning shot in the championship game against Susan Carol's beloved Duke Blue Devils. Even she had admitted to being happy with that outcome.

Stevie and Susan Carol had gotten a lot of media attention for their involvement—what his father called their "fifteen minutes of fame." They even got to go on Letterman together. That was the last time he had seen her, but they IM'd all the time.

Now she was typing a long answer to his question about what she was doing, and Stevie could almost see her smiling at him through the computer screen.

"Really exciting news," she said. "I convinced the spts. ed. at the Fayetteville paper to credential me to go to U.S. Open tennis next week. School doesn't start until week after. Dad and Mom said I can stay w/my uncle in Manhattan!"

Stevie stared at the screen, instantly envious of the Instant Message. He knew Susan Carol loved tennis almost as much as she loved basketball. He was more into golf than tennis, but he did follow it, even though his father insisted the game hadn't been the same since the retirements of John McEnroe and Jimmy Connors. He was too young to remember either of them as players, but he thought McEnroe was good on television. His favorite tennis player, by far, was Nadia Symanova. He had a poster of her hanging over his bed to prove it. She was another in the recent line of gorgeous Russian players—following in the footsteps of

Anna Kournikova and Maria Sharapova, among others—who had shot up the world rankings. She was sixteen and had been the talk of Wimbledon after getting to the semifinals, only to lose in three sets to Venus Williams.

Stevie did *not* have a crush on Symanova. That would have implied that he knew her or might somehow have a chance someday to even meet her. What's more, if Susan Carol was too tall for him at five foot eight, then what was Symanova, who was six feet tall? Besides, every time Stevie picked up a magazine he saw Symanova walking into or out of a party with some movie star or famous young athlete. Now Susan Carol was going to get to go to New York and see Symanova and the rest of the U.S. Open from up close.

"Great news," he finally typed. He thought for a second and then added, "I'm jealous."

Susan Carol's answer came flying back. "U shud go 2."

He was baffled by that one. "How?" he answered.

"EZ. Write to Kelleher. I still have his e-mail if U don't. Ask him to help U get a credential. U can help him or something. He knows everyone."

It wasn't a bad idea. Bobby Kelleher was a columnist for the *Washington Herald* who had helped Stevie and Susan Carol immensely in New Orleans. The chances were good he would be covering the Open. "Worth a shot," he wrote back. "What's his e-mail?"

She sent it to him: "UVA0.9@aol.com." He actually knew what that meant because Kelleher had told him that when he played basketball at the University of Virginia, his career scoring average had been 0.9 points per game. "I'll let U know," he said.

"Tell your parents U can stay with me at my uncle's apartment," she wrote back. "He's divorced so he has lots of room."

Another good idea. His parents certainly wouldn't let him go to New York for a week and stay in a hotel alone. And he knew neither of his parents could take a week off from work since they had just gotten back from vacationing at the beach. Staying in Susan Carol's uncle's apartment had one other benefit: he would get to spend more time with her.

He just hoped she hadn't gotten any taller.

✗ ✗ ✗

Stevie sent the e-mail to Kelleher, asking him to write him back whenever he got a chance. The Open started in five days. He was afraid he might be asking too late. A couple of hours later he was sitting on the family room couch watching his favorite TV show, *Daily News Live*. The show aired on weekdays and featured Michael Barkann and three sportswriters—different ones each day—from the *Philadelphia Daily News*. Stevie liked the show for two reasons: First, the *Daily News* guys always had opinions and were very willing to share them, even to the point of occasionally shouting at guests while asking them questions. Second, he knew several of the show's regulars: Dick Jerardi had been the first reporter to help him out when he began trying to go to local sporting events and learn about journalism. Through Jerardi he had met writers he had read locally for years, including the deans of Philadelphia sports journalism: Bill Conlin and Stan Hochman of the *Daily News* and Bill Lyon of the *Philadelphia Inquirer*. Jerardi had even invited him to sit on the set during the show once and introduced him to Barkann.

Conlin and Jerardi were having a heated debate about whether or not baseball players who used steroids should be in the Hall of Fame when Stevie's mom walked into the living room carrying the phone. He had been so caught up in the show he hadn't heard it ring. "It's Bobby Kelleher," she said.

Surprised, Stevie took the phone. "Let me guess," Kelleher said without saying hello. "Susan Carol figured out a way to get to the Open and you want to come too."

Stevie felt his face flush. "How'd you know that?" he said.

"I remember how my mind worked when I was a teenager," Kelleher said.

"Actually, it was her idea that I contact you," Stevie said. "I didn't know you had my phone number."

"You gave it to me in New Orleans, remember? Anyway, she's a smart girl, because not only can I get you in, but I'd be happy to have you come up and give me some help the first week."

"Wow!" Stevie said, forgetting for an instant that he was trying very hard to remove that word from his vocabulary. "You're sure you can do that?"

"Easily," Kelleher said. "The guy who runs public relations

for the USTA is an old friend—Ed Fabricius. In fact, he's a Philly guy—worked at Penn for years. I'll bet he knows just who you are. It won't be a problem at all. My guess is Fab's only condition will be that he gets to meet you guys."

Stevie had been amazed after the Letterman appearance how often people recognized him. He had become an instant celebrity in school. Even Andrea Fassler, the eighth-grade girl every eighth-grade boy wanted to go out with, had started being friendly to him. But a lot of that had faded with time, and he heard himself laughing at the notion that the USTA's public relations honcho would want to meet him. "Well, if you really can get me in . . . ," he said.

"Consider it done," Kelleher said. "I'll send you an e-mail with my cell phone number and all the details, since my guess is you're watching *Daily News Live* right now and you don't have a pen."

"How'd you know that?"

"Because whenever I'm in Philly I watch it too. I'll see you Monday."

Stevie's mom walked back in, a quizzical look on her face. "Why was Bobby Kelleher calling you?" she asked.

Stevie hadn't said anything about the possibility of going to New York—he figured there wasn't any point until he heard back from Kelleher. Now he told his mother what was going on.

"Did you discuss this with your father?" she asked.

"No," he said. "It happened after we played golf and he'd already gone back to the office."

She sighed. "Well, I'm sure he'll say yes, because he loves

the idea of you becoming a sportswriter and this would be an adventure," she said. "I think he'll want to check with Susan Carol's dad to make sure it really is okay for you to stay with her uncle. I think a grown-up should invite you, not Susan Carol."

Stevie rolled his eyes a little but he knew he was in good shape if the only thing standing between him and the trip to New York was a call from his dad to Susan Carol's dad. He had been to New York before but it had mostly been to do sightseeing: Statue of Liberty, Empire State Building, several of the museums, and, just a few months before 9/11, the family had eaten dinner at Windows on the World atop the World Trade Center. He still shuddered a little when he thought about that.

But he'd never gotten to see any sports in New York. The timing was always wrong. His mom had always taken the position that since he went to sports events all the time in Philadelphia, he should do more "cultural" things while they were in New York. He didn't mind all culture: *The Lion King* had actually been kind of cool. But he could certainly have lived without the museums.

Now he would be going to New York and there would be no culture to deal with. Just covering tennis while hanging out with Susan Carol. Maybe, he thought, he'd get to meet Nadia Symanova. Now, *that* would be cultural.

2: NEW YORK, NEW YORK

STEVIE FELT both very adult and a little bit nervous when his mom dropped him off at 30th Street Station for the train ride to New York. It was one thing to have the independence to ride his bike pretty much wherever he wanted in the neighborhood; it was another to board a train that would drop him off smack in the middle of Manhattan. Once he was on the train, though, he began to feel a lot more confident. It was a beautiful Sunday afternoon and the heat and August humidity seemed to have disappeared just in time for the U.S. Open. The train wasn't very crowded, so he had an empty seat next to him, where he piled up the Sunday editions of the *Philadelphia Inquirer* and the *New York Times* as he read through them. He had felt quite cool buying the

Times—even if it did cost four dollars—in the lobby of the train station.

The trip took a little more than an hour. Penn Station was a lot more crowded and, it seemed to Stevie, quite a bit dirtier than 30th Street Station. He followed his father's instructions to look for signs for the Eighth Avenue exit. "There will be fewer people lined up for cabs there," he had said. "And the cabs are pointed uptown, which is where you're going."

He got a cab in no time and told the driver he needed to go to 52 Riverside Drive, adding, "It's between Seventy-seventh and Seventy-eighth streets," as he had been told to do by Susan Carol. If the driver either needed or did not need that piece of information, Stevie couldn't tell. He simply turned on the meter and began rocketing up Eighth Avenue, dodging between cars as if he was on a NASCAR track. In less than fifteen minutes, the cab pulled up in front of an elegant-looking older building. To his left, Stevie could see a small park. As he climbed out of the cab, he saw Susan Carol Anderson and a tall man who looked to be about his father's age standing on the sidewalk waiting for him. Stevie's dad had finally broken down and gotten him a cell phone for this trip, figuring it wasn't a bad idea to have one while traveling. He had called Susan Carol from the train station to say he was en route.

"Stevie, you got *tall*!" Susan Carol said as soon as he took his suitcase from the cabbie and turned to greet his two hosts. She ran up and threw her arms around him in a hug.

She had her long brown hair tied back in a ponytail and was wearing what Stevie had come to think of as the teenage girl's summer uniform: a pullover shirt, white shorts, and flip-flops. The difference was that she looked a lot better in the uniform than most of the girls back home. In spite of her claim about Stevie's newfound height, she was still at least two or maybe even three inches taller than Stevie. Still, he was pleased that she'd noticed he was at least closing the gap. When they untangled from their brief embrace, she turned to the man with her.

"Uncle Brendan, this is Stevie Thomas," she said. "Stevie, this is my uncle, Brendan Gibson."

Brendan Gibson had the same sort of easy smile that Susan Carol did. "I know all about Stevie Thomas," he said, pumping his hand. "It is a pleasure to finally meet you. Come on in."

Stevie wondered what Susan Carol had told her uncle about him but didn't think this was the time to ask. Susan Carol was giving him the big smile he had seen disarm so many people in New Orleans—oh yeah, he still had a crush on her. Brendan Gibson turned around and punched buttons on the keypad next to the door and it buzzed to let them in. A few minutes later, they were on the fourteenth floor and Susan Carol was showing Stevie to a bedroom that had a view up and down the Hudson River.

"Pretty spectacular," Stevie said as a Circle Line boat went past. He remembered taking a ride around Manhattan on one of them with his parents when he was ten.

"I know," Susan Carol said. "I was here once before, but I was little—I think I was eight. I had forgotten how nice it is around here."

Stevie started to laugh. Since they communicated exclusively by e-mail, he hadn't actually heard her voice for months and he had almost forgotten just how Southern she could sound.

"What's so funny?" she asked.

"Nothing."

"Steven Thomas, don't start with me."

He laughed again. "Jeez, Scarlett, you're starting to talk like my mother. I'd just forgotten about your accent."

"My"—she actually said "ma"—"accent? What about *your* accent?"

"I have no accent."

"Of course not. Northern is the way normal people talk, right? Everyone else has an accent."

He rolled his eyes. She hadn't changed even a little bit since New Orleans. She was still very tall, very pretty, very Southern, and very smart. Too smart.

She gave him a playful shove. "Let's go find out about dinner. We have a whole week to fight."

She was right about that. Verbal sparring with her wasn't easy. But he had to admit it was fun.

✗   ✗   ✗

Dinner turned out to be pizza. Stevie, Susan Carol, and Mr. Gibson—who had ordered Stevie to call him Brendan—walked two blocks to Broadway to an old-fashioned pizza joint. They sat at a table and Brendan, who was the younger brother of Susan Carol's mom, told Stevie a little bit about himself. It turned out that some of Susan Carol's love of sports came from her uncle. He grew up in North Carolina but somehow became fascinated by hockey at an early age. "We had to get up at five in the morning because there were only two rinks in Greensboro and that was the only ice-time we could get," he said. "But I loved it and stuck with it."

Hockey and good grades got him into Harvard. He also went to law school at Harvard and worked for a big New York firm until three years earlier. "Then I got bored and decided it was time to try something new," he said.

His new thing was, as he called it, "player representation," which Stevie knew meant he was now an agent. He had used his old hockey contacts to get the business started, and he was now the CEO of a small company called ISM. The company represented basketball players, tennis players, and a handful of golfers.

"What does ISM stand for?" Stevie asked, picking up a third slice of the pizza, which was better than anything he could remember tasting in Philadelphia. When Gibson said ISM stood for Integrity Sports Management, Stevie must have made a face.

Susan Carol noticed. "My dad says integrity in sports management is a bigger oxymoron than jumbo shrimp. But Uncle Brendan isn't like other agents, right, Uncle Brendan?"

Brendan Gibson laughed. "Our business can be pretty dirty, I've learned that," he said. "But we do try to do things a little bit differently. We rarely recruit big stars—we recruit young athletes who really need some help. And when they sign a contract with us, athletes agree to do a certain amount of charity work every year. How much they do depends on how much money we make for them."

Stevie had to admit that sounded like a pretty good idea. He had been around enough sportswriters to know that most agents couldn't be trusted to give you an honest answer if you asked them the day of the week. Stevie remembered Dick Weiss, his escort at the Final Four, pointing out one big-time agent and saying, "If that guy tells you the sun will rise in the east tomorrow, bet everything you've got it'll come up in the west."

Brendan Gibson seemed different from that. And, he figured, if he was Susan Carol's uncle, he couldn't be all bad. Plus, he was putting him up for a week.

"We've got a few clients playing in the Open," he was saying. "We'll make plans to meet out there and I'll introduce you to some of them."

"Anyone I've ever heard of?" Stevie asked.

"Probably not yet. There's one girl I have a lot of hope for, though, who you'd like. She's just a little older than you guys, and she isn't a star yet only because her parents have kept her in school. She only plays during the summer, unlike most teenage prodigies, who play tennis first and foremost. They won't even hire a coach to travel with her yet. They want everything low-key for her. She's jumped sixty spots in the rankings in seven tournaments this summer."

"What's her name?"

"Evelyn Rubin. She's fifteen, she's from Chicago, and she can really play. This is her first major championship, so we're all eager to see her do well."

"And," Susan Carol added, "she's very, very pretty."

"Very, very pretty, huh?" Stevie said. "Like Nadia Symanova very, very pretty?"

"Better than that," Susan Carol said. "Symanova wears all that makeup like Anna Kournikova used to do. She's too obvious. Evelyn doesn't have flash and dash, but trust me, you'll like her."

"When have you seen her?" Stevie said.

"She played an exhibition in Charlotte this summer that Uncle Brendan helped organize. I met her there."

"So is she taller than I am?"

"I don't think so," Susan Carol laughed. "I'd say she's about five five or five six."

"I'm taller than that," Stevie said defensively, although anything over five six might be stretching it.

"I know you are," Susan Carol said. "Why, you're just about as tall as I am, I think."

"Susan Carol, it's me, Stevie," he said.

"Okay, okay," she said. "But you are catching up—seriously."

"And how tall are you now?" he asked.

"Um, maybe five nine."

"And still growing," Brendan put in, causing his niece to blush.

"I hope I'm not," Susan Carol said, the red still in her cheeks.

"Me too," said Stevie, and they all laughed while Stevie reached for slice number four.

✗ ✗ ✗

Stevie went to bed with a stomachache but slept soundly anyway and was awakened at seven-thirty by Susan Carol peeking in the door to his room to say, "Rise and shine, there's work to be done."

"Why do I think that's something your mom says to you in the morning?" Stevie said, suppressing a yawn and rubbing his eyes as he sat up.

"Close," she said. "My dad. Now come on!"

She pulled the door closed. They left the apartment about an hour later. Susan Carol had told him that Bobby Kelleher had offered to give them a ride to the National Tennis Center as long as they got to the apartment he was staying in by nine o'clock. "It's on Forty-eighth Street and Third Avenue," she said. "Uncle Brendan says it's too far to walk. He said if we walk over to West End Avenue, we'll catch a cab."

Stevie was amazed at Susan Carol's whistling ability. She spotted a cab turning the corner onto 78th Street and brought it to a halt with a whistle Stevie figured could be heard in Queens. "Where'd you learn that?" Stevie said as they climbed into the back of the cab.

"My swim coach," she said.

Stevie had a tendency to forget that his friend was a ranked age-group swimmer. Maybe he forgot because she'd had more success athletically than he had. He was hoping to make the freshman basketball team this fall but knew it was probably a long shot.

The cab ride didn't take long. The cabbie worked his way over to Central Park and then went right through the park on 66th Street, no doubt saving a lot of time. He kept going east until he reached Lexington Avenue. He turned right there and made every light until he turned left on 48th Street. He pulled up in front of the apartment building about ten minutes after he had picked them up. Stevie was a bit dizzy.

"Welcome to New York," Susan Carol said, laughing as she handed the cabbie a $10 bill for an $8 fare.

Stevie offered to split it, but she just said, "We'll take turns."

Stevie's dad had given him $250 in cash—telling him to use no more than $50 to buy an Open souvenir and try to get through the week without phoning home for more money. Stevie knew from his experience at the Final Four that he could easily spend the $50 on a hat and a T-shirt. Anything beyond that would undoubtedly break his budget.

Bobby Kelleher was standing in the lobby of the apartment building talking on a cell phone when they walked in the door. He waved at the doorman to indicate Stevie and Susan Carol were with him, then smiled and held up one finger to say he would just be a minute. In many ways, Kelleher was what Stevie wanted to be. He was, Stevie guessed, about thirty-five. He was fairly tall, probably about six one, and lean—unlike a lot of the sportswriters he had met.

Stevie had Googled him after the Final Four and learned that he had been a star high school basketball player who had ended up going to the University of Virginia, where he had hardly played at all. One of the quotes Stevie remembered about Kelleher's college career went something like, "I was the only player in the history of the Atlantic Coast Conference to go four years without needing a postgame shower." That would be a fairly apt description, unfortunately, of Stevie's junior high school career.

Kelleher had spent several years covering politics and then, after leaving the *Washington Herald* briefly, had returned there as a sports columnist not long after breaking a major story involving a recruiting scandal. Stevie remembered some of the grim details: an assistant coach who had been a friend of Kelleher's had been murdered and Kelleher had helped solve the crime while revealing that Brickley Shoes and the University of Louisiana were trying to buy the services of a star high school player from Lithuania. That had been a couple of years back. Stevie couldn't remember the player's name.

Kelleher snapped his phone shut. "Perfect timing. I just called the garage to bring over the car," he said. He gave Susan Carol a hug and shook hands with Stevie.

"So, how are my two favorite media stars?" he asked.

"Let's put it this way," Susan Carol answered. "We're not expecting the Open to be anything like the Final Four."

Kelleher laughed. "We can only hope," he said. He held up the phone. "Sorry about this. That was my wife. You'll meet her this afternoon. She's on her way up from Washington." Stevie hadn't been aware that Kelleher was married. In fact, he hadn't given it any thought one way or the other.

"Is she coming to watch?" Susan Carol asked.

"Coming to work," Kelleher said. "She's a sportswriter too. Writes a column for the *Washington Post*."

That surprised Stevie. He often read the *Post* online so he could read Tony Kornheiser and Michael Wilbon, his heroes—mostly because they had their own TV show. He didn't remember seeing anyone named Kelleher among the bylines.

"Wait a minute," Susan Carol said. "Are you married to Tamara Mearns?" Stevie knew Susan Carol read the *Post* too because they frequently discussed things they read there in their IMs. If Kelleher was Stevie's role model, Tamara Mearns was Susan Carol's. In fact, he had seen her on Wilbon and Kornheiser's show on numerous occasions. She was smart and *very* good-looking.

"Yes, I am," Kelleher said. "Tough being the second-best writer in your own family."

"She *is* very good," Susan Carol said, awestruck, then rushed to add, "not that you aren't, Bobby."

Kelleher laughed. "Nice catch, Susan Carol. Don't worry, I'm like Stevie—I enjoy hanging around smart women. Oh, look, here's the car."

Stevie looked outside to see a black Jeep Grand Cherokee pulling up. "Is that a rental car?" he asked as they walked out the door.

"Nope, it's mine," Kelleher said. "I have a five-hour rule when it comes to airports: if I can drive someplace in under five hours and avoid an airport, I do it. It's less than four hours from our house to here, and now I've got the car for the whole tournament."

"Isn't it expensive to park in New York?" Susan Carol said.

"It's ridiculous to park in New York," Kelleher said. "That's why God invented expense accounts. Plus, I always stay in this apartment during the Open, which saves the paper a lot of money. It belongs to a buddy of mine, Jeff Roddin, but he's always out in the Hamptons until the end of the Open."

Susan Carol gave Stevie the front seat for the ride out to Queens. Traffic was relatively light leaving the city at the end of morning rush hour. Kelleher took the Midtown Tunnel, whisked through the toll thanks to E-ZPass—"greatest invention since the wheel," he said—and a few minutes later a security guard was waving them into a lot right across the street from the main stadium of the National Tennis Center. "What did you have to do to get to park *here?*" Stevie asked. He knew how hard it was to find parking at big sporting events. Once, he and his dad had made the mistake of driving to a Philadelphia Eagles game. For twenty-five dollars they had parked a good fifteen-minute walk—in frigid weather—from the gate where they entered the stadium.

"Actually, Stevie, it's that Philadelphia connection I told you about," Kelleher said as they climbed out of the car. Each of them had computer bags. Susan Carol was supposed to write a story for the Fayetteville paper every day. Stevie had no idea what—if anything—he would be writing, but he had brought his computer to be safe. "Ed Fabricius, the USTA's public relations boss. When he was at Penn, UVA played them my junior year and I met him. When I became a reporter, he was in tennis, but he remembered me. I think he feels like we're bonded because we're both old basketball guys."

"Nice bond to have," Susan Carol said.

"Yeah, especially these two weeks," Kelleher said. "Without Fab, I would either have to pay twelve bucks to park on the other side of the boardwalk near Shea Stadium—*if* there was space—or ride the shuttle bus every day."

"Is the shuttle that bad?" Stevie said.

"It isn't bad *if* it shows up and *if* the Fifty-ninth Street Bridge isn't packed," Kelleher said. "But those two things both happen almost as often as leap year."

While they were talking, they had walked around the stadium to a small office with a sign that said CREDENTIALS.

Kelleher pointed them inside a small room that was teeming with people. There were signs over the various desks: MEDIA, OFFICIALS, PLAYERS. They were starting to turn left to the side of the room that had the sign for media when Stevie heard someone on the far side of the room say, "Well, this must be a big event. Bobby Kelleher's here."

In the next instant, Stevie thought he heard a tiny little shriek come out of Susan Carol's mouth. He looked in the direction of the voice and saw Andy Roddick walking toward them with a big smile on his face. "And don't ever forget it," Kelleher said in response to Roddick's jibe. Roddick was putting a credential around his neck that had his picture on it and a large "A," which was apparently the designation given to players. He and Kelleher shook hands and Kelleher turned toward Susan Carol and Stevie.

"Andy, I want you to meet a couple of future stars in my business," he said. "This is Susan Carol Anderson and Stevie Thomas."

Stevie looked at Susan Carol. He had never seen her quite so pale. The number four tennis player in the world smiled at both of them. "Aspiring reporters, huh?" He shook both their hands. "Is it too late to convince you guys to go straight and pursue real work when you get older?"

Stevie liked him right away. This was a big star, a past U.S. Open champion, a Wimbledon finalist, and there were no airs about him—or so it seemed. Susan Carol was on the verge, he thought, of hyperventilating. "Andy, it is *so* nice to m-meet you again," she stammered. "I mean, to meet you. I just feel . . . as if . . . well, as if I know you. I've watched you play so many times and . . ."

"I hope not against Federer," Roddick said, clearly sensing her distress. Roger Federer was the world's number one player and Roddick's on-court nemesis.

"Well, yes, I mean, well, I still remember the Ferrero match like it was yesterday."

Stevie couldn't help but notice that her full Southern accent was working. The "I's" were all "aah's" and "Ferrero" had about fourteen R's in it. Juan Carlos Ferrero was the player Roddick had beaten in the Open final in 2003.

Roddick laughed. "That was years ago. Back when I was young." He turned to Kelleher. "So, you giving the kids some kind of tour?"

"Actually, they're working," Kelleher said. "Susan Carol is filing for her paper back in North Carolina, and Stevie is going to help me out with news and notes the first week. You might remember them, Andy, since you're a hoops fan. They're the kids who saved Chip Graber at the Final Four."

Roddick's eyes went wide. "That's why the names rang a bell. Of course. Wow. I should be asking *you* guys for an autograph. That was great work."

Stevie was just about convinced Susan Carol was going to faint. "Oh, Andy, we were *so* lucky," she said. "In fact, if not for Bobby, it might have turned out a lot different."

"All I remember," Roddick said, "is that a bunch of sleazoids from Minnesota State were trying to blackmail their best player to throw the title game and you guys stopped it."

"With help from a lot of people," Stevie said, thinking if he heard one more breathless answer from Susan Carol, *he* would become faint.

"Well, anyway, it is great to meet a couple of true heroes," Roddick said. "You guys aren't exactly your run-of-the-mill Bobby Kellehers, that's for sure."

"You got that right," Kelleher said. "You play Wednesday night, right?"

Roddick nodded. "Yeah, long time to wait for round one. But the USTA always has to get the names on at night, right? Forget the daytime fans—this is about what TV wants."

"Tell me about it," Kelleher said.

"Well," Roddick said, "I'm going to go hit for a while, get the feel of the place." He shook hands with them all again, waved, and headed through the door.

"What you just saw," Kelleher said, "was an aberration. Most tennis players would sooner cut off their serving arm than talk to reporters. Andy's different. He hasn't lost all sense of reality. He's still a pretty good guy."

"Not to mention being gorgeous," Susan Carol sighed.

"Oh God," Stevie said. "Does this mean you're never going to wash that hand again? I thought you might pass out for a minute there."

Her response was to whack him on the shoulder with that hand. "I wasn't *that* breathless. Come on."

"Oh, Andeeee, aah am *so* glad to meet you. . . ."

Kelleher cut him off. "Cool it, Stevie," he said. "Or we'll head straight for the players' lounge and I'll introduce you to Symanova."

Stevie cooled it. He knew when he was overmatched.

3: CELEBRITIES

IT DIDN'T take them long to get their credentials. There were only a couple of people in line ahead of them and, even though Stevie and Susan Carol had to have photos taken, that only delayed them a couple of minutes.

"Ten o'clock," Kelleher said, looking at his watch as they walked out the door, each of them now wearing a credential with a giant "B" and the small word "Media" below it around their necks. "We've got an hour until they actually start playing tennis. If we'd gotten here fifteen minutes later, we would have had to wait awhile." Stevie could see he was right. Since they had arrived, the line to pick up media credentials had grown to about twenty-five people.

They had to pause at the entrance gate so the guards could look through their computer bags and wand them, much the way they had done at the Final Four. Once they were inside, Stevie could see that the vast grounds of the tennis center were still virtually empty. "Public can't come in until ten-thirty," Kelleher said, as if reading Stevie's mind. "This is my favorite time of day to walk around out here. In fact, let's put our stuff down and then walk over to the practice courts. We might run into some people. Once the crowds come in, you can't get close to anything over there if one of the names is practicing."

"You mean like Andy Roddick?" Susan Carol asked.

"You got it."

They were walking with the main stadium, which Stevie could see was huge, to their left. To their right were the practice courts Kelleher had been referring to. In front of them, Stevie could see what looked like a large open plaza, with a fountain bubbling up in the middle.

"Where are all the other courts?" Stevie said.

"You can't see them from here," Kelleher said. "I'll show you once we drop our stuff off in the media room. The smaller stadium and the Grandstand court are around to the left. The outside courts are over on the right, beyond the plaza. They're the best place to watch the first week, because you can practically walk right up to the court since the area around each of them is so small. The players hate playing there because they feel like the fans are right on top of them."

They didn't have to walk far to get to the glass doors with a sign that said MEDIA CENTER. There were two guards on the door, neither of whom had an answer for Kelleher's "Good morning." They eyed everyone's badge, then stepped out of the way. Walking inside, Stevie could see a cafeteria on the left. To the right was the entrance to the media work area. Even an hour before the matches began, it was humming with life. As they walked by the front desk, Stevie could hear shouting in what sounded like at least three different languages.

"Annual battle," Kelleher said, again seeming to know what Stevie was wondering. "Foreign media get upset when one of their stars gets put on an outside court—which the USTA always does. Today, they'll be angry because Nadal's out on court twelve. There will be a riot out there with people trying to find a place to sit."

"Rafael Nadal is the number two player in the world," Susan Carol said. "He won the French Open. Why in the world would they put him on an outside court?"

Kelleher, who was leading them through a maze of desks, nodding hello to people as he went, smiled. "Because of tennis politics. You go to the French Open or Wimbledon, they'll take Roddick or the Williams sisters and stick them on an outside court. The French are notorious for it. They'll put French qualifiers on center court and stick an American star way outside. Pete Sampras's last match at Wimbledon was on court two."

"I remember that," Stevie said. "He lost in the second round, didn't he?"

"Yeah," Kelleher said. "Then he had to fight through the

crowds to get back to the locker room because only center court and court one are accessible from the locker room without going out among the masses."

"Guess that's what they mean by 'going outside,' huh?" Susan Carol said. "Court two's the one they call the graveyard of champions, right?"

"Very good, Susan Carol," Kelleher said with a smile. "Lot of big upsets have taken place out there. And, to be fair, the Brits always stick players outside. But Pete Sampras? He won the event seven times!"

"So the Americans get even at the Open," Stevie said.

"Yup," Kelleher said. "Nadal is really a tough one because it isn't just the Spanish media that has to cover him, it's everyone from Europe. Take a look at the schedule on the Armstrong Court. They've got Nick Nocera there. I mean, who wants to watch Nick Nocera besides friends, family, and his agent?"

Stevie didn't even know the name. Naturally, Susan Carol did. "Didn't he make the semis here last year?" she said. "And he beat Roddick in Indianapolis."

"Jeez, Susan Carol, what *don't* you know?" Kelleher said. "Yes, he had a great tournament last year here because the draw opened up. And he did beat Roddick in Indy. That jumped him to about twenty-fifth in the world. You and I and Bud Collins know who he is and that's about it. That may change, but as of this moment—"

He was interrupted by someone shouting, "Robertino! Robertino!"

A huge smile came across Kelleher's face as the shouter

approached, arms open wide. Stevie did a double take. It was the man Kelleher had just been talking about—Bud Collins.

"Colleeny!" Kelleher shouted with as much enthusiasm as Collins had shown. *"Ciao, caro!"*

The two men hugged. "And?" Collins asked. "Where is the fair Tamara?"

"Be here this afternoon," Kelleher said. "Hey, I want you to meet a couple of people."

He put an arm around Collins's shoulders. "Stevie, Susan Carol, I want you to meet the one and only Bud Collins. Bud, this is Stevie Thomas and Susan Carol Anderson."

"Wonderful to meet you both," Collins said. He gave Stevie a warm handshake, then kissed Susan Carol on both cheeks, the way it was done in Europe.

"So these are the two young saviors you told me about from New Orleans, eh, Robertino?" Collins said. "My goodness, you two were heroic. I read all about you. Read your stuff too. You two have accomplished more at thirteen than most of us will in a lifetime."

Stevie felt himself flush. He couldn't believe Bud Collins had read anything he had written. When he had first watched Wimbledon on TV with his father, he had immediately noticed Collins, the man with the warm smile, the white beard, and the pants that were almost blinding to look at. Collins reminded him in many ways of Dick Vitale, the college basketball announcer whose enthusiasm was legendary. Stevie had met him in New Orleans and his ears were still ringing. Collins wasn't as loud as Vitale but he was similarly enthusiastic about his sport. Stevie's dad had told him that Collins had been the first man *ever* to broadcast tennis on television, back in the 1960s, when the PBS station in Boston decided to telecast the local tournament played there. He had gone on to become "the voice of tennis" on NBC. Stevie hadn't realized that he was friends with Kelleher.

"Mr. Collins, I've watched you since I was a baby," Susan Carol was saying. "And I really loved reading your book."

She had him there. Stevie didn't know Collins had written a book.

"My book!" Collins screamed. "You read my book! I wrote it before you were born! Wait one second."

He scurried to a desk a few yards away from Kelleher's that was marked BOSTON GLOBE and began burrowing through a gigantic bag. "Aha, knew I had one." He pulled a book out of the bag, opened it, and quickly scribbled something inside. He walked back and handed it to Susan Carol. Stevie could see a picture of Collins on the cover and could see the title, My Life with the Pros.

"Stevie, I'm sorry, I only have one," Collins said. "I will track one down for you too."

Before Stevie could say anything, Susan Carol was hugging Collins to say thank you. Stevie was embarrassed he hadn't known about the book. "Thank you so much," she said.

"No, no, thank *you*," Collins said. "It's been years since anyone mentioned it. Always thought the book would have done better if they'd stayed with my title."

"What was that?" Stevie asked.

"What a Sweet Racquet," Collins said.

"Oh, that's a *much* better title," Susan Carol said. Stevie would have thought she was sucking up, but this was Bud Collins, so it was not only okay, it was appropriate.

"So, Robertino, who are these two young mavens going to write about today?" Collins said.

"Haven't asked yet," Kelleher said. "Guys?"

Stevie had figured he'd be going wherever Kelleher needed him, so he hadn't studied the schedule that closely. He *did* know that he wanted to see Symanova play, if possible, and that her first-round match was later in the day. She was one of the few stars playing on the afternoon program the first day. He had read a story in the Sunday paper about the U.S. Tennis Association dragging the first round out over three days so that the men's semifinals wouldn't be played until the second Saturday—to accommodate TV. Every other Grand Slam event played the men's semis on Friday.

Susan Carol—naturally—knew the schedule by heart. "Well, I was hoping to go see Evelyn Rubin play at eleven o'clock," she said. "She's on an outside court, I forget which number. And then I saw that Symanova is playing over on Louis Armstrong late this afternoon and I *know* Stevie wants to see that."

"Stevie and every red-blooded American or non-American male on the grounds," Collins said, laughing. "Why do you want to see Rubin play, my dear? I hear she's quite good, but what's your interest?"

"My uncle is her agent."

Collins did a double take. "Your uncle is an agent? But you seem like such a nice girl."

Kelleher laughed. "Now, Bud, you can't choose your relatives."

"You can't?" Collins said. "I've chosen three wives—and here comes one of them now."

Stevie saw a tall, elegant-looking woman walking up to them. It turned out she *was* his wife, Anita Klaussen. "Bud, don't go agent bashing again," she said, walking up.

"What's not to bash?" Kelleher said.

"Are they that bad?" Susan Carol asked.

"Well, I don't know your uncle, so I'll presume he's a fine fellow," Collins said. "But agents are responsible for most of the ills of tennis, and the ills of tennis are endless."

"But you love tennis," Stevie said.

"I do. I just don't love the people running it," Collins said. "Look, you all *must* have dinner with us one night. We'll talk more. Right now, I have to go figure out who to write about today. Stevie, Susan Carol, you keep an eye on Robertino for me."

He trundled off with Anita right behind.

"Why 'Robertino'?" Stevie asked Kelleher.

Kelleher smiled. "Bud loves all things Italian. Spends a month in Italy every year. He would rather speak Italian than English. So he Italianizes everyone's name. Guaranteed, the next time you see him he'll call you Stefano."

"What about me?" Susan Carol asked.

"He'll probably stick to *cara*," Kelleher said. "That's Italian for 'darling.'"

Susan Carol looked at her watch. "The matches will be starting soon," she said.

"You're right," Kelleher said. "I have to go to the Grandstand and watch Paul Goldstein play. He's a D.C. kid, and if I don't write about him today, he might be gone by tomorrow. Are you serious about going to see your uncle's client?"

Susan Carol nodded. "Yes. I think she might be a good story for me the first day. No one knows her and she's playing someone who is seeded. I think it's Maggie Maleeva."

"Maggie Maleeva?" Kelleher said. "I swear she played against Billie Jean King. She must be a hundred years old."

He picked up a schedule and scanned it. "You've got it— Maggie Maleeva, court 18—it's way out on the far end of the grounds. Shows you what they think of Maggie Maleeva. She's the number twenty-two seed, playing a young American, and they have her playing halfway to New Jersey. Do you think you can find it?"

"I can find it," Susan Carol said. "Stevie, you gonna go with me?"

Stevie looked at Kelleher. "What do you need me to do?" he asked.

"For right now, you can go with Susan Carol," he said. "Keep that cell phone of yours on. If something's happening and I need you to get to a match, I'll call you. With so few seeded players playing this afternoon, we need to wait and see what develops."

"Can I watch Symanova later?" he asked.

Kelleher smiled. "Unless something crazy happens, sure," he said. "I wouldn't deny you that. In fact, I have no plans to deny myself that either."

Susan Carol sighed. "*Why* are boys so predictable?" she said.

For once, she had thrown Stevie a hanging curveball. "Oh, Andy, aah am *so* thrilled to meet you. . . ."

She turned bright red, which pleased him to no end. "Okay, okay, I give. Come on, let's go. Apparently we've got a long way to walk."

✗ ✗ ✗

Kelleher had not exaggerated about court 18 being at the far end of the grounds. They walked out of the press center, went past the practice courts, and crossed the plaza—Collins no doubt would have called it a piazza. The plaza was surrounded by merchandise kiosks. Just about every corporate name connected to sports seemed to have a place to sell its wares: Nike, Reebok, Adidas, and Prince were names that jumped out at him right away. There was a place where you could test the speed of your serve and another where you could buy "official" USTA merchandise. Stevie knew from his Final Four experience that that would be the most expensive stuff on the grounds. As they crossed the plaza, they could smell food straight ahead. Stevie saw a sign that said FOOD COURT. It was only eleven o'clock, but the smell of grilling hamburgers made him hungry. Below the arrow pointing to the food court were more arrows pointing people in various directions: stadium, Louis Armstrong, corporate village, practice courts. At the bottom one of them said COURTS 10–18, guiding them to turn right and head away from the main stadium, which people were now starting to make their way into since the gates were open.

"That reminds me," he said as they began picking their way through people to follow the sign leading them to the outside courts. "What's with Louis Armstrong?"

She sighed as if he had asked who Andy Roddick was. "When they first moved here from Forest Hills in 1978, the main stadium was named after Louis Armstrong," she said.

"What does Louis Armstrong have to do with tennis?" he asked.

"Nothing. But the stadium was once used as a place for concerts. Since Louis Armstrong had lived near here, they named it for him. Before that, it had been used during the World's Fair. . . ."

"Okay, fine, but what about the tennis played in there?"

"I'm getting to that. When they built the new stadium"— she paused and pointed over her shoulder at Arthur Ashe Stadium—"they took the upper deck off of Louis Armstrong"—she turned again and pointed briefly at a much smaller structure about a hundred yards from the main stadium—"and made it into the number one side court. It seats, I think, about ten thousand."

"I have one more question."

"What?"

"Is there anything you *don't* know?"

She smiled. "Yes. Why you never bother to know anything."

The crowds thinned as they approached court 18. Most people were walking in the opposite direction from Stevie and Susan Carol. Court 18 was up against a fence that separated the tennis center from a local park. There was seating around it, but not much—two tiers of bleachers on either side of the court. Still, that was plenty of room for the crowd on hand. Stevie guessed there were fewer than a hundred people watching the match.

It was 2–2 in the first set when Stevie and Susan Carol quietly slid into seats on the bleachers. Evelyn Rubin was wearing a white baseball cap and had light brown hair pulled back in a ponytail. Stevie guessed she was about his height. She was already glistening with perspiration in the morning heat as she and Maggie Maleeva stood at the baseline blasting ground strokes at one another. Maleeva held serve for 3–2 and the two players walked to their chairs to change sides, no more than fifteen feet from where Stevie and Susan Carol were sitting.

Rubin sat down and took a long sip of water. She took her cap off and pulled the elastic out of her ponytail to reknot it, and for a moment her hair fell to her shoulders. She was close enough that Stevie could see she had enormous brown eyes.

"Wow," he said, forgetting where he was.

"I told you," Susan Carol said.

Stevie caught himself. He wasn't going to go breathless and give up his Andy Roddick advantage. He would at least save that for Symanova.

"She's pretty," he said. "But she isn't any prettier than you."

He couldn't tell if Susan Carol was blushing, because she had put on a cap too. "Why, Steven Richman Thomas, I do declare that is the *nicest* thing you've ever said to me."

She was doing her Southern belle routine. He wished he had never told her his middle name. It was his mother's maiden name. "I try, Scarlett," he said, smiling nevertheless as the players stood to resume the match.

They ended up in a tiebreak in the first set. Rubin was a lot stronger than she looked. She blasted her ground strokes off both her forehand and her backhand and was quick enough to chase down balls that appeared to be winners. Twice, she saved set points by racing into the corner to turn what looked like a Maleeva winner into a crosscourt winner of her own—once off the forehand, the other off the backhand.

"Your uncle wasn't kidding," Stevie whispered. "She can play."

"The only thing she can't do well is volley," Susan Carol said. "But very few of the women can volley."

Stevie nodded. Maleeva had no more interest in getting to the net than Rubin did. They both treated the area close to the net as if it was radioactive. In the end, Rubin saved a total of five set points and won the tiebreak, 12–10. Maleeva looked like she might cry—which reminded Stevie of something he *had* read once about the three Maleeva sisters who had played on tour. All of them, it seemed, had a penchant for crying when things didn't go well, so they had been nicknamed the Boo-Hoo Sisters.

As the players changed sides before the start of the second set, he mentioned the nickname to Susan Carol, who giggled.

"Actually, they were called Boo-Hoo One, Boo-Hoo Two, and Boo-Hoo Three," a voice said behind them.

Stevie looked up and saw Brendan Gibson walking toward them, dressed in a snappy blue suit with a white shirt and a red-striped tie. The fancy getup looked out of place among the tennis outfits and the T-shirts and shorts that most people were wearing. Susan Carol was wearing a tennis skirt and sneakers. She fit right in.

"Uncle Brendan, why are you so dressed up in this heat?" Susan Carol asked.

"This is what's called the agent's uniform," Brendan said. "Makes the clients feel better that their agent cares enough to dress up. It also makes it easier for them to pick you out in the crowd so they can see that you're there to support them."

"Well, in this crowd you won't be tough to pick out," Stevie said, waving his hand at the hundred or so spectators scattered around them. Across the way, he saw another man in a suit. "Hey, is that an agent too?" He pointed at the suit.

"As a matter of fact, it is," Brendan Gibson said. "And he doesn't represent Maleeva. He's checking Evelyn out."

"But don't you have a contract with her?" Susan Carol said.

"Yeah, I do," Brendan said. "Which means exactly nothing to the competition." He dropped his voice to a whisper as his client prepared to serve. "If someone thinks Evelyn's a rising star, they'll try to figure out a way to steal her from me."

"Nice business," Stevie said, remembering what Bud Collins had said.

The second set didn't take very long. Losing the long tiebreak seemed to take the heart out of Maleeva, who clearly had no interest in playing three sets against a teenager with boundless energy on a day that was getting hotter by the minute. Rubin won the second set 6–1, serving an ace on match point. She came off the court with a big smile, pausing to point her racquet directly at Brendan Gibson as if to say, "I did it."

"Come on, I'll introduce you," Gibson said. The three of them worked their way down to the side of the court, which was separated from the stands by only a low fence. There were two security guards standing on the court behind the umpire's chair. Stevie guessed one of them was there to escort each player through the crowds and back to the locker rooms. Clearly, no one thought that Maggie Maleeva or Evelyn Rubin needed much protection.

Rubin gathered her racquets and walked over to where Stevie, Susan Carol, and her agent were standing. Gibson leaned over the low fence to give her a kiss on the cheek. "What a great win!" he said, squeezing her very sweaty shoulder.

Rubin was glowing. "I know," she said. "The first set, I was *so* nervous I felt like I couldn't hit a ball. But I knew if I kept her out there, she'd wear down. I think she's like thirty-two or something."

"God, I didn't know anyone was *that* old," Gibson said wryly. "Evelyn, I think you met Susan Carol Anderson in Charlotte. This is her friend Steve Thomas."

The two girls shook hands, and Susan Carol offered her congratulations. Evelyn Rubin then turned to Stevie with a smile so bright Stevie almost blinked. "It's so nice of you guys to come watch me play way out here on this back court," she said. She swept her hand around the bleachers. "I guess the good news is you didn't have any trouble finding a seat."

She had one of those flat Midwestern accents in which the word "back" became "be-ack" and "fact" became "fe-act." Stevie was hypnotized by her smile.

"You played so well today, I'll bet there will be a lot more people watching the next time you play," he said.

Gibson jumped back in. "Evelyn, a couple of reporters told me they wanted to talk to you if you won," he said. "But I don't see them out here. Can I call you on your cell when I track them down?"

"Oh sure," she said. "I'm going to shower and eat something, so I'll be here awhile."

She turned back to Stevie and Susan Carol. "I hope I see you guys again soon." They all shook hands once more, and she began walking to the court exit, the security guard a half step behind her.

"And you thought I was bad with Roddick."

"Hey, she's pretty and she's nice," Stevie said. "Should I not like someone who is pretty and nice *and* can play?"

"Oh, Evelyn, I just know there will be more people watching the next time you play. . . ."

Stevie smiled.

"Okay, Scarlett," he said. "We'll call it deuce."

4: NADIA SYMANOVA

THE MEDIA center was packed by the time they made the long walk back.

"Lunchtime frenzy," Bobby Kelleher said when they found him at his desk. He had just finished a phone call.

"So, what's the scouting report on Evelyn Rubin?" he asked. "I saw the end of the match on one of the TV monitors. I see she made Boo-Hoo Three cry."

"Stevie's in love with her," Susan Carol reported.

"I am *not!*" Stevie said. "She can really play, though. Great ground strokes and she's fast."

Susan Carol was grinning. "*And* a beautiful smile."

"An older woman, huh, Stevie?" Kelleher said, smiling. Without giving Stevie a chance to respond, he gestured at the TV screen propped on the corner of his desk. "The match before Symanova out on Armstrong is just about over. If you guys want good seats, we probably ought to walk over there."

"Do we have time to eat something?" Susan Carol said.

Kelleher shook his head. "No. It's packed in the cafeteria right now. If you want to eat, we probably won't get into the press section."

"I'm not that hungry," Stevie said.

"That figures," Susan Carol answered, rolling her eyes.

"Bud wants to come too," Kelleher said. "In fact, he might have a sandwich or something—he's always carrying food. You guys can grab a soda on the way out."

Kelleher turned out to be right. Collins was more than happy to offer up a choice of sandwiches. Stevie and Susan Carol each grabbed one and quickly disposed of them. They grabbed cups of Coke and made their way back outside. The temperature had gone up at least ten degrees and the number of people appeared to have doubled. Kelleher led the way, with Stevie and Susan Carol behind him and Collins, hat pulled low over his head, right behind them. Even with the cap, people were constantly screaming Collins's name. He answered everyone but kept moving, his hand on Stevie's shoulder to make sure he stayed close to him.

"Gotta keep moving!" he said. "If Nadia's boyfriend isn't there when the match starts, she'll be very upset."

"Where? Who?" everyone kept asking.

"Right here in front of me," Collins would reply. "Young Steven Thomas. Don't you read the tabloids?"

Given that Symanova was three years older than Stevie

and about a half foot taller, the notion of them as an item was pretty outrageous. But such was the power of Bud that few fans seemed skeptical. One woman wearing a tennis dress even asked Stevie for his autograph. "Not right now," Collins said. "After the match. He's got his game face on."

They made it to the entrance and walked under the stands to the far side, where a small sign with an arrow said MEDIA SEATING. They went up a short flight of steps and came out in a section that was almost directly behind the court—which was empty at the moment. Apparently the prior match had ended. The stands were almost full and there were no more than ten seats left in the media seating area, which Stevie estimated had about a hundred and fifty seats.

"Just in time," Kelleher said.

A security guard stood at the top of the steps checking badges. He gave Stevie a skeptical look and twice looked at the photo on Stevie's badge and then back at him. Having been through the same sort of thing at the Final Four, Stevie said nothing. When the guard went back for a third look, Kelleher couldn't take it. "You can look at the photo a hundred times and it's going to be him," he said. "He's working with me. He's legit."

"Whaddya think, workin' with you makes the kid legit?" the guard said in one of those unmistakable New York accents. "I'm just doin' my job here, okay?"

"Fine," Kelleher said. "Are you done doing your job now?"

"You want I should just throw youse bot' out?" the guard said.

Before Kelleher could respond, Collins, a step behind Kelleher, jumped in. "Fellas, fellas, let's all be friends here," he said. "Mr. . . . ?"

"Shapiro," the guard said. "Max Shapiro."

"Max, nice to meet you," Collins said, shaking hands with the guard as if they were long-lost friends. "This is Bobby Kelleher. He's the leading tennis writer in the country, and this is his assistant, Steven Thomas. They're just like you and me, here to see Symanova. No one wants any trouble."

Shapiro eyed Stevie and Kelleher for another moment. "Okay, Bud," he said. "Seein' that it's you, okay. But the kid don't look older than thirteen."

"Well, they do get younger-looking all the time," Collins said.

That seemed to satisfy Max, who moved aside. Stevie heard someone several rows up shouting Kelleher's name.

"Kelleher, right here—I was about to give up on you guys!"

Stevie looked in the direction of the voice—which was very familiar—and did a double take. It was Mary Carillo, the CBS tennis commentator who he knew also worked for ESPN. His dad had told him on more than one occasion that if his mother ever ran off with George Clooney, the first person he would pursue was Carillo.

Carillo had black hair and big brown eyes. Her distinctively deep voice sounded exactly as it did on television. She was wearing a collared white shirt and shorts, and Stevie was surprised at how tall she was when she stood up to greet their group. It looked to him as if she and Susan Carol were about the same height. He had never thought of her as tall, but then he had only seen her on TV.

"The love of my life," she said, throwing her arms around Kelleher as they walked up to greet her. "Only for you and Bud would I have fought off the masses to save these seats. Who've we got here?"

Kelleher introduced her to Susan Carol and Stevie. "I can't tell you what a big fan I am," Susan Carol said. "I love listening to you talk about tennis."

"Learned it all from the master," Carillo said, hugging Collins. "Right, master?"

"You never needed to learn a thing," Collins said. "You were born knowing everything about tennis."

Stevie, feeling a little bit left out, heard himself blurt, "My dad thinks you're hot."

Carillo laughed, a musical laugh that was filled with joy. "Thank you, Stevie," she said. "I will take that as a compliment. And tell your dad thank you."

They all maneuvered into the seats Carillo had saved for them. Others were right behind them searching for seats in the fast-filling media section.

"How soon?" Kelleher said, settling in between Carillo and Stevie.

"They announced players on court to warm up at two o'clock," Carillo said. "I've got one fifty-five. Hey, did you see the Rubin kid beat Boo-Hoo Three? She could play Symanova in the third round."

"Didn't see it," Kelleher said. "But Susan Carol and Stevie did."

"What'd you think?" Carillo said, turning to Stevie as if they were peers.

Feeling quite expert, Stevie said, "Well, she's very good from the back of the court, but she doesn't volley at all."

"Sweetie, no one volleys in women's tennis," Carillo said in a tone that somehow didn't make it sound like a put-down, even though he knew she was right.

"We haven't had a true serve-and-volleyer since Martina," Collins said.

A murmur ran through the crowd and Stevie saw a TV cameraman backing out of the tunnel that was right in the middle of the stands across from the umpire's chair. A moment later, a security guy came out onto the court followed by a short, dark-haired player carrying an enormous racquet bag who Stevie knew had to be Joanne Walsh, Symanova's opponent. Stevie knew nothing about her other than what he had seen in the newspaper that morning. She was twenty-four years old and ranked ninety-sixth in the world. The paper had referred to her as a "veteran," which in women's tennis meant anyone over twenty-one. A second security man walked right behind Walsh.

Stevie realized he was standing up, craning his neck for a view of Symanova. Walsh kept walking across the court to the players' chairs but the cameraman remained poised just outside the tunnel, waiting for Symanova. Stevie waited. So did everyone else.

"Where is she?" Susan Carol asked. The crowd was beginning to buzz. Walsh had reached her seat and was unzipping her racquet bag. Still no one else came out of the tunnel.

"Maybe she stopped to check her makeup," Collins said.

Kelleher laughed. "There is that little bathroom right off the court."

"Yeah," Carillo said. "Remember when this was the stadium court and Lendl used to jump in there and change so he could go straight to the parking lot without going back to the locker room?"

"We used to call him Ivan the Unshowered," Collins said.

The buzz was growing. There was still no sign of Symanova. Walsh was now standing, holding her racquet, looking up at the umpire. The umpire had put her hand over the microphone and was leaning down to talk to Walsh.

"This is now officially getting strange," Carillo said.

"Check this out," Collins said, pointing in the direction of the tunnel.

A gaggle of security men came sprinting from the tunnel—Stevie counted one, two, three, four, five of them—followed by two men in blazers, both of them barking into walkie-talkies.

"Uh-oh," Kelleher said. "Something's up, something big-time."

"She must be hurt," Collins said. "But how do you get hurt walking over to the court?"

"Tripped on her stilettos?" Susan Carol asked.

"She's wearing sneakers!" Stevie said, thinking that was a

dumb comment until he realized she was being sarcastic. "Nice, she's hurt and you're making jokes."

"Calm down, Stefano, I'm sure your betrothed is fine," Collins said, smiling.

The new group of security men had gone directly to Walsh and spoken to her. Whatever they said, she walked quickly back to her chair, zippered her racquet back into her bag, and began walking back across the court with no fewer than eight blue-shirted security men surrounding her. Seeing this, the crowd began whistling—the tennis equivalent of booing.

"Walsh is leaving," Stevie said. "Symanova must be hurt."

Kelleher was shaking his head. "If she's hurt, what's with all the security people around Walsh? Something's up. Come on, guys, we need to get out of here."

"Now?" Susan Carol said.

"Yup," Kelleher said, "right now."

He pointed at the two walkie-talkie guys who were talking intently to the umpire. "Soon as they make an announcement, all hell is going to break loose here. We need to get moving so we don't get trapped in the stampede for the exits. Come on."

"I need to stay," Carillo said. "I'll see you guys later."

"I better stay too," Collins said. "You young guns start chasing this down."

Kelleher shrugged and made his way to the aisle. Stevie kind of wanted to stay too, but he trusted Kelleher's instincts. Susan Carol seemed to agree, because she was standing, ready to move. The three of them started down the steps while others in the media section were standing up and consulting with one another. They bolted past Max Shapiro and down the steps leading under the stadium. They were under the stands and sprinting through an almost empty concourse when they heard what had to be the umpire's voice on the PA system. She wasn't calling out any score.

"Ladies and gentlemen, we regret to announce that the scheduled match between Joanne Walsh and Nadia Symanova has been postponed until a later time." Stevie could hear groans and shouts coming from inside as the umpire forged on. "More details will be announced when they become available. Thank you for your patience and indulgence."

Kelleher turned to Stevie and Susan Carol, shaking his head. "There's *nothing* in the rules about postponing a match. If she's hurt, she defaults. Something crazy's going on here."

They made it out onto the courtyard between the two stadiums. There were security people and police all over the place, blocking the most direct path back to the main stadium. When a security guard stopped Kelleher, he held up his media badge. "We're media," he said. "We have to get back to the media center."

"I don't care who you are," the security man said. "You can go through the food court like everyone else and you'll get there eventually. This area's frozen right now."

Stevie could see two cops right behind the security guy, ready to back him up. People were being herded from the area very quickly by security and police, all of them being pushed toward the food court. Kelleher could clearly see this was an argument he wasn't going to win—even if Collins had been there.

He took one swipe at getting something accomplished. "Can't you at least tell us what in the world is going on?" he said.

One of the cops answered, stepping in front of the security guard. "Here's what I can tell you, pal: if you don't get moving right now, you're going to jail. How's that for telling you something?"

Stevie could see Kelleher redden a little and bite his lip. He turned to Stevie and Susan Carol. "Come on," he said, pointing them toward the food court. The good news was that because they had beaten the crowd out of Louis Armstrong, they were able to maneuver their way through the food court fairly quickly.

"I'm not sure who is worse to deal with," Kelleher said when they finally reached the other side and were back within sight of the entrance to the media center. "The security guys are just rent-a-cops, know-nothings given a little bit of authority. The cops know what they're doing, but they see a media credential and it's like waving red at a bull."

"Why is that?" Susan Carol asked.

"It's just a natural adversarial thing," Kelleher said. "Sometimes cops help reporters, but they also like to remind you they're in charge whenever they get a chance."

"Kind of tough to argue with guys when they have guns," Stevie said.

"No kidding." Kelleher pulled open the door that led back inside with a frustrated yank. The scene inside the building was chaotic. People were running in and out of the entrance to the media center shouting, as far as Stevie could tell, in a variety of languages.

"Okay," Kelleher said, pausing just outside the pressroom entrance. "We need a strategy of some kind. I think we should split up—"

He broke off in midsentence as a middle-aged man with graying hair ducked out of the media center and made a quick turn away from them.

"Arlen!" Kelleher said, heading toward the man. "Arlen, hang on a second!"

The man half turned, still walking, and waved a hand as if to say, "Go away." "Not now, Bobby. I can't talk. We're organizing a press conference. We'll let you know what's going on in a while."

He had slowed down enough that Kelleher was able to catch up to him. Stevie and Susan Carol followed at what they hoped was a discreet distance.

"In a while?" Kelleher said. "Come on, Arlen, give me a break. Don't give me that press conference crap. What happened out there? Where the hell is Symanova?"

The man stopped and turned to face Kelleher. Stevie noticed he was quite pale. He looked around as if to be sure no one could hear him and dropped his voice to a whisper so that Stevie, standing right behind Kelleher, could barely hear.

"We don't know," he said.

For a second, Kelleher just stared at him. "What do you mean, you don't know? How can you not know? Wasn't she on her way over to Armstrong with Walsh?"

"Yes! She was!" Arlen said, clearly exasperated, still looking around as if he was afraid someone would hear him. "They were on their way over there and she disappeared."

"Disappeared!" Kelleher shouted.

"Bobby, please," Arlen hissed, signaling Kelleher to keep his voice down. "Yes, she disappeared. You know what it's like out there between the stadiums. We had four security guys surrounding the two players. A group of people cut across their path, headed for the food court. The security guys got jostled. Walsh and her two guys kept going—no one bumped them. By the time Symanova's guys got untangled, she was gone."

"But how is that possible?"

Arlen held up his hand. "For crying out loud, Bobby, if we knew, she wouldn't be missing, would she? We've sealed all the exits from the place, but that's the problem—we're right on the edge of a park. There are plenty of ways to get off the property without walking through an exit." He looked around again. "I've got to go. There's a meeting in about two minutes. I've told you everything I know."

"Okay, okay," Kelleher said. "Can I quote you on this stuff?"

Arlen smiled wanly. "At this point, that's the least of my worries." He turned and walked down the hallway.

"Who was that?" Stevie asked.

"Arlen Kantarian," Kelleher said. "He's the CEO of professional tennis for the U.S. Tennis Association. It means he's in charge of the tournament. He talks to me because his brother Harry's a friend of mine." He took a deep breath.

"Okay, this story is officially huge. Beyond huge. We've got a big leg up on people right now—let's do something with it."

"Like what?" Susan Carol said, for once looking as baffled as Stevie felt.

Kelleher took a deep breath. "Good question," he said. Then he snapped his fingers. "Listen, Susan Carol, *you* can get into the junior girls' locker room."

"What's that?" she asked.

"I'll give you the short version," Kelleher said. "There are so many girls under eighteen in the event that they have a separate locker room that the media isn't allowed into because the parents freak out about men seeing their daughters half-dressed. Since female reporters are allowed in the men's locker room, male reporters are allowed into the women's. But not where there are women under the age of eighteen. It's been a huge controversy for years because all the players freak out about us being in the locker room. The point is the junior locker room door's not even marked and they usually don't even have a guard on it because they don't want to call attention to it. If you take your press credential off, you can probably walk in there like you're a player."

"How do *you* know where it is?" Susan Carol said.

"Carillo showed me. Come on, let's start walking. I'll show you where it is. Meantime, Stevie, I want you in the players' lounge. Once you're past the guard, take your credential off and just walk around and listen. I'm going to the men's locker room. We'll meet back here in thirty minutes and compare notes."

"What exactly are we listening for?" Stevie asked as they started to walk down the long hallway.

Kelleher shook his head. "I have no idea, Stevie," he said. "But people will be talking and someone must know *something*."

"And what do I do if I manage to get in?" Susan Carol said. "Won't the other players know I'm a fraud right away?"

"Sit in front of an empty locker as if it's yours and listen. You're dressed like a player. There are so many different events going on here at once that no one knows everybody. You never know when you're going to be in the right place at the right time. If we're in three different places, our chances are three times as good of hearing something helpful."

"But what do we think is going on here?" Stevie asked.

"That," Kelleher said, "is the multimillion-dollar question."

5: KIDNAPPED

STEVIE HADN'T been in the hallway under the main stadium yet. Like the media center, it was filled with people running in different directions shouting at one another.

"Keep your heads down, keep walking, and act like nothing's going on," Kelleher said.

"Aren't we allowed in here?" Susan Carol asked.

"Yes, we are," he said. "But everything changes when the most famous female player in the world has just gone missing."

There were signs on all the walls pointing out where different things were. When they reached a point that would have been a four-way stop with traffic coming in all directions, Stevie noticed a sign pointing to the left that said STADIUM COURT.

"Turn right," Kelleher said. They turned and walked halfway down the hall, where Kelleher stopped. "Okay, Susan Carol," he said. "Right around the corner there, you'll see an unmarked door." He glanced around. No one was paying attention to them. "Okay, take your credential off. *If* there's a guard on the door, just say you left your player badge inside your locker."

"And what if he won't let me in?" she said.

"We'll wait here until we know you're in," Kelleher said.

She nodded and started walking. Stevie had been tempted to make fun of her in the morning for wearing a tennis outfit. Now it seemed like an awfully good idea. She disappeared around the corner and Stevie held his breath. "We'll know quickly," Kelleher said.

They waited a full minute. They heard and saw nothing.

"Stevie, walk to the end of the hall and turn the corner," Kelleher said. "If you see a guard and no Susan Carol, act as if you made a wrong turn and come right back."

Stevie followed orders. As soon as he rounded the corner, he saw a guard. No sign of Susan Carol. The guard looked at him. "I'm trying to find the stadium court," he said.

"You took a wrong turn," the guard said. "All the way at the other end of the hall."

"Thanks," Stevie said. He walked back to Kelleher. "She's in," he said.

"Was there a guard?"

Stevie nodded. "Yup. But there's never been a guard born she can't talk her way past."

Kelleher laughed. "Come on, we've got work to do."

The two of them made their way back down the maze of hallways until they came to a large double door on the left. "I'll wait to make sure you get in," Kelleher said. There were two security guards on this door. People were whizzing past them and, surprisingly, they didn't seem to be checking badges that carefully. Kelleher noticed too. "I'm guessing they're more concerned about people going out than in right now," he said. "Get going."

Stevie squared his shoulders, then tried to relax so he could look casual. He waited to let a couple of people he assumed were players get in front of him and then walked up to the doors, giving one guard a nod and a quick "Hey." The guard didn't even look at him, which was fortunate because if he had he might have seen how terrified Stevie was. Worse, he might've heard his heart pounding. Stevie walked inside and stopped to look around. There were tables and couches all over the vast room and people sitting or lying everywhere. Most wore tennis clothes, but some were dressed more formally. There were several offices that ran along the inside wall of the lounge, which all had large windows, so Stevie could see inside. In one of them, Kelleher's friend Arlen Kantarian was seated behind the desk, surrounded by at least fifteen people who had crowded into the room.

Rather than get caught staring, Stevie kept walking. He could smell food coming from the far end of the room and saw that there was a dining area with a number of people waiting in line at a buffet. He heard an announcement over the PA system: "Ms. Hetherington and Ms. Russell, please report to court 14. Ms. Hetherington and Ms. Russell, court 14, please."

He hadn't really given any thought as to whether matches were still being played, but realized that not only was the tournament still going on, the people in this room might not even be aware yet that Symanova was missing. He looked at his watch. It was 2:20. He remembered that the players had been due on court at two o'clock, so it had only been twenty minutes since she had disappeared.

If anyone in the lounge cared that he was there, they didn't show it. People were chattering away in different languages, and when Stevie walked by, even if he looked right at them, they looked either past him or through him. He realized that to these people he was completely invisible. Which, for the moment, was a good thing.

There was an empty table in the dining area, and Stevie thought maybe he could sit down there and pick up conversations around him. He took a bottle of water from a cooler and sat at the table sipping from it, trying to look as if he belonged. He realized that he had forgotten to follow Kelleher's instructions to take off his media credential once inside, but he was afraid if he took it off at that moment it would look suspicious. Then again, it was possible that even if he took off all his clothes no one would notice. He slipped the credential off, hoping no one would see him do it.

But someone did.

"Are you going undercover?" a voice said behind him.

Stevie froze, convinced he was about to get thrown out. He turned and saw Evelyn Rubin holding a tray of food, standing next to him. "Mind if I join you?" she said.

"Oh, um, of course, I mean, no, not at all," he said, stumbling all over himself because of nerves and because of her smile.

She sat down and unloaded her tray. Her lunch consisted of a salad, some kind of green vegetable, and two bottles of Gatorade.

"Is that all you're eating?" he said.

"I save myself for dinner," she said. "The Gatorade fills me up and I'm a little dehydrated from the heat and a long shower."

He was struck again by how pretty she was. Her hair was still wet from her shower and she had it tied back, but her eyes were almost mesmerizing. She took a couple of quick bites of her salad, put her fork down, looked around to make sure no one was listening, and leaned closer to Stevie.

"Did you hear what's going on?" she said in a whisper just loud enough for Stevie to hear.

Stevie looked around too, then remembered that he was invisible. "You mean about Symanova?" he said.

She nodded. "I was just getting out of the shower when Joanne Walsh's agent came in looking for Arlen Kantarian's assistant, who was making sure that all the other under-eighteen girls were okay and letting us know they were going to keep playing matches," she said. "So as soon as this agent came in, the assistant—I think her name is Cindy—

said, 'Jeannie, what are you doing in here? You know agents can't come in this locker room.'

"Well, Jeannie didn't really want to hear that. She started screaming at her, demanding to know where Arlen was and how come Symanova hasn't been defaulted for not showing up for the match.

"So Cindy started *pushing* the agent toward the door, saying, 'We aren't going to discuss it here, Jeannie. Arlen's in a meeting about it right now.'

"Jeannie starts screaming, 'Meeting, *meeting*, what's to meet about? What are you guys hiding? Are you protecting that spoiled little Russian brat? Rules are rules, Cindy, and Arlen knows that!'

"At which point Cindy, who is a lot bigger than Jeannie, practically picked her up and carried her out the door. The last thing I heard her say was, 'Will you just shut up, we've got a crisis here.' "

Stevie was trying to comprehend the idea of an agent demanding a default because her client's opponent had vanished, when he noticed Rubin looking over his shoulder. He turned and noticed a TV set that was behind them. On the screen were the words "Symanova update."

"Someone turn the sound up," he heard a player at a nearby table say. Magically, the sound came up as a sober-looking Michael Barkann came on camera. This wasn't the Barkann Stevie was used to seeing on *Daily News Live*. The room was suddenly quiet as Barkann's voice became audible: ". . . we will of course keep you updated, but, to repeat, tournament officials say they are in touch with Symanova's agents, trying to determine exactly what happened that kept her from reaching the court for her first-round match with Joanne Walsh this afternoon. They have told us that as far as they know, Symanova is not injured and there is no health issue involved. Elise Burgin is standing by right now with Hughes Norwood, who represents Symanova for the Stars Management Group. Elise?"

Barkann disappeared and was replaced on the screen by Elise Burgin, who had once been a top doubles player. Burgin was short and had dark hair and was, Stevie guessed, in her mid-thirties. The man standing next to her looked to Stevie as if he was about the same age as his dad. He wore wire-rimmed glasses and a scowl.

"The Master of Disaster," Rubin hissed as Norwood came on-screen.

"They call him that?" Stevie said.

"Uh-huh. Because dealing with him in a negotiation is a disaster and he thinks he's master of the tennis universe. Everyone hates him—except his clients."

Burgin was attempting to ask the Master of Disaster where Nadia Symanova was.

"I can't discuss that at this time," Norwood said.

"Is she going to play in the tournament?" Burgin asked.

"I can't discuss that at this time."

Burgin began to look a bit exasperated.

"Can you give us some idea—*any* idea—why she didn't show up on court as scheduled today?"

"I can't discuss that at this time."

This time Burgin paused for a moment as if deciding what to ask next.

"Just to save time, Mr. Norwood, what *can* you discuss?"

Norwood almost smiled.

"I can tell you that my first concern and SMG's first concern, as always, is the welfare of our client. That's the way we have always conducted business."

"Can you tell us if your client's welfare is in jeopardy at this moment?" Burgin asked.

"I can't discuss that."

Burgin sighed and turned back to the camera. "Michael," she said, "sorry to have wasted your time."

Stevie was surprised by that bit of honesty. Barkann was shaking his head when he came back on camera. "Well, Elise, you tried," he said. "We're now told that the USTA has scheduled a press conference for three-thirty to update everyone on the situation. We will cover that for you live. In the meantime, let's go back to the stadium court and Bill Macatee and John McEnroe."

As magically as the sound had come up, it was turned down.

"Did you see her before she went on court?" Stevie asked Rubin, realizing that Symanova would have been in her locker room.

"Just for a minute," Rubin said. "I came back in and she was getting ready to go out. I wished her luck and she said to me, 'I'm playing Joanne Walsh. She's the one who needs luck.' She's always like that, very confident."

"Sounds arrogant to me."

"Maybe, but she's sixth in the world at age sixteen. She was smiling when she said it."

"You say anything else to her?"

Rubin shook her head. "Didn't get a chance to. The guard came over and told her that Mr. Norwood was waiting outside the door to talk to her and she jumped up and left. That's when I went in and took my shower."

Stevie saw Brendan Gibson walking through the room in their direction. His usual smile was missing as he sat down. He didn't even greet Stevie or Evelyn. "This is just awful," he said. "How can the USTA let someone just grab a player en route to play a match?"

"So you're convinced she was kidnapped?" Stevie said.

Gibson nodded. "It's already being reported on CNN, MSNBC, and Fox News. The only one not reporting it that way is USA Network and that's because they don't want the USTA to be upset with them the next time they renegotiate their contract."

"How can they keep playing with this going on?" Stevie asked.

"Because if they stop playing, it would cost them millions of dollars," Gibson said.

Rubin frowned. "Well, I really hope she's okay," she said. "I want to play her in the third round—if I can get there."

Stevie had forgotten that Rubin and Symanova might meet in the third round. "But kidnapping," Stevie said. "Does it make you nervous?"

Rubin thought a moment, then shook her head. "She's

beautiful and famous and wealthy. I'm not even close to her in those categories. If I disappeared, Brendan would notice and that would be about it."

"I'd notice," Stevie said—too quickly, he thought as soon as the words were out of his mouth.

"You're sweet," she said. He felt himself redden.

Brendan Gibson brought him back to planet Earth. "I'd like you to play her too," he said to Rubin. "Right now, though, the issue isn't whether she'll play tennis this week, but whether she's still alive."

The thought that Nadia Symanova might be dead had never occurred to Stevie. Now he stopped for a moment to consider it. No, it couldn't be possible. Then he had another thought: kidnapping a player in front of thousands of witnesses wasn't possible either.

And yet, it had just happened.

✗ ✗ ✗

Stevie realized that it had been more than thirty minutes since he had left Kelleher. He asked Rubin and Gibson what their plans were for the rest of the day. "We're getting out of here," Gibson said. "They weren't letting anyone leave for a little while, but now they're letting player courtesy cars through. I'm going to see Evelyn back to her hotel. I'm assuming you and Susan Carol will stick around for the press conference?"

"Oh yeah," Stevie said. He had no idea what the rest of the day would hold, but he certainly wasn't leaving the premises unless someone told him he had to. He said goodbye to Rubin and Gibson and picked his way back to the double doors. When he walked outside, he saw Hughes Norwood standing in a corner, bathed in TV lights, surrounded by a gaggle of reporters. Stevie listened for a moment until he realized Norwood was giving the same nonanswers he had given Burgin. He followed the signs back to the media center, where he found Kelleher and Susan Carol sitting at a table in the media dining area. Both of them had plates of food in front of them.

"Where've you been?" Kelleher said. "I was about to walk down and look for you, but Susan Carol said you were probably in there breaking the story."

Stevie shook his head. "Nothing like that," he said. "But I was talking to Evelyn Rubin and Susan Carol's uncle."

"They know anything?" Kelleher said.

"Not much," Stevie said. "I guess it's all over TV that Symanova was kidnapped. Evelyn said she talked to her just before she left to go to the court."

"Did she say anything?" Susan Carol asked.

"Only that she didn't think she'd have much trouble with Joanne Walsh. Then she went outside for a minute to talk to that agent of hers."

Kelleher gave Stevie a look. "She was talking to Norwood just before she left to go play?"

"That's what Evelyn said. Why? Does it mean anything?"

"Probably not. But agents don't usually mess with their players just before a match. I can't imagine what Norwood would need to talk about right at that moment."

"Well, I wouldn't waste your time asking him," Stevie said.

Kelleher laughed. "The Master himself? You got that right. But there may be some other people we can ask. Everyone in that business loves to gossip."

"Did you guys find anything out?" Stevie asked.

Susan Carol shook her head. "Not much," she answered. "When I walked in, everyone was talking about Walsh's agent. I must have just missed a big scene. Then they were all wondering how long the USTA could wait before they default Symanova."

"What about the guys?" Stevie asked Kelleher.

Kelleher shook his head. "Nothing going on in there," he said. "The main question was if this meant the schedule on Armstrong would be moved up for the rest of the day. It was pretty shocking, really."

Stevie realized he was starving and headed for the grill only to learn that a hamburger cost $8.50. He was going to run out of money very quickly. He was about halfway through his burger when Bud Collins burst in the door and pulled up a chair. He was out of breath and clearly excited.

"I just talked to the kid's father," he said. "He says he knows what happened."

"So she wasn't kidnapped?" Kelleher said.

"Oh, she was kidnapped, all right," Collins said. "But not by your everyday, 'send us a few bucks' kidnappers."

"Who, then?" Susan Carol asked.

"The SVR," Collins said. "That's the Russian CIA, or in the old Soviet days, it would have been the KGB. Misha is sure they have his daughter."

6: THE SEARCH

THE WAY Bud Collins told the story, he had spotted Symanova's parents in the stands shortly after Stevie, Susan Carol, and Kelleher had left. "I went down to talk to them and they were in a state of panic. Misha kept saying, 'I knew they would do something.' Security came to walk the parents out of the stadium. I finally asked Misha who 'they' were when he calmed down a little. By then, we were walking with security. They tried to shoo me away, but Misha told them I was his friend. I've known him since the kid was twelve. So I walked back with him and his wife with about six security guards around us. He told me that Nadia is going to apply for American citizenship. The Russians don't want that, *really* don't want that. They don't care if their players live here as long as they represent Russia in the Olympics and the Federation Cup and have 'Russia' after their names when they play. But if this girl becomes an American citizen and plays for the U.S., they will be extremely upset."

"Upset, I understand," Kelleher said. "But kidnapping? Isn't that a bit of an overreaction?"

Collins shrugged. "Remember, they think this kid is going to be bigger than Kournikova and Sharapova. She's got the game and the looks and she's going to start winning majors very soon. Maybe at this tournament. She becomes an American, the Russians consider that a humiliation."

"I thought the Cold War was over," Susan Carol said. "Isn't this more like what would have happened before the Soviet Union split up?"

"Things aren't all that different," Collins said. "I was there last summer. It isn't so much communist anymore, but they still regard us as a major rival—especially when it comes to sports."

"Duke and North Carolina are rivals," Stevie said. "This goes beyond a rivalry."

"True," Collins said. "But Misha is convinced that's what this is about. He's not one of these crazy tennis fathers—he's a pretty good guy. He thinks they'll release her as soon as he agrees not to put in the papers for citizenship."

"But what's to stop them from applying later—after they set her free?" Susan Carol said.

"I asked him that," Collins said. "He almost laughed at

me, and said, 'They've made their point, Bud. They can get to her anytime, anyplace. If we try again, they will come after us again.'"

"Does that mean he's going to give in?" Kelleher said.

"Don't know," Collins said. "I was about to ask him his next step when we got to the players' lounge and about five SMG operatives showed up and spirited him away. Norwood stopped long enough to poke his finger at me and say, 'Anything he said to you is off the record.'"

"What'd you say to that?" Stevie asked.

"I told him the day I took orders from him would be the same day he was caught in a truth."

Kelleher pursed his lips. "The question is, if we *do* write it, are we endangering Nadia?"

"True," Collins said. "We should try to talk to him again."

The PA was making pinging noises to indicate an announcement was about to be made. Stevie looked at his watch. It was exactly three-thirty.

"The USTA press conference will begin in three minutes," the voice on the PA said. "Three minutes in the main interview room."

"We better get in there," Kelleher said. "It's bound to be a zoo."

He wasn't exaggerating. At the door to the interview room, a security guard, a police officer, and a USTA public relations person stood carefully checking credentials.

"Jordan, why do we have to show credentials to get in here when we've already cleared security to get into the media center?" Kelleher asked the PR guy, who seemed a lot more relaxed than most of the people Stevie had met during the day.

Jordan smiled. "Because in the last hour we've had calls from every news network, every tabloid, and every magazine in the world wanting credentials to come on the grounds. Some are too legit to turn down. PBS is sending Charlie Rose. Are we supposed to turn him down? CBS is sending Katie Couric out here because—I swear to God, this is what the producer said—'Katie just interviewed Nadia last week and she's *very* upset about this.' We're giving priority in here to people like you who are actually here to cover the tournament. That's why we're checking credentials."

Kelleher clapped Jordan on the shoulder. "Good answer," he said. "Three times longer than necessary, but a good answer."

"Hey, I'm a lawyer in real life," Jordan said. "What do you expect?"

"Is he really a lawyer?" Susan Carol asked as they found seats in a rapidly filling room.

"Actually, he is," Kelleher said. "He's been volunteering out here for years."

Carillo walked in a few seconds after they had been seated, the cheery smile she had worn earlier nowhere to be found. She slid into an empty seat next to Stevie and leaned over so she could whisper to the group. "I just talked to one of the SMG boys," she said. "He's claiming the Russians did this."

Kelleher nodded. "He probably got that from the father. That's what he told Bud."

"Last I saw Misha, the FBI was taking him someplace," Carillo said.

People were walking onto the podium. Stevie recognized Arlen Kantarian and Hughes Norwood. There was another man in a dark suit, who Stevie immediately guessed was with the FBI, and a fourth man who was wearing a blazer that said USTA on the breast pocket.

"Ladies and gentlemen, if you can settle down, please, we'll get started," Arlen Kantarian said. "As you know, an event has occurred here today that, to be honest, we are still trying to sort out. But to cut right to the heart of the matter, Nadia Symanova disappeared en route to her match to be played in Louis Armstrong Stadium just before two o'clock this afternoon. At this moment, given the circumstances and in the absence of any other theories, we believe it is possible she was kidnapped. Sitting on my far left is Special Agent Bob Campbell from the New York field office of the FBI. Next to him is Hughes Norwood, who, as most of you know, represents Ms. Symanova, and on my right is Dana Loconto, our tournament director. We aren't going to take many questions, because, as I said, we really don't have many answers at this moment, but we will take a few."

As soon as he finished, it sounded as if a hundred people were talking at once. Kantarian looked stunned for a second, then put his hands out, palms down, to ask for quiet. "Folks, we need you to follow our normal procedures in here even though this isn't a normal situation. We've got three people with mikes. Call for a mike and I'll call on you from there."

The noise broke out again, people screaming for mikes. Kantarian finally pointed at a man who was holding one of the mikes.

"Can someone *please* tell us exactly how this happened in broad daylight?"

"I'll take that." It was Loconto, who Stevie noticed had an accent similar to Susan Carol's.

He explained that the security procedures for matches on outside courts varied, depending on who was playing. "The standard is one player, one security guard," he said. "Basically, we're just trying to make sure the players can get through the crowds unimpeded. Most fans, when they see security people coming with a player, get out of the way. With a well-known player, we usually add a second security person. In the case of someone like Symanova, who attracts a lot of attention, we add a third guard. That was the case here—she had three security guards with her."

"To follow up, then, what in the world happened?"

Loconto smiled wanly and looked at Kantarian to see if he should continue. Kantarian nodded. "There was a commotion," Loconto said. "Several people walked across the path of the players, and all the security guards got jostled. It isn't all that unusual for that to happen, especially near the entrance to Armstrong before a big match, when people are bunched up trying to get inside. When the security guys got untangled, they looked around and Symanova was gone."

"Just like that?" It was the same questioner, still holding his mike. No one objected. He was asking the right questions.

Loconto nodded. "No one really knew what had happened. The security people thought perhaps she'd fallen or gotten too far ahead of them. By the time they realized she wasn't anywhere in their vicinity, the crowds appeared to have swallowed her. Her racquet bag was found a few yards from where all this happened, but we haven't found anyone who can remember seeing her drop it."

"Isn't that kind of remarkable?" the reporter with the microphone asked—as if reading Stevie's mind.

"Yes, it is," Loconto said. "This whole day has been remarkable."

Someone on the other side of the room had a mike. "Agent Campbell, is the FBI looking at this as a kidnapping?"

"We aren't looking at it as anything yet, but we have to consider kidnapping a possibility," he said. "We're still in the process of interviewing her family, other players, and"— he nodded at Norwood—"her agents. The NYPD did its best to seal exits and check people leaving as soon as the incident occurred, but in a place this size, if someone is trying to sneak out, they probably can do it—especially if this was a preplanned event."

"Arlen, are you going to stop play?"

It was Collins, violating the rule about being at a microphone. No one seemed to mind.

"No, Bud, we're not," Kantarian said. "We've spoken to the Symanovs and they want play to continue. We're in agreement with the FBI that it doesn't help the investigation to stop play. If the FBI told us it would help, we'd stop, but they don't think it will." He paused and smiled for a moment, which surprised Stevie. "We get criticized by you people quite a lot because it takes us three days to play the first round. This is one time where it helps us. If we can find Nadia in the next forty-eight hours, assuming she's up to it, we can reschedule her first-round match and it will be as if this never happened. That's what we're hoping for."

Someone brought up Joanne Walsh. "We understand she and her agent think the match should have been defaulted."

"I think once Joanne understands the unique circumstances here, she will feel differently," Kantarian said. He stood up, indicating the press conference was over. "We'll keep you informed as we know more."

The babble of voices broke out again, people trying to shout questions. One voice, clearly British, kept asking loudly if anyone knew where "R.J." was and had he been informed.

"Who is R.J.?" Stevie asked.

Susan Carol rolled her eyes. "R.J. is R.J. Tenuto, the lead singer for Boys-in-Demand—they're a kind of teen hip-hop band. He's Symanova's boyfriend."

Stevie knew she was on the cover of a lot of teen magazines but he didn't actually *read* any of them. "How long has this been going on?" he asked, wondering just how out of it he was.

"Oh, not long," Susan Carol said. "At Wimbledon she was with someone else."

"Yeah," Carillo said. "That someone else was Prince Harry's best friend."

Susan Carol nodded. "I know, Sir something. I didn't think he was very cute."

"Me neither," Carillo said. "But then, neither is R.J."

"Yeah, but he can really dance."

"*Enough!*" Kelleher exploded as if reading Stevie's mind. "We need to decide what to do next." He looked at Susan Carol and Stevie. "You guys still up for working on this?"

"Are you kidding?" Stevie said. "Of course we are. Intrigue is our specialty, don't you remember?"

Kelleher nodded. "I was in New Orleans, Stevie. I remember," he said. "But down there, you and Susan Carol were the only ones who knew something was wrong. This is different. One of the most famous athletes in the world has been kidnapped and this place is going to be crawling with every kind of media you can think of until she's found."

"So it's a different challenge," Susan Carol said, smiling.

"I'd say so," Kelleher said. "But if you guys are up for it, we'll see what we can do."

"Isn't this the part where someone tells you to let the FBI do its job?" Carillo said. "If the Russians *are* involved, I don't think you should be putting yourself at risk, much less a couple of thirteen-year-olds."

"I have no intention of putting anyone at risk," Kelleher said. "But there's no harm in asking questions."

A slender woman with wavy brown hair and light blue eyes had walked up during the conversation and was now standing next to Kelleher. She was about Stevie's height and was wearing a white tennis shirt, shorts, and sneakers, almost identical to the outfit Susan Carol was wearing.

"Yeah, but what questions do you want to ask and who are you going to get to talk to you, hotshot?" she said to Kelleher.

A look of delight crossed Kelleher's face. "About time you got here," he said, giving her a hug and a kiss.

"Stevie, Susan Carol—meet my wife, Tamara Mearns."

"I know just who these guys are," Mearns said, smiling to reveal remarkable dimples. "Bobby gave me the blow-by-blow on what you did at the Final Four. I'm glad you're on our side."

"Stevie and I both read your column—I am a huge fan," said Susan Carol.

"Can we focus on the crisis at hand?" Kelleher said. "Hold the lovefest for later."

"Okay, Kelleher, what've you got?" Mearns said.

"We've got a big-time mystery here," Kelleher said. "Bud and Mary have both got to go do TV stuff, so it's the four of us for now. I think you and Susan Carol need to go work the women's locker room. Find out what they're saying in there. By now everyone will be talking about it. When Susan Carol, Stevie, and I skulked around earlier, a lot of people were just finding out."

"The locker room," Mearns said. "Oh, joy."

"I know, I know," Kelleher said. "But it has to be done."

"What are you going to do?" Mearns asked.

"I'm going to talk to Arlen again. By now he's undoubtedly heard what Misha thinks about the SVR. He'll have talked to the FBI too. And I'm sending Stevie to talk to Ross."

Mearns smiled again. "Little Tom? That's a good idea. He may not know anything, but he'll certainly talk."

"Who are we talking about?" Stevie said.

"Tom Ross," Kelleher said. "He's an agent, but in spite of that he's a pretty good guy. He's been in tennis forever. Knows everyone. You tell him you're working with me and he'll tell you what he knows."

"Send Susan Carol with Stevie," Mearns said. "It'll soften Tom up—he's got daughters. One of us in the locker room is enough."

"Good idea," Kelleher said. "Let's get going. We need to find *anyone* who talked to Symanova today or even saw her. Any little bit of information can help."

Stevie looked at Susan Carol to see if any of this was making her nervous. She seemed fine with it all.

"So *we're* going to find Symanova?" he said to Kelleher.

"Find her?" Kelleher said. "Not likely. But find out what happened to her? Yeah, I think we can do that."

7: TOM ROSS

THE GOOD news was that Kelleher was convinced they would find Tom Ross in the players' lounge. At least Stevie knew his way around in there.

"That's his office," Kelleher said as they walked back down the now-familiar hallway. "He likes to call himself the dealmaker. He sits in there most of the day making deals."

"With who?"

"With whom!" Susan Carol corrected.

"Everyone in tennis," Kelleher said. "Clothing company reps, shoe company reps, tournament directors . . ."

"Tournament directors?" Stevie asked. "What kind of deals would he make with tournament directors?"

"To pay his players under the table to play in their tournaments," Kelleher said.

Stevie was about to ask if he was serious but saw he was by the look on his face. They reached the hallway intersection where Kelleher and his wife had to go in one direction to the locker rooms while Stevie and Susan Carol went in another to the lounge. "Are you guys okay on your own?" Tamara asked.

Kelleher laughed in response. "These two? Are you kidding? They can handle themselves better than we can."

Stevie wasn't sure that was the case, but he was glad Mearns had suggested that he and Susan Carol stick together. Knowing her ability to charm people, he would feel a lot more confident going back into that lounge with Susan Carol.

"Should we make a plan to meet at some time?" Susan Carol asked.

Kelleher looked at his watch. "It's four-fifteen," he said. "Let's all be back in the media center no later than five-thirty. Got your phones turned on?"

"I do," Susan Carol said, and Stevie nodded.

"Anything happens or you need help, call me or Tamara," he said.

They quickly exchanged numbers with Tamara and then it was time to go.

"Okay, then," Kelleher said. "Good luck, guys."

Since Stevie knew the way, he led Susan Carol to the lounge. Kelleher had told them to look for "a slightly overweight Ken doll." He wasn't absolutely certain what a Ken doll looked like, but Susan Carol seemed to know exactly what that meant. "If you don't see him, just ask people," Kelleher said. "Everyone in there will know him."

The lounge was absolutely packed when they walked in, more crowded than when Stevie had been there earlier. Every few seconds, it seemed, the PA was calling another match. "Mr. Nocera and Mr. Johansson, please report to security to be escorted to Louis Armstrong" was one announcement.

"I wonder if that's the way they were calling people before this happened," Susan Carol said.

"You mean 'report to security'?" Stevie said. "It wasn't when I was in here earlier."

They made their way through the lounge, finding a staircase Stevie hadn't seen before and going up it to a second floor that was just about as crowded as the first. If Ross was on either level, they didn't spot him. "None of these guys looks like a Ken doll to you?" Stevie said.

Susan Carol shook her head. "Not even close. We better start asking people."

They looked around until Susan Carol spotted a guy in a suit on a cell phone. He reeked of being an agent. When he saw her walking toward him, a smile crossed his face and he put down the phone. "Can I help you with something, young lady?"

"I hope so," Susan Carol said. "Do you happen to know Tom Ross?"

The suit grunted. "I was just with him a few minutes ago. He was trying to convince me to give one of his players a wild card to my tournament."

So, Stevie thought, he's a tournament director, not an agent. They all looked the same, apparently.

"What's a wild card?" Susan Carol asked.

The tournament director smiled at her, the way you smile at someone who doesn't know something everyone knows. He eyed her credential. "Up-and-coming young reporter, huh?" he said. "Well, you should know this, then. Every tennis tournament has several spots that are saved for players who aren't ranked highly enough to be automatically entered. They're called wild cards because the tournament director—in San Jose, that would be me—gets to pick whomever they want. It can be a young player, an old player, or just someone I like. If a player doesn't have a high enough ranking to get in and doesn't get a wild card, they have to play in a qualifier to get into the tournament. One way agents impress young players is by telling them they can get them wild cards and save them from playing qualifiers all the time. Tom was pitching me on one of their young players."

"Will you take him?" Susan Carol asked, even though it was irrelevant.

"Doubt it," the tournament director said. "*Unless* Ross can deliver one of his name guys as part of a package deal. Then I might do it."

Stevie was relieved when Susan Carol didn't ask any more questions on the subject of wild cards. "Do you know where Mr. Ross might be?" she asked.

The tournament director laughed. "I know *exactly* where he is. They just called Nick Nocera onto the Armstrong court. He'll be over there babysitting. Unless, of course, someone kidnapped Nocera en route to the match."

Apparently the tournament director thought that was funny. "Just a little joke," he said, perhaps noting the fact that neither of his listeners was doubled over with laughter. He reached into his pocket and took out a card and handed it to Susan Carol. "If you ever come to San Jose"—he peered a little more closely at Susan Carol's credential— "Ms. Anderson, you call me. Come cover our tournament if you want. You can bring your young friend." He nodded at Stevie.

"Actually, we're the same age," Susan Carol said.

The tournament director stared in disbelief for a second, then recovered and smiled again. "Well, good luck finding Tom," he said. "I'm sure he'll be glad to tell you everything you never wanted to know about Nick Nocera."

He turned and walked away. Susan Carol handed the card to Stevie: RON GRINKOFF—TOURNAMENT DIRECTOR, DUNKIN' DONUTS OPEN. "Hmm," Stevie said. "Might be worth going. Free doughnuts every day in the pressroom, I'm sure."

"I think I can skip it," she said. "Come on, let's get back over to Armstrong and see if we can find Tom Ross."

"That's a big place," he said.

"My guess is there won't be all that many people watching Nick Nocera and Thomas Johansson, especially this close to dinnertime," she said.

"Yeah, and probably not many in suits," Stevie said, remembering what Brendan Gibson had said about the agent's uniform.

They made their way out of the lounge and followed signs that led them out of the catacombs of the main stadium back onto the main plaza. It was crowded. A lot of people were heading for the exits with the day program beginning to wind down. The area that had been blocked off earlier when they had left Armstrong after Symanova's disappearance had been reopened. They traced their path back under the stands and decided to go in at one of the regular public entrances to the seating area. Stevie liked that idea, if only because he had no desire to encounter Max Shapiro again without Collins along to protect them. They walked up the ramp and found a rope across the entranceway.

"You have to wait here until the changeover," an usher told them quietly.

Susan Carol had been right about the crowd. There couldn't have been more than three or four hundred people, and in a stadium that seated ten thousand, the crowd seemed even smaller. Stevie looked up at the big scoreboard at the far end of the stadium. It was 5–all in the first set, Nocera serving at 30–all. Since the players changed ends every two games beginning after the first game of each set, they would be changing at the end of this game. Stevie watched Nocera as he prepared to serve. He had long dark hair and wore a sleeveless shirt, no doubt to show off his impressive arms. He tossed the ball high in the air and served a bullet that cracked the net cord. The scoreboard said the serve had been traveling 139 miles per hour. Impressive, but it didn't matter. It was still a fault. Nocera twisted in a second serve and Johansson, going for a passing shot as Nocera tried to come in, pushed a backhand wide. Nocera got two new balls from a ball boy, pocketed one, tugged at his racquet strings, and served again. This time, the serve cleared the net and one-hopped to the fence, untouched by a lunging Johansson. An ace.

"Game Nocera," the umpire said. "He leads, 6–5."

A cheer rose from the right corner of the stadium and Stevie saw about a half-dozen people in the front row standing to cheer Nocera on. The usher had moved the rope and Susan Carol immediately started walking in that direction. "I think I see him," she said.

They walked to a section of seats near the baseline that was virtually empty. Since there were so few people in the stands, the ushers really didn't care where anyone sat. Behind the Nocera cheerleaders, Stevie saw a man in a suit, sitting with his legs crossed. He had sandy hair and a large briefcase on his lap. He looked, Stevie guessed, like a slightly overweight Ken doll. Susan Carol got to him first. "Mr. Ross?" she said.

Ross looked up, clearly surprised to be recognized. "Hi," he said. "How do you know me?"

"I'm Susan Carol Anderson," she said. "This is Steve Thomas. Bobby Kelleher sent us to talk to you."

"Me?" Ross said. "Kelleher sent you to talk to me?"

Stevie heard the umpire say, 'Time,' and saw the players get out of their seats and head back onto the court.

"Grab a seat," Ross said. "We can talk as soon as the set's over. Either Nick will break here or it will go to a tiebreak."

Down 40–30, Nocera crushed a perfect forehand crosscourt to tie the game at deuce. Neither player seemed able to win two straight points to win the game. Finally, on the fifth deuce, Johansson served a winner and then watched Nocera hit a forehand long on the next point, giving him the game and a 6–6 tie in the set. That meant a tiebreak, and Stevie was squirming throughout, wanting it to be over. Ross kept adjusting and readjusting his tie, and after every point, he would lean forward and say something to the group in front of them: "I love it when he goes down the line."

Or: "Johansson can't volley—he should drop-shot him once in a while."

Nocera seemed to read his agent's mind. Leading six points to five, meaning he had set point, he stood at the baseline, slugging it out with Johansson. Finally, when it seemed the point might never end, he flicked a delicate forehand that just cleared the net. Johansson took one step toward it, then stopped, knowing he couldn't get to the ball.

"Game and first set Nocera," the umpire said.

"*Yes,*" Ross said, pumping a fist. The most enthusiastic member of Nocera's cheering squad was a heavily made-up woman who was wearing a tight-fitting halter top and very short shorts.

"Who do you think *she* is?" Stevie whispered to Susan Carol.

"I'm betting girlfriend," Susan Carol whispered back.

"Listen, guys," Ross said to the group. "I have to go talk to these two reporters for five minutes. I'll be back at the next changeover."

One of the men eyed Ross suspiciously. "Not talking

about another client, are you, Tom?" he said. "You wouldn't walk out on Nicky to do that, would you?"

"No, Mr. Nocera, I certainly wouldn't," Ross said. "Actually, they want to talk about Nick, right, guys?"

Susan Carol jumped in. "Oh, absolutely," she said. "I'm writing about unsung stars for my newspaper."

That seemed to satisfy everyone—except perhaps the girlfriend, who didn't even crack a smile.

"Be right back," Ross said, and he bounded up the steps toward the exit, with Stevie and Susan Carol following. Once they were under the stands, he stopped and loosened his tie.

"Okay," he said. "I hope this is important, because Mr. Nocera probably wants to kill me right now."

"For missing two games?" Stevie said.

"Oh yeah," Ross said. "Long story. Tara's actually worse."

"Who's Tara?" Susan Carol asked.

Ross looked surprised. "You didn't recognize Tara Beauregard? I thought every teenager knew her. She's in that show on the CW, what's it called, *Uncovered*? She plays a teenage hooker."

"A hooker?" Stevie said.

"A teenager?" Susan Carol said. "That woman plays a teenager? You're kidding, right?"

Ross looked nervously at his watch. "Tell me what you guys need so I can get back."

Susan Carol nodded. "We want to know what you've heard about the Symanova kidnapping."

Ross suddenly began looking in all directions as if afraid someone might be listening. There wasn't anyone in sight. "Why would I know anything about that?" he said. "She's not my client."

Susan Carol nodded. "We know. But Bobby says you know every rumor there is in tennis. He wants to know what you've heard."

Ross looked around again. Stevie was beginning to think there were invisible people watching them.

"Okay, okay," he said, pulling on his tie again. "All I know is this. The SMG people are telling everyone the Russians did it and that the father is hysterical that they're going to do something awful if he doesn't agree not to go through with the citizenship thing."

"We already know that," Stevie said, trying not to sound impatient.

From the court they heard the umpire say, "Game Johansson."

Ross twitched again. "Oh my God," he said. "I really need to get back in there. Look, I'm sure you know that because that's the big talk in the lounge. But here's what's strange: the SMG people *never* share information. Hughes Norwood usually won't tell you the time. Now they're all running around in circles saying, 'It's the SVR, it's the SVR.' It just isn't the way they do business."

"So what do you think is up?" Susan Carol asked.

Ross's eyes were darting all over the place now. "I'm not sure. But here's the one thing I'm convinced of, and I'm not the only one who thinks this: if SMG says it's the SVR, they're probably the only people you can be sure *didn't* do it."

Stevie and Susan Carol looked at each other.

"Okay, then who?"

Ross shook his head. "That I don't know. But if I was trying to figure it out, the first thing I'd do is look at a draw sheet."

"Why?" they both asked.

"Someone benefits if Symanova is gone. They can only wait two days before they have to default her and move on with the tournament. Most people think she should have been defaulted already. I'd sure like to know which player that helps the most."

"Joanne Walsh?" Stevie said.

"No," Ross said firmly. "She wins one match, it's worth a few thousand dollars to her. But she isn't going any further than that. Look a round or two—or more—down the road. Symanova is ready to win. She's been the best player all summer. Someone is afraid of her. If you figure out who it is, I think you figure out who kidnapped her."

"You mean a player had her kidnapped?" Susan Carol said.

"I doubt it," Ross said as the umpire's voice told them it was now 2–0 Johansson in the second set. "Oh God, Mr. Nocera's going to blame me because Nick got broken. No, not a player, probably. An agent maybe. A clothing company rep with a big contract at stake if his player wins here. Even a national federation. It could be anyone."

"Do you represent any women in contention here?" Stevie asked.

Ross actually smiled. "I only rep men," he said. "I have an alibi."

"You might be the only one," Susan Carol said.

"Too true," he said.

"Game Johansson," they heard from inside. "He leads 3–0."

"Oh my God!" Ross screamed. "I'm fired. Gotta go."

He bolted back to the court.

Stevie looked at Susan Carol. "Did that help us?" he asked.

She smiled. "Only if being totally confused helps," she said. "Come on. I left my draw sheet in the media center. Let's go find another one."

8: YOU CANNOT BE SERIOUS

STEVIE AND Susan Carol walked back out into the plaza, which was now half-empty. Someone with a megaphone was urging everyone to exit to the right and reminding them that once they left the grounds they would not be allowed back unless they had tickets for the evening session.

They found a stack of draw sheets next to a stand where someone was trying to sell programs. Stevie couldn't help but notice the price: fifteen dollars. Remarkably, the draw sheets were free. Susan Carol picked one up and said, "Let's go sit at a table in the food court. It's not very busy right now."

She was right. The afternoon crowd was leaving and the evening crowd hadn't been let in yet since there were still afternoon matches being completed. As soon as they sat down, Stevie was almost overwhelmed by the smell of hamburgers being grilled a few yards away from them. "I'm starving," he said. "I'm getting a hamburger."

"You just ate one a couple of hours ago."

"I know. My mother says it's a thirteen-year-old-boy thing. I get hungry very quickly. You want anything?"

"Bottle of water?" she said.

He walked over to a counter and asked for a hamburger and two bottles of water. All around him were other counters offering food. Stevie noticed a sushi bar, a place selling lobster and shrimp sandwiches, and another counter offering cookies and ice cream. The man he had ordered from nodded at him and said, "That'll be eighteen dollars."

Stevie was stunned. "Eighteen dollars for a hamburger and two waters?" he asked.

The man shrugged. "Yup," he said. "That's all it is. Nine dollars for the burger and four-fifty a pop for the waters."

"Hang on," Stevie said. "I had a hamburger in the media dining room a while ago and it was only eight-fifty." He realized as soon as he said it how ridiculous it sounded to say that a hamburger was "only eight-fifty."

"I guess they give the media a discount," the guy said. "You want the food or not?"

"I want it," Stevie said, digging into his pocket for the money. The man gave him a tray to carry everything on for no extra charge. Stevie walked back to Susan Carol, who was intently studying the draw sheet, and handed her her water. "Drink it all," he said. "It costs about fifty cents a sip."

"Welcome to New York," she said with a laugh.

"You find anything?" he asked, sitting down and digging in to the hamburger, which, regardless of price, was delicious.

"Don't know," she said. "She's supposed to play the winner of a match between two nonranked players in the second round, and then if your new girlfriend Evelyn Rubin wins her next match, she could play Symanova in the third round."

"You think your uncle Brendan kidnapped Symanova?" Stevie said.

"Oh sure, very likely. She's probably back at Uncle Brendan's apartment right now. It gets more interesting later in the tournament. She could play Serena Williams in the fourth round. I doubt the Williamses are all that concerned with Symanova since they're already making millions in endorsements and are about as famous as you can get."

"Yeah," Stevie said. "Once you've got your own reality show, what's left to accomplish in life?"

She gave him a look but nodded in agreement. "Have you ever seen it?" she asked.

"If a reality show ever appeared on a TV in our house, I think my father would blow up the set," Stevie said. "He says reality shows are proof that our country is in deep trouble."

"There's more proof than that," Susan Carol said. "Back to the draw. She's a long way from it, but she could play Elena Makarova in the quarters."

Stevie knew the name. "Another Russian," he said. "Another *young* Russian."

Susan Carol nodded. "She's two years older than Symanova, but she was a late bloomer. I remember reading that some people think she's a better player but not as pretty, so Nadia gets all the magazine covers. Makarova made the final in Paris this year."

"Hmmm." Stevie was looking at the side of the draw sheet where the seedings were listed. Makarova was the number three seed on the women's side. "Makarova's seeded higher than Symanova."

"And yet receives only a fraction of the attention. And, unlike Symanova, she and her family still live in Russia. Of course, if that's a factor, it could bring the SVR back into play. It makes sense they would want to see Makarova do better than Symanova, even if she wasn't filing for citizenship."

"How old was Symanova when her family moved to California?"

"I think eleven. Might have been ten. It was young enough that she speaks English with almost no accent."

"How's Makarova's English?"

"Good question. I'm not sure I've ever heard her talk. I think we need to find out more about her."

"More about who?" a voice said from behind Stevie.

He turned and saw Evelyn Rubin standing behind him with that spectacular smile on her face. He certainly wasn't unhappy to see her, but he was surprised that she kept turning up.

Susan Carol seemed to read his mind. "Hey, Evelyn, how are you?" she said. "Stevie said he ran into you in the players' lounge and that you and Uncle Brendan were getting ready to head out. Are you stalking my friend?"

Evelyn Rubin laughed. "Well, he *is* awfully cute," she said. "Do you guys mind if I join you?"

Stevie knew his face had turned bright red. He could tell both girls were getting quite a kick out of his obvious embarrassment.

Evelyn sat down next to Stevie. "Brendan didn't realize I have to play doubles tonight," she said. "I never left. But if I spent one more minute in that players' lounge, I thought I'd lose my mind. So I decided to go for a walk."

"What's so bad about the players' lounge?" Susan Carol said.

"Too crowded. Too many people who look bored out of their minds. Too noisy to read a book." She held up a copy of *Wuthering Heights*. "Summer reading for school. I've been traveling so much, I never got a chance to read this and school starts next week. I thought I'd sit out here and read, until I saw you guys."

"Why *does* everyone look so bored in there?" Stevie said, remembering all the blank looks he had encountered.

"They *are* bored. They have to show up way before their matches start in case there's a short match or a default or"— she paused and smiled—"a kidnapping." She made sure that got a laugh before continuing. "Most of them are high school dropouts who don't know about anything but tennis. So if they aren't playing or practicing, there's really not anything for them to do except watch television or play a video game. But the tournament's always on in the lounge and tennis players almost never watch tennis—it makes them nervous—so they just sit around looking bored."

"Doesn't sound like much of a life, does it?" Susan Carol said.

"It isn't. I remember reading in a book about the tour one time that out of all the players in the French Open one year, *two* had visited the Louvre—*ever*. Can you imagine going to Paris *once* and not going to the Louvre? These guys see three things when they travel: airports, hotels, and a tennis court. Maybe an occasional restaurant. That's it. If I ever play in the French, the first place I'm going is the Louvre."

Stevie wasn't exactly a museum aficionado, the forced trips to the New York museums aside. But he *did* know what the Louvre was, if only because he knew the *Mona Lisa* was there.

"Don't get me wrong, I love tennis," Rubin continued. "But I don't want it to be the only thing I love. Anyway, enough about me—what were you guys talking about before I interrupted?"

"Elena Makarova," Susan Carol said. "Do you know her at all?"

Rubin rolled her eyes. "You might say that. I played her in San Diego a few weeks ago. She drilled me, one and one."

Stevie knew in tennis lingo that meant Makarova had won the match 6–1, 6–1—which *was* a drilling.

"Did you talk to her at all?" Susan Carol asked.

"Not really. She doesn't speak much English. She was nice, though. After the match, she said, 'You were just on lucky today.' Which I think meant I was *unlucky*. I was *unlucky*—that I had to play her. She's really good. My ground strokes are pretty good, but hers are better. And her serve is almost impossible to break—I think she served a ball one hundred thirty-eight miles per hour this summer. She's strong. Why do you want to know about her?"

"We were just looking over the draw," Susan Carol said. "You could play her in the quarters."

Stevie knew from the answer that Susan Carol didn't want to share too much with Rubin, whose eyes went wide when Susan Carol mentioned the quarters.

"I'm a *long* way from the quarters," she said. "Lisa Raymond next round is no walkover and then, assuming she's okay, I'd play Symanova. And even if something *does* happen with Symanova or if I somehow beat her, there'd be the little matter of Serena Williams."

If nothing else, she knew what her draw was off the top of her head. Stevie guessed most players would. "You hear anything new about Symanova?" Susan Carol asked.

Rubin shook her head. "No, not really. Just the same SVR rumor. Someone *did* say that the USTA told Joanne Walsh's people they would wait until Thursday if they had to, which I guess made them go crazy again."

"Thursday?" Stevie said. "Isn't the first round supposed to be over by Wednesday?"

"Yeah. But they could play Thursday morning and then the winner would play a second-round match at night on Friday. That would give her plenty of rest. They want her in this tournament by hook or by crook."

"And the question is," Susan Carol said, "who are the crooks trying to give her the hook?"

It was a clever line, Stevie thought. But there wasn't a hint of a smile on her face when she said it.

✗ ✗ ✗

It was after six o'clock when they got back to the media center. Kelleher was frowning when they walked in. "I was just about to call you guys," he said. "Where've you been?"

"Lost track of the time," Susan Carol said. "You guys hear anything?"

"A little," Kelleher said. "Arlen told me they're not going to default her before Thursday. Tamara heard something about some of the women threatening a boycott or something if they do that."

"Very sympathetic of them, huh?" said Bud Collins, who had joined the conversation just as Kelleher started talking.

"Yeah, well, we know how selfless tennis players are, don't we?" Kelleher said. "Survival of the fittest out here. Even doubles partners don't get along half the time. Bud, the SVR story seems to be everywhere. Does that surprise you at all?"

"It does," Collins said. "But Misha was so hyper, maybe he's just telling people."

"Or maybe that's not the real story," Susan Carol said.

They both looked at her quizzically. She and Stevie filled Kelleher and Collins in on what Ross had said and what they had gleaned from studying the draw. "That could just be agent talk," Kelleher said. "But at this point, we probably need to check everything out—which, Susan Carol, means we probably need to check not only on Makarova, but also on your uncle—no offense. Bud, who is Makarova's agent?"

"You know, that's a good question. I have no idea. But I'm sure we can find out."

He walked down the aisle, yelling something that sounded like Russian. "He's going to ask the Russian media guys," Kelleher said.

Tamara Mearns walked up. "Bobby, are we still going into town to meet the Mayers for dinner, or are we going to cancel?"

Kelleher shook his head. "I don't know about you, but I still have to write."

"Oh gosh," Susan Carol said. "So do I. I completely forgot to check in with the newspaper. I'm not close to done either."

"I'll tell them another night." Tamara sighed. "This has already been a long tournament."

Stevie looked at Kelleher. "Is there anything you want me to write?" he asked.

"You got any good notes?" he said.

"I could write about Evelyn Rubin."

"Mmm-hmm," Susan Carol said. "She thinks Stevie's cute."

He was turning red again. "Scarlett . . . ," he said.

"Okay, okay," Susan Carol said. "We can fight later. I have to figure out what to write."

Collins came back, appearing excited. "I don't know if this is interesting or not interesting," he said. "Makarova *was* represented by SMG."

"*Was?*" Kelleher said.

He nodded. "Yes, *was*. Apparently her father decided they weren't doing a good enough job for her because they were spending too much time making deals for Symanova."

"Nothing new there," Mearns said. "Parents always get into a snit about their kids not getting enough attention from their agents."

"Absolutely," Collins said. "Some other agent comes along, offers them the world, and they jump. Happens all the time."

"So who did Makarova jump to?" Kelleher asked.

Collins glanced at Susan Carol. "It probably means nothing," he said. "It hasn't been announced yet, but they say she's about to jump to Brendan Gibson at ISM."

✗   ✗   ✗

In all the time he had spent with Susan Carol, including a two-hour period when they had been tied to chairs and left alone with an armed thug in a hotel room, Stevie had never seen her so unnerved. "It probably does mean nothing," she said to Stevie after all the grown-ups had given her the "Don't worry about a thing" talk and gone off to write. "But isn't it strange that Evelyn never mentioned it when we were asking her about Makarova?"

It was strange. "Maybe she doesn't know yet?" he said.

"I suppose so. But why wouldn't my uncle tell us last night

when you were asking him how he was doing as an agent? That's kind of a coup."

"Maybe it's still a secret."

"Maybe. But I've got a lot of questions for him when we get home. Let's write and get out of here."

That was fine with Stevie. He pulled his computer out from under Kelleher's desk and found an empty desk in the back row, which was apparently kept empty for overflow writers who showed up on the last weekend and didn't have assigned spots. When he had finished his glowing account of Evelyn Rubin's upset of Maggie Maleeva—including her desire to go to the Louvre and her attempt to finish her summer reading for school—he brought his computer to Kelleher so he could help him file. Kelleher stopped what he was doing long enough to scroll through the story. "It's good," he said. "But you've written twenty-four inches. We'll be lucky if they give you sixteen. You want to cut it or let them do it in the office?"

Stevie decided he'd rather cut his own stuff. It was painful. Every time he cut a sentence or a paragraph, he was convinced he had to be down to sixteen inches. Then he pressed the count key and the computer told him he was still way over the right length. He gave up when he finally got to eighteen inches and presented it to Kelleher again. "There's not a cuttable sentence in there," he said.

"No doubt true," Kelleher said. "But trust me, they'll cut it anyway."

It was after eight o'clock by the time all four of them were finished. The room was buzzing with people writing, people asking one another questions—every thirty seconds or so someone would shout a question at Collins, who either knew the answer or stopped his work to look it up in the myriad of books he had sitting at his feet. The room began to clear when the night match on the stadium court, featuring Andre Agassi, the ageless wonder, got under way.

Kelleher, Mearns, Susan Carol, and Stevie convened around Kelleher's desk to figure out what to do next. "First thing we need to do is get something to eat," Kelleher said. "Let's walk over to Slew's."

"What's Slew's?" Stevie asked, wondering if he could get another hamburger there.

"It's a little restaurant named after Slew Hester. He was the USTA president who came up with the idea of moving here from Forest Hills in 1978. Bud says he was a good guy."

"Bud says everyone's a good guy," Mearns said, causing Collins to look up from his computer a few yards away.

"That's not true," he said. "I thought Hitler and Mussolini were terrible guys. Of course, Mussolini did get the trains running on time. Maybe he wasn't so bad." He went back to writing.

"Anyway," Kelleher continued, "you need a badge to get in, so it isn't so crowded."

They walked across the plaza for what felt like the hundredth time that day, angling left to follow the curve of the stadium. It took them past some glass doors marked U.S. OPEN CLUB to a smaller door that said SLEW'S PLACE.

It was almost empty. There were only a handful of matches

being played at night and almost everyone left on the grounds was watching tennis. When they were handed menus, Stevie's eyes grew wide when he got to what was called the "Slew-burger." Here, the price of a hamburger had risen to twelve dollars.

"Think I should drink a ten-dollar beer?" Kelleher asked Mearns.

"No. Because you'll want a second one."

"Good point."

Once they had ordered, Kelleher said, "So, anyone got any ideas?"

Stevie wasn't even a little surprised when Susan Carol said, "I do."

Kelleher smiled. "You ready to get your uncle to confess?" he asked.

"Sort of," she said. "I think I should ask him directly about what's going on with Makarova."

"I think you ought to just ask him what he knows about her," Stevie said, jumping in. "See what he says."

Susan Carol looked at him angrily. "He won't lie."

"Susan Carol, we can't be sure of anything," Mearns said gently. "I don't think we want to show anyone our cards right now—even your uncle. We need to use what we know to find out what others know. I'm sure you're right that he won't lie. But let's find out."

Susan Carol nodded, still looking distressed.

"What else?" Kelleher said.

"I think we need to find out more about why SMG is pushing the SVR story so hard," Susan Carol said.

"I agree," Kelleher said.

"I still have some NYPD sources from my stint at *Newsday*," Tamara said. "I'll call them in the morning, see what they're saying."

"Good," Kelleher said. "I'll see if I can call in a favor with a friend at the FBI. Stevie, Susan Carol, I think you ought to nose around early at the U.N. Plaza before coming back out here."

"The U.N. Plaza? What's that?" Stevie asked.

"It's the hotel where most of the players stay. Very posh. All the agents have suites where they hold meetings, have refreshments for players who want to hang out, things like that. Usually everyone's around in the morning. I'll call Ross to make sure you guys can get around the hotel unhassled."

"If Ross is an agent, why is he your friend?" Stevie asked. "You don't like agents."

Kelleher shrugged. "It's sort of like having a pet. Even if you don't like dogs, you like *your* dog. Tom's *my* agent."

Mearns laughed. "You always forget that cuts both ways," she said. "I'm sure Tom sees you as *his* reporter."

"Probably true," Kelleher said. "I'll call him first thing in the morning. He's always up early. Unless you guys hear different from me, take a cab to the hotel and I'll have Tom meet you in the lobby at eight-thirty."

"When do you think I should talk to my uncle?" Susan Carol said.

"First chance you get," Kelleher said.

"Bobby, there's one thing you need to understand," Susan Carol said, looking as serious as Stevie had ever seen her.

"What's that?"

"Uncle Brendan is *my* agent."

Kelleher nodded. "Understood. But let's find out if he's Elena Makarova's agent too."

9: SURPRISE VISITORS

BRENDAN GIBSON wasn't home when Kelleher dropped Stevie and Susan Carol off in front of 52 Riverside Drive, but Susan Carol had the code to get into the building and a key to the apartment. There was a note in the kitchen that said simply: "Home late. See you in the morning."

Susan Carol had been very quiet on the car ride home, and Stevie wasn't sure how or if he should bring up the subject of her uncle possibly being involved in Nadia Symanova's disappearance. He decided to try and use the old reporting tactic of asking soft questions first to see if they might set up the harder questions. Dick Jerardi, who had become a mentor to him back home, always told him to save the toughest questions for last.

"So how close are you to your uncle?" he asked casually as they sat at the kitchen table munching on some pretzels and chips that she had found in one of the cabinets.

"Don't you play reporter's tricks with me, Stevie Thomas," she said, her eyes flashing anger again. "I know *exactly* where you're going with this."

That figured, he thought. Trying to outsmart her was a waste of time. "Okay, okay," he said. "I can understand why you'd feel this way, but . . ."

"No buts, Stevie," she said. "My uncle isn't a kidnapper."

"Can I ask one question?" he said.

"Maybe," she answered.

"Three years ago, if someone had said your uncle would become an agent, would you have believed it possible?"

She stared at him for a few seconds, then stood up from the table. It looked like she was going to say something. Then her eyes welled up with tears. "You know, it *really* doesn't bother me that Bobby and Tamara might think Uncle Brendan could be involved in this," she said. "They've never met him and they've had years to build up their distrust of agents. But *you?* Not only have you met him, not only are you staying in his apartment, but how could you so doubt *me?*"

He started to answer but she was gone, stalking past him while he was trying to swallow a pretzel. He heard the door to her bedroom slam. Then the door opened again and she was back. "To answer your question, no, I wouldn't have thought he would become an agent. But I also wouldn't as-sume it was a dishonorable thing to do."

She turned and stalked out again. The door slammed one more time.

"Okay, then," he said to the empty kitchen. "I think that went well."

He got up to go to bed, walking past the entryway to the apartment, when he heard voices in the hallway. He paused for a second and then heard a key being put into the door. Instinctively, he ran for cover, perhaps because he didn't want to explain why he was still up and Susan Carol wasn't. He went into the hall and stood listening, figuring he would run into his bedroom if anyone came in his direction. He wondered if Susan Carol would come out of her room, hearing the voices, but he thought he heard a shower coming from there. He heard Brendan Gibson's voice as the door was closing. "This is a lot better than the hotel," he was saying. "Much more private."

"What about your niece and her friend?" a man's voice said in response. The voice was heavily accented. Stevie thought he might be imagining things, but it sounded Russian.

"I'm sure they're asleep," Gibson answered. "They had a long day, especially with the kidnapping."

"Us too," said a female voice, also accented. "People were everywhere. All the questions and rumors. Such craziness."

"I know," Gibson said. "Why don't we sit in the living room? What can I get you two to drink?"

"You have Stolichnaya?" the man's voice said.

"As it happens, I do," Gibson said. "My favorite vodka. Mrs. Makarova?"

Stevie almost shouted, *What?* Or, more appropriately, he thought, clapping a hand over his mouth, *Who?*

"Yes, please, me also," he heard Mrs. Makarova say.

He slunk back against the wall as the man and the woman crossed the foyer and went into the living room. He could hear Gibson rustling around in the kitchen. He was tempted to knock on Susan Carol's door so she could hear what was going on, but he was afraid any noise at all might alert Gibson. When he heard Gibson saying something as he walked—Stevie assumed—into the living room, he crept forward as far as he dared. There was no door, just an entry-way, and the acoustics of the apartment were such that he could hear pretty clearly from his hiding spot. He even heard glasses clinking.

"To a new relationship," Gibson said.

Bud Collins's information had been accurate. Of course, that didn't mean Gibson or the Makarovs had anything to do with Symanova's disappearance. He kept listening.

Mr. Makarov was talking now. One thing Stevie had learned during the day was that Russian women's names all ended in *-ova* but the men didn't add the *-a*. "As we told you, Brendan, we have done—work at home—on you?"

"Homework, I think you mean," Gibson said. "Which is good—you should do that before making a decision as big as this."

"The people at SMG are not happy with us at all," Mr. Makarov said. "Mr. Norwood was very unpleasant today."

"I would think Mr. Norwood had other things on his mind today," Gibson said.

Stevie leaned forward a little more, not wanting to miss a word at this stage of the conversation.

"Yes, you would think so, no? I was very surprised. I have seen him soon after the girl disappears and he starts shouting at me that I am a terrible man and my daughter will pay for this."

"Maybe he said this because what happened upset him," Mrs. Makarova said.

"Don't worry about him, he's just flailing," Gibson answered.

"What is this 'flailing'?" Mrs. Makarova said.

"Swinging wildly when you don't know what to do," Gibson said. "When Elena wins this tournament, which she's going to, he'll really be flailing."

"I wish she would get to play Symanova in quarters," Mr. Makarov said. "Then people would see she is much better player. I hope she is found soon."

At that moment Stevie felt a cough coming on. He tried to stop it, but before he could get his hand over his mouth the cough came out. The voices in the other room stopped. For an instant, Stevie thought about sprinting to his bedroom. That wouldn't work. Clearly, he'd been heard. As he saw Brendan Gibson bolting through the entryway into the foyer, he took a long step into the foyer himself, angling toward the kitchen.

"Stevie," Gibson said, looking unnerved. "I didn't think you guys were up. What's going on?"

"Got a cough," Stevie said. "I was going to see if there was any Coke in the refrigerator. It helps when I have a scratchy throat."

"Um, I'm sure we do," Gibson said, half pulling him in the direction of the kitchen, clearly not wanting him in the living room.

"You have guests?" Stevie asked. "I heard voices."

"Oh yeah. Friends. Old friends. They were at the matches tonight, so I brought them back here for a drink. They live right nearby. They'll be leaving very soon."

He pulled a can of Coke from the refrigerator. "You need a glass?"

Stevie was tempted to stall to see if one of the Makarovs would come into the kitchen. But even if they did, Brendan Gibson could just introduce them by another name and they would be smart enough, he figured, to say nothing.

"No, this is fine. Thanks."

Gibson walked him back into the foyer and down the hall to his room as if to make sure he didn't accidentally veer into the living room. "I'll see you in the morning," he said. "Get some sleep. Susan Carol's got a head start on you."

"Yeah, sure," Stevie said. "Good night."

"Good night, Stevie," Gibson said, then headed back down the hallway.

Stevie stood by the door for a moment and tried to listen. He heard footsteps again. It sounded like the little party was breaking up. He quickly stepped into his room and sat on the edge of the bed. He realized his heart was pounding. He wanted to rush in and tell Susan Carol what he had just heard but he figured that was a bad idea. Gibson might hear them talking and know something was up. Plus, he could see it was almost midnight. It had been a long day. Based on what he had just heard, tomorrow might be even longer.

✗ ✗ ✗

He fell asleep a lot faster than he thought he might, so exhausted that even trying to piece together the conversation between Gibson and the Makarovs didn't keep him awake. The next thing he knew there was a soft knocking on his door. He glanced at the clock next to the bed: it was a quarter to eight.

"Stevie," he heard Susan Carol say. "You need to wake up. We have to leave here by eight-fifteen."

"I'm up," he called back groggily. "I'll be in the kitchen in fifteen minutes."

He got up, took a fast shower, and got dressed. Susan Carol was sitting in the kitchen drinking from a coffee mug when he walked in.

"Still drinking coffee?" he said, remembering she'd given him some in New Orleans.

"Only when there isn't a grown-up around."

"Where's your uncle?"

"Left ten minutes ago. But I talked to him about Makarova and he laughed when I told him that one of the rumors going around last night was that he was going to represent her."

"Laughed?" Stevie was too stunned to object.

"He said *everyone's* trying to represent Makarova and he

made a pitch to them like everyone else. Then he asked me why Makarova changing agents would come up in conversation."

"What'd you tell him?"

"The truth—that SMG seemed to be a little too eager to spread the idea that the SVR did this and we were wondering who might benefit if Symanova was out of the tournament."

"What did he think about that?"

"I think the word he used, once he stopped laughing, was 'absurd.' He said Makarova was a better player than Symanova and *he* had heard that she's dying to play her because she's tired of Symanova getting all the deals and the publicity because of her looks."

"Wonder where he heard that."

Susan Carol gave him a look. "What do you mean?"

"Nothing. I just wonder where he heard it."

"Anywhere. Everywhere. It's all over. We made the same assumption, didn't we?"

While he was trying to decide how to tell her what he'd overheard, she said, "God, I'm so relieved. I feel so much better knowing the whole Makarova thing was just another wild rumor. I mean, I *knew* my uncle wasn't involved in anything bad, but now there's no reason to even think about it."

"Quick bowl of cereal and we're out of here," he said, deciding this wasn't the time to tell her that her uncle was a flat-out liar.

She tossed a newspaper in his direction as he sat down.

Much to his surprise, he saw that it was the *Washington Herald*. There was a headline on the front page, just underneath a story about Congress and the president battling over the budget, that said VANISHED. Underneath was a photo of Nadia Symanova.

"Your story is on page three of the sports section," she said. "Uncle Brendan made arrangements to have it delivered here all week so you could see your stuff. I guess that's more proof of what a bad guy he is."

"I never said he was a bad guy," he said, more defensively than was probably necessary. He knew if he told her now she probably wouldn't even believe him.

"Is there anything new on Symanova this morning?" he asked.

She shook her head. "I was listening to the radio when I woke up. Everyone is reporting that it's the SVR. The Russian government is expressing outrage that anyone would think they had anything to do with it. Apparently Larry King did his whole show on it last night. The guy I was listening to on the radio said that King referred to the Lindbergh kidnapping as the most famous kidnapping in history—before yesterday."

"So people are being calm and rational about it, huh?"

She gave him a no-kidding look. He opened the sports section and there it was. The headline read RUBIN PULLS FIRST UPSET OF TOURNAMENT. The byline underneath it said, "by Steven Thomas—Special to the *Herald*." It gave him chills to see his name in print that way. He was about to start reading when Susan Carol stood up.

"Sorry, Ace, you'll have to read yourself later. We've got to get going."

She bounced out of the kitchen, clearly pumped to go and find out what had happened to Symanova—now that she knew her uncle was in the clear.

10: WILD-GOOSE CHASE

JUST AS they had done the day before, they walked to West End Avenue, where Susan Carol whistled down a cab. They pulled into the small circular driveway of the U.N. Plaza Hotel at precisely eight-thirty and found Tom Ross standing right behind the doorman who opened the cab door for them. "I figured I'd meet you guys out here," he said. "The security is so tight around here, they won't even let you in the lobby without a key."

He was already dressed in his agent's uniform and tightening his tie every few seconds, which Stevie had now decided was a nervous tic. He led them through the revolving doors and then explained to the security man inside the door that the two teenagers were, in fact, with him. "Just visiting for a little while," he said, as if the security man actually cared.

"You guys had breakfast?" he asked. "I'll buy you breakfast if you want."

"We're fine," Susan Carol said. "We just need some idea of how to get to the agents' suites."

Ross was nodding and shaking his head all at once. "Okay, okay, I told Bobby I could help you with that. But there's a limit to how *much* I can help you. I can get you guys upstairs to the floor where all the suites are, but once you're up there, you're on your own. I can't exactly go waltzing into another agency's suite."

"That's all right," Susan Carol said. "We have a plan."

"We do?" Stevie said. She hadn't said a word to him in the cab, so this was news to him.

"You mind if I ask what it is?" Ross said. "Because you can't just wander in with those computer bags slung over your shoulders."

"We'll ditch the bags in your suite," Susan Carol said. "And then we'll pose as junior players. They hold a tournament here next week for the juniors, right? We'll just say we came in early to watch the first week and we wanted to learn more about agents for down the line."

Ross was shaking his head before she had finished. "Won't work," he said. "Bobby said you guys are fourteen, right?"

"Almost fourteen," Stevie said.

"Okay. The point is this: there's no way a top junior is unknown to the agencies by the time he or she is thirteen—

especially the girls. You go in there claiming you're junior players, they'll ask your names, look you up, and know you're phonies."

"What if we just give them the names of real junior players?" Susan Carol asked.

"Won't work. Chances are good someone in every one of those suites will have seen those kids play. You need a better idea."

Susan Carol put her hands on her hips and for a minute Stevie thought she was going to get angry with Ross. They were standing near the elevator bank now, people whizzing by them, some of them carrying racquet bags. Most of those who appeared to be players, Stevie noticed, were wearing headphones to shut out the world around them.

"What about this?" Susan Carol said. "We can be someone's relatives."

"Like who?" Ross said. "It would have to be someone they don't represent because they'd know about brothers and sisters of their clients."

"How about Evelyn Rubin?" Susan Carol said. "My uncle is her agent. They won't know much about her."

Ross looked surprised. "Gibson is your uncle? Kelleher didn't tell me that. Wow. Is it true he's got the Makarovs wrapped up?"

Susan Carol's eyes flashed again. "No, it's not true."

"Okay, fine, just a rumor," Ross said, hands up in defense. "Being Evelyn's brother and sister could work. She's not a big name yet but everyone in the business knows she has potential. That's worth a shot. Tell them you're looking for

Pete Lawler. He's their lead recruiter for up-and-coming girls. He'll know who Evelyn is. They'll be nice to relatives of hers for sure."

"Why would they want to be nice?" Stevie said. "Doesn't she have a contract with Susan Carol's uncle? Why do we tell them we're hanging out in SMG's suite?"

"Because Gibson doesn't have a suite," Ross said. "Look, contracts mean nothing in the agent business. There's almost always a way out. Trust me, I've been on both sides. Even if there's not, no one ever has a contract for more than three or four years. At some point, she'll be on the market again, and if she keeps getting better, everyone will be after her. She's got what we call 'upside,' because if she becomes a good player, she can make a lot of money off the court.

"She's fifteen, right? How old are you guys going to be if someone asks? You certainly can't pass for twins."

Stevie didn't know if that was an insult or not.

"I'll say I'm sixteen—people always think I'm older than my age—and Stevie can be thirteen," Susan Carol said. "Big sister and little brother."

Stevie was a little hurt that he had to be his real age while Susan Carol pretended to be older. But there was no doubting the fact that she could easily pass for sixteen and he could easily pass for thirteen—in part because he *was* thirteen.

"Tell me one more thing," Ross said, now walking toward the elevators. "What are you hoping to find out up there?"

"Gossip," Susan Carol said. "Rumors. See if anyone in the SMG suite says something they shouldn't. See if they *really* think it was the SVR or if they've got other ideas. If you were them, wouldn't you be wondering about a ransom note by now?"

"I'd be wondering a lot of things," Ross said as the elevator arrived.

They got in and Ross put his key card into a slot and pressed a button for thirty-six. "If you want, I'll take you into our suite and you can get something to eat or drink first and see what the setup looks like," he said. "They're all about the same."

Susan Carol shook her head. "Just point us to SMG. That's where we need to go."

✗ ✗ ✗

When the elevator reached thirty-six, they all got off. As it turned out, there were signs pointing to the various agencies' suites. "That's so players or families know where to go," Ross said, reading their minds. "We're down here to the right. Your guys are all the way down the hall in the end suite. They always get that one to show off. It has the most spectacular view."

They thanked Ross for his help and he took charge of their computer bags. He told them he wouldn't be heading to the tennis center until late morning and they could find him in the Octagon suite when they wanted their computers back. "Be careful," he said as he shook their hands. "I know Bobby thinks all agents are evil, but these guys are a different level. They're the best because they're the most ruthless."

Stevie felt a little chill go through him. As usual, Susan Carol appeared to be totally calm. As they walked down the hall she said quietly, "Remember, we're brother and sister, so act like you like me."

"I *do* like you," he said.

"Oh yeah, I forgot. I'm the one who's angry." She almost smiled when she said it. Stevie decided that was a good sign.

The doors to the SMG suite were open wide. An attractive blond woman sat behind a large desk, talking on the phone as Stevie and Susan Carol walked in. Even from across the room, Stevie could see that the suite had a spectacular view of Manhattan, looking west. The woman on the phone was wrapping up her conversation. "That's right, there will be four tickets at Will Call for you in our box in the stadium for the night session." She paused for a moment. "No, Agassi played last night." She shuffled through some papers. "Sharapova's playing the first match tonight, and then James Blake plays after that. It should be great tennis." Another pause, followed by a frown. "No. We haven't heard anything new." More talking on the other end. "Yes, it certainly is terrifying. It's been on TV nonstop. My boss is walking in, Mrs. Andreu. We're all excited about Matthew playing his first match tomorrow. If you need me for *anything,* please call."

She hung up and took a deep breath. "Long morning," she said, smiling at them. "Players' parents. They're all concerned about what happened. Anyway, how can I help you?"

As always, Susan Carol took the lead. "My name is Susan

Rubin and this is my brother Steve," she said. "You may know our sister, Evelyn? She beat Maggie Maleeva yesterday. We were supposed to be meeting her now to go out to the tennis center but she just called"—she held up her cell phone for emphasis—"and said she's running late coming back from a hit and suggested we might come up here to get a drink or something. She said to tell Mr. Lawler who we were."

If the woman was skeptical about this story, she didn't show it. Stevie was trying to figure out exactly what a hit was, but evidently it made sense to the woman. "Pete's actually in a meeting right now, but I'm sure he'd love to say hello if you guys are going to be here for a few minutes," she said. "In the meantime, of course you're welcome to come on in and have something to eat. We've got a nice buffet set up. My name's Melissa—if I can be of any help at all, let me know."

Stevie had to give Tom Ross credit: he knew the people in his business. The mention of Evelyn Rubin seemed to work wonders. Stevie never would have guessed that a company as powerful as SMG would be that fired up about someone ranked forty-eighth in the world. Apparently he was wrong.

"Thanks so much," Susan Carol said, shaking hands with Melissa, who then offered her hand and a smile to Stevie. As often seemed to happen to him when Susan Carol was charming someone, he couldn't think of a thing to say.

"Um, hi, Steve," he said.

Melissa nodded, smiled again, and then picked up the phone that had mercifully started ringing again.

Stevie followed Susan Carol into the suite, which appeared to have one huge room, surrounded by doors leading elsewhere. There were two open doors leading to bathrooms and two closed doors leading into what were no doubt meeting rooms. A number of people, including several players, were sitting on couches listening to headphones or sitting at small tables that had been set up near the buffet.

"Let's get something to eat," Susan Carol said quietly. "Then we can sit down and keep our eyes and ears open."

"I still don't know what we're looking for," Stevie said.

"Me neither. Let's just try and look like everyone else."

She was leaning down so she could speak softly to him and her hair fell across his shoulder. She pulled it back and smiled at him. For a split second he wanted to tell her about the Makarovs and her uncle, but he decided just as quickly this wasn't the time or place. Then again, he wasn't sure he'd ever find the right time or place to break her heart.

The buffet had enough food on it to feed a small country. Stevie simply could not turn down French toast, so he put a couple of pieces on his plate and poured some syrup. He put some eggs carefully on the side of the plate and then tossed three strips of bacon on top of the eggs. He glanced at Susan Carol, who had taken a small portion of eggs and an orange juice. "Ravenous again?" she said as he put his plate down on an empty table and went back for orange juice. They sat down and looked around the room. Stevie recognized no one. It had struck him the day before in the players' lounge that even though he thought he knew a fair bit about tennis, there were very few players he actually recognized. There were 128 players in each singles draw, so it would be next to impossible to know half of them, much less all of them.

There were TV sets positioned around the room, tuned to different stations. On CNN, one of the anchors was interviewing someone who was identified as an "SVR expert." On MSNBC, Don Imus was talking to Sally Jenkins of the *Washington Post*, who was describing her visit to Symanova's home in California earlier in the summer. On the third set, Matt Lauer was talking to the Symanovs about their daughter. "We are grateful for all the concern people have shown," Misha Symanov said. "We pray for the best." Yolanda Symanova had tears in her eyes as she spoke, and at one point Lauer leaned over to give her a comforting pat on the leg. Stevie noticed that at the bottom of the screen in small lettering were the words "Taped earlier today," meaning, he figured, this was probably the second time this morning that NBC had aired the interview.

Susan Carol noticed him staring at the TVs. "All Nadia all the time," she said. She had that right.

Stevie was digging into his French toast when he heard Susan Carol make some kind of hissing sound to get his attention. He looked up and saw Hughes Norwood walking toward them. Stevie almost choked on his food. Norwood walked up, glanced at Stevie's plate, then turned to Susan

Carol. "Melissa tells me you are Evelyn Rubin's sister and . . . little brother."

"Why, yes, we are," Susan Carol said, cool as ever. "I'm Susan and this is Steve."

"*Very* nice to meet you both. I'm Hughes Norwood," he said, surprising Stevie by actually smiling. He shook hands with the two of them. "You are *always* welcome here, throughout the two weeks. And please tell Evelyn to feel free to stop by anytime she wants. I think Melissa told you Pete's in a meeting right now, but if you're here for a few minutes, I'm sure he'd love to say hello."

"Oh, that is *so* nice of you," Susan Carol said, noticeably toning down her Southern accent—a good move since Evelyn was from the Midwest. "We'll be sure to tell Evelyn we saw you and how kind you were."

Norwood beamed to the point where Stevie wondered if he was really the same guy he had seen yesterday.

"And we're *so* sorry about Nadia. We hope she's going to be found soon and that she's okay."

Norwood nodded. "Yes, it's been tough for everyone. SVR, bad group of people, you know."

There he went again, pinning it on the SVR. "So that's really true?" Stevie asked. "Wow. We could hardly believe it. Have you heard anything from them? Has there been a ransom note?"

"No, nothing that specific—yet," Norwood said. "Mr. Symanov is convinced they're making him twist in the wind for a day or two before they tell him what they want. Well, we all know what they want."

"Will Mr. Symanov give in?" Susan Carol asked, still the picture of concern.

"I don't know," Norwood said. "He was so upset yesterday. It's hard to believe this could go on in today's world." He sighed, heavily burdened. "One would hope sports and politics wouldn't mix, but I guess that's naive." He looked at his watch. "You tell Evelyn good luck against Raymond in the second round. And tell her we'll be watching her when she plays Nadia in the third round. . . ." He paused a minute. "Of course we *hope* they play in the third round."

"Yes, of course. Very nice to meet you," Susan Carol said.

He smiled, seemed to catch someone's eye, and said, "Jorge, *hola!*" and raced across the room to hug a man who had been sitting by the window.

"Just a wild guess," Stevie said as he left. "Jorge's a player's father."

"No doubt," Susan Carol said. "You breathing yet?"

"Barely. Did you notice he knew just who Evelyn was playing in the second round?"

"He could have looked it up on the draw sheet when Melissa told him about us," she said. "Still, Tom Ross was right. It's pretty obvious they would *love* to get Evelyn away from my uncle. And we would have been toast trying to pose as players."

There was no arguing with that. Stevie had been convinced the day before that Hughes Norwood's face would break if he smiled. Now, among clients and potential clients—or their siblings—he couldn't stop beaming.

Stevie wanted more French toast. He stood up to go back

to the buffet. "You aren't going to eat *more*, are you?" Susan Carol said. "Have you got a hole in your stomach?"

"I'm still growing, remember?" Stevie said. "And the prices in here are a lot better than out at the tennis center."

She opened her mouth to say something, then stopped. The room had suddenly gone quiet. Stevie looked in the direction of the door and saw why: Misha and Yolanda Symanov were walking in the door. They stopped to exchange kisses on both cheeks with Melissa and were then greeted with hugs by Hughes Norwood. He led them to a table in the corner and waved a much younger man over. He whispered to him for a moment and the younger man bolted to the buffet table and began loading two plates with food. Stevie realized he was staring. He looked around and saw that everyone else in the room was doing the same thing. The Symanovs looked remarkably composed under the circumstances. Norwood's man Friday brought food to the table and then scurried back to get drinks.

Some of the other people in the room walked over to the table to greet the Symanovs. There were more hugs and kisses and lots of quiet talking. Stevie was still standing, having forgotten about his French toast. Suddenly he saw Norwood turn and wave in their direction. His heart started racing again. "Steve, Susan—can you come over here for a moment?"

Susan Carol gave him a stay-calm look as she stood and walked to the table, followed by Stevie.

"The Symanovs just wanted to say hello to you two," Norwood said. "They've seen your sister play."

"She is very good player," Misha Symanov said as he shook hands with each of them. "She will be champion, I think, someday."

"Might make good doubles partners," Norwood said. "Contrasting styles, not to mention backgrounds."

"Yes, I think maybe. Nadia is tall, can play the net. Evelyn is more ground stroker, no?"

"Yes, she is," Susan Carol said. "Right now, though, we're only concerned with seeing Nadia safe."

Mrs. Symanova had started to cry again. "Thank you, my dear," she said. "You are very kind."

"Will you go out to the matches today?" Susan Carol said. "Or stay here?"

"We are not certain yet," Mr. Symanov said. "There is *so* much media there. We did four TV interviews this morning. Maybe later, if we are needed, we will go out there. For now, I think we stay here and rest once we have eaten."

"It seems like the entire world is following this story," Susan Carol said.

"Yes. We are grateful for all the concern people have shown. Maybe this will show the SVR they cannot get away with this. The whole world knows what they are attempting. We pray for the best."

Stevie thought he had heard those words before. Then it hit him: he *had* heard them just a few minutes ago, watching the *Today* show interview.

"Please," Mrs. Symanova said, "give our best to your sister."

"Yes," Norwood said. "Please do. And tell her to think

about Nadia as a doubles partner in the future. They'd be a great team—on and off the court."

Stevie saw Mrs. Symanova's eyes cloud again. "She'll be okay," Norwood said to her. "Have faith."

"And pray for the best," Susan Carol said.

Stevie wondered if he should say "amen." He decided against it.

11: WHAT NEXT?

THEY DECIDED it was time to make a graceful exit from the SMG suite while they were still ahead. Stevie's only regret was the second plate of French toast he didn't have. They walked quickly down the hallway to the elevator bank and Stevie turned to press a button. Susan Carol waved him off.

"Where are we going now?" he asked.

"We have to get our computers back. Plus, I want to see what Tom Ross thinks about all this."

They continued down the hall, past the suite marked INTER-NATIONAL MANAGEMENT GROUP and the one marked SFX, until they arrived at the last one, which was marked OCTA-GON INC.

A smiling woman with short dark hair greeted them at the door. "Hi, can I help you?" she said.

"We're looking for Tom Ross," Susan Carol said.

"Oh, he's in a meeting," she said. "I'm Kelly Wolf, his assistant. Can I be of help?"

Susan Carol shook her head. "No, we really need to talk to Tom. It's kind of an emergency. Could you possibly tell him that Susan Carol and Steve are here?"

Kelly Wolf eyed Susan Carol for a minute, clearly unsure of why she would have an emergency involving her boss. "Hang on one second," she said. "Let me see."

She walked to a closed door at the back of the suite and walked inside. A moment later Tom Ross, looking nervous and harried, emerged.

"Guys, I'm in the middle of a tough negotiation on a shoe contract," he said. "Are you sure this can't wait?"

"Can we have three minutes?" Susan Carol said.

He did the tie thing again, pulling it tight one more time. "Okay, okay." He glanced around, looking for a private spot. The Octagon lounge was at least as crowded as the SMG lounge.

"The hallway?" Stevie suggested.

"Too public," Ross said. "Follow me."

He walked them across the room, opened a door, and ushered them into a bathroom. "Sorry," he said. "This is the best I can do. At least it's a big one."

He sat on the sink and listened while Susan Carol filled him in on their visit to SMG.

"Hughes's behavior with you isn't surprising at all," he said. He shook his head. "That old trick about playing doubles, though, that went out years ago. No one cares about doubles anymore. . . ."

"That doesn't matter," Susan Carol said. "What matters, I think, is that he and the father are both acting as if this is an inconvenience, while the mother is clearly hysterical."

Ross looked at Stevie. "Did it seem that way to you too?" he asked.

Stevie was glad someone cared about his opinion. "It just felt like they knew something she didn't," he said.

"Exactly," Susan Carol put in.

"I think you're onto something," Ross said. "Problem is, I don't know what. Maybe they're just trying to be calm for the mom's sake. Or maybe they've heard something but for some reason aren't telling her."

"Like what?" Susan Carol asked.

"No idea. But if I'm not back in that room in about thirty seconds, I'm going to blow a multimillion-dollar deal. Look, here's my card. That's my cell number on the bottom. Call me this afternoon."

Susan Carol took the card and put it in her pocket. When they walked out of the bathroom, Stevie noticed several people giving them funny looks. They picked up their computer bags, which were behind the front desk, thanked Kelly Wolf, and walked back to the elevators. In parting, Ross had recommended they walk three blocks over to Grand Central Station and take the subway out to Flushing rather than wait for the next courtesy bus from the hotel.

"You just missed the ten-thirty. Next one isn't until eleven. With traffic, it'll be noon before you get there. The subway will take you forty-five minutes."

Stevie had never been on the New York City subway but figured it would be fine during the daytime. Susan Carol wasn't as sure. "I've heard all the stories," she said as they walked to Lexington Avenue and turned left to walk two blocks down to 42nd Street.

"Come on," he said. "It'll be an adventure."

"Just what we need," she said. "More adventures."

✗ ✗ ✗

He was right about the subway being fine. They didn't have any trouble finding the number 7 train, but when they got to the platform it was jammed with people clearly headed for the tennis tournament. Stevie knew this because many of them were wearing tennis outfits—especially the women. Still, somehow the train swallowed them all up and there was room to stand even if there were no seats. The train was quiet—Stevie wondered if that was the nature of a tennis crowd, or if perhaps the fans were thinking about Nadia Symanova. After the second stop in Queens, the train came out of the tunnel and became elevated. Stevie liked that. In just under thirty minutes, they were at the station marked SHEA STADIUM/WILLETS POINT and saw the smaller signs pointing to NATIONAL TENNIS CENTER. They spilled out of the train along with just about everyone else and followed the crowds across the street and up onto the boardwalk that led from Shea Stadium to the tennis center. It was teeming with fans and vendors selling everything from T-shirts to caps to tennis bags. There were also the inevitable ticket scalpers, all of them yelling, "Anyone selling tickets?"

Stevie knew from his experience at the Final Four that this was code to let people know they had tickets without taking a chance on being accused of scalping by a passing policeman. As they came down the steps onto the promenade outside the gates, Stevie could see that part of the area had been roped off so that TV crews could set up platforms to do live shots. Stevie saw signs for CNN, MSNBC, Fox News, ESPN, Fox Sports, and E! There were roving crews doing stand-ups in the middle of the crowd without benefit of a platform. "The whole world is here," he said to Susan Carol.

"And then some," she said.

They put on their press credentials so they could go in the gate marked PLAYERS/OFFICIALS/MEDIA. Stevie's shoulder was aching a little bit from carrying his computer bag. They had come in at the opposite end of the grounds from where they had arrived the day before with Kelleher, so they had to trek all the way across the plaza to the media center. Stevie was breathing hard by the time they arrived.

"Let me guess," Susan Carol said. "You're hungry?"

"Always," Stevie said.

That would have to wait. Kelleher and Mearns were waiting to debrief them. Stevie said nothing when Susan Carol reported her uncle's response to her questions about Evelyn Rubin. Kelleher and Mearns were far more interested in their experience in the SMG suite than anything else.

"Here's what Arlen told me just a few minutes ago," Kelleher said. "Norwood called and told him they had been contacted by the SVR. Their demands are very simple: make a public announcement that Nadia will represent Russia in the Fed Cup and the Olympics for the rest of her career and she'll be returned immediately. Do it by midnight tomorrow or they'll have her on a plane to Russia."

"Can they get away with that?" Stevie asked.

Kelleher shrugged. "Arlen seems to think they can."

"Have they thought about getting our government involved?" Susan Carol asked.

Kelleher shook his head. "That's what's interesting," he said. "I talked to my FBI guy and he said they have no evidence at all that the SVR's involved."

"What about the police?" Stevie asked, looking at Mearns.

"Same thing," Mearns said. "The witnesses they talked to all had different versions. But nothing of any substance. None of their sources seem to have any serious clues."

Stevie was wondering when the Symanovs had heard from the SVR. Maybe that was what they were going to talk to Norwood about in the SMG suite. But if they were discussing something that serious, why would Norwood have waved them over to make his little recruiting pitch to the brother and sister of Evelyn Rubin? And where, he wondered, did Brendan Gibson and the Makarovs fit in to all this? He felt dazed.

"So what do we do next?" Susan Carol wondered. "Just wait?"

"That's probably not a good idea," Bud Collins said, walking up. "It sounds like this kid is in serious trouble."

The discussion about what to do next continued while Stevie picked up a match schedule for the day. One match caught his eye: the second match on court 3, the Grandstand court. Elena Makarova would play Kristen Stafford. It was about twelve-thirty and the opening matches had started at eleven o'clock. Stevie turned to the computer behind him and saw that the first match on the Grandstand was over. It looked as if Makarova and Stafford had just started.

"I'm going for a walk," he announced. "I want to watch some tennis. I need to clear my head for a little while."

Kelleher wanted to stay near the press center in case something broke. Mearns and Collins were going to walk out to court 11 to watch Jonas Björkman play Greg Rusedski. "Played each other in the semis five years ago," Collins said. "Now they're playing on an outside court in the first round. In fact, Björkman had to make it through qualifying just to get here."

"How many matches do you have to win to qualify?" Stevie asked.

"Three," Collins said. "They start with sixty-four players and sixteen get into the tournament. That tournament is probably a better story than the real one. You lose in the first round this week, you still make ten thousand dollars. The real pressure is to get into the first round."

"I can see why a wild card is a big deal," Stevie said. "How many are there here?"

"Eight," Collins said. "And you're right. That's why the agents beg for them."

Stevie started for the door.

"You mind if I go with you?" Susan Carol said.

That was a dicey question. She just now seemed to be getting over being angry with him. If he took her with him, she was going to be angry all over again. "I was sort of going to just go watch the match on the Grandstand court a little," Stevie fumbled. "I haven't been in there yet. But I'm going to get a hamburger first."

She had been looking at him suspiciously until he brought up the hamburger. Now she rolled her eyes.

"You're unbelievable," she said.

Maybe. But she did seem to believe him.

✗　✗　✗

Stevie walked briskly across the plaza and back under Louis Armstrong Stadium. He remembered seeing signs the day before that said GRANDSTAND COURT, so he knew he was going in the right direction. He could hear the sounds of the match being played on Louis Armstrong as he walked and noticed there were long lines of people waiting to get into the court. He glanced at the schedule he had put into his back pocket and saw why: Roger Federer, the number one player in the world, was playing his first match. He now understood why the people who ran the French Open and Wimbledon would stick Americans on outside courts. How could Federer, the defending champion, *not* play his first match on the biggest court on the grounds?

Maybe he would write about that later in the day. For the moment, he followed the signs that took him around the Armstrong hallways until he saw a sign that told him that if he went up a flight of steps and turned right he would reach the Grandstand. When he got to the top of the steps, he could see that the Grandstand court was actually attached to the side of Armstrong and there were walkways that allowed people to go back and forth between the two courts.

He turned right and walked to the corner of the court, where he was stopped by ushers and told to wait for the changeover. He looked at the scoreboard and saw that Makarova was already leading 3–1 in the first set. She was serving at his end of the court. Stevie studied her as she tossed the ball and served with a twisting topspin so that it high-hopped Stafford, forcing her to lunge and hit her return awkwardly into the net.

"Thirty–love," he heard the umpire say.

Makarova wasn't, as far as Stevie could tell, nearly as tall or as attractive as Symanova. She was probably five foot seven and, if truth be told, a tad on the chunky side for a tennis player. But Stevie could see she had great power and was surprisingly quick as she sprang to the net to put away a volley that made it 40–love.

The changeover could come on the next point. Stevie turned his attention from the court to the stands, which were no more than half-full—a fact that would no doubt annoy the Makarovs. There was a small media section only a few feet from where he was standing but there was no one there whom he recognized. He searched the stands, hoping he would get lucky—and he did. Sitting directly across from where he was standing, about three-quarters of the way up, all by himself, was Brendan Gibson. He was easy to pick out because there was no one around him and he was wearing the agent's uniform. Stevie knew there had to be a family-seating section someplace close to the court, but he figured Gibson wouldn't be seen with the Makarovs in public just yet.

"Okay, kid, you can go now."

It was the usher. He looked up and saw the two players walking to their chairs. Makarova had held serve to lead 4–1. He walked quickly behind the court and began climbing up the stairs to where Gibson sat. When Gibson saw him, his face registered surprise. Then he gave him a big smile. "Hey, Stevie, what brings you out here?" he said, waving him to come join him. "What have you done with my niece?"

Stevie tried to make sure he returned the smile. He was remembering the old reporting adage about asking the easy questions first. "I just went out to get a hamburger and she wasn't hungry," he said. "And I wanted to see Makarova play a little."

"Well, you better watch fast," he said. "I don't think this match will take very long." He pointed at a clock on the scoreboard that showed how long the match had been going on. It was just flipping to :20, meaning Makarova was on her way to winning the match in under an hour if this continued.

Stevie sat down in the empty area near Gibson. The upper part of the stands was just plastic benches without chair backs. The view was very good, though—the Grandstand probably didn't seat more than four thousand, so their angle looking down from twenty rows up was just about perfect. He heard the umpire call "Time," so he dropped his voice as Stafford lined up her first serve. She hit what looked to Stevie like a pretty good serve, only to watch as Makarova stepped into it and slugged a crosscourt backhand winner that Stafford didn't even bother trying to chase down.

"Love–15," the umpire said.

"So what brings *you* out to this match?" Stevie said quietly.

Brendan Gibson was staring at the court. "Huh? Oh. Just a little scouting mission."

Since he knew Susan Carol had already asked him about the Makarova rumors, there was no sense playing completely dumb. "You mean because Makarova's available?"

"Uh-huh. But don't believe the rumors I know you and Susan Carol have heard. We're a small agency. She's a very big fish. One of the giants will reel her in."

"Really? Sounded like you had a pretty good hook in last night."

What the hell, Stevie figured as he watched Makarova crush another forehand. Might as well go for it.

Gibson's eyes narrowed as he turned to look at Stevie. "What in the world are you talking about?"

"I was still awake when you got home last night."

Brendan Gibson looked at him as if trying to decide what to say or do next.

"Game Makarova. She leads 5–1."

"I know that. I got you a Coke. So what?"

"So I heard you talking to the Makarovs. I heard you toasting your new relationship."

"Didn't your parents ever tell you it's wrong to eavesdrop?"

"Didn't *your* parents tell you it's wrong to lie—especially to a niece who worships you!"

Stevie knew his voice, even though he was speaking in a loud whisper, was too loud. He could feel his heart pounding. He had never called a grown-up a liar before.

Much to his surprise, Gibson smiled. "Look, Stevie, you don't understand my business. Nothing has been signed yet. If it gets out that the Makarovs are going to go with me before they actually sign the contract, the other agencies will come in and try to blow me out of the water. They'll offer to cut their fees and they'll tell the Makarovs that I'm not experienced enough to get them the kind of deals and publicity they're looking for."

"So that means it's okay to lie to Susan Carol? Why didn't you just ask her to keep it quiet? She thinks you're the coolest guy going. She'd do anything for you."

"Does she know you're here cross-examining me as if I committed a crime?"

"*No.* She's angry with me for even questioning you."

"Game and first set Makarova."

The applause rose as the players started to change ends again. It had taken Makarova twenty-seven minutes to win the first set.

"Maybe you're right, Stevie," Gibson said, picking up as soon as the umpire stopped talking. "Maybe I should have confided in Susan Carol. But what's the big deal? I'm just starting in this business, and getting Makarova would be a huge hit for me. Why does that matter so much to you?"

"Because I'd like to know just how huge a hit it would be," he said, feeling himself start to sweat profusely. "And just what you would do to get the Makarovs to sign with you."

Brendan Gibson's eyes opened wide. He had figured out where Stevie was going with this. "Are you actually accusing me of kidnapping?" he said. "Susan Carol said something about people thinking me being involved with the Makarovs might somehow be tied to Symanova's disappearance. Now I know where she got it, from the wild and overheated imagination of her rude—not to mention completely out of his mind—friend!"

He stood up just as the umpire called "Time" again. "I'm going to sit someplace else," he said. "I'd recommend you find someplace else to stay. You're really not welcome in my home. I'm sure you can stay with your boy Kelleher or someone else."

He was gone before Stevie could get another word out of his mouth. He sat and stared at Gibson's back as he walked down the stairs. What had he just done? Had he flushed a guilty conscience? Or had he genuinely angered an innocent man?

He was sure of only two things: he needed to find a place to sleep tonight, and he needed to talk to Susan Carol before her uncle did. Because if he didn't, she might not speak to him.

Ever.

12: OLD FRIENDS . . . AND NEW

STEVIE WAS relieved when he saw that Brendan Gibson wasn't leaving the match, merely changing seats to get away from him. He watched him pick out another empty spot at the far end of the court. That meant he had a chance to find Susan Carol and talk to her before her uncle did.

He waited impatiently until the next changeover so he could leave. Naturally, leading 2–0, Makarova struggled in the next game. She played through three deuces before finally hitting a gorgeous drop shot to make it 3–0, allowing Stevie to get up and leave. He glanced in the direction of Gibson as he walked out, wondering if he was watching him. He couldn't tell—he was talking on a cell phone, which was technically against the rules. Whoo boy, Stevie thought, if he's on the phone with Susan Carol, I'm a dead man.

He practically sprinted back across the plaza, almost knocking people over on several occasions and eliciting commentary that would not have been allowed on network TV. He thought about calling Susan Carol on his cell phone but then remembered it was tucked safely—and uselessly—inside his computer bag. Breathing hard, he charged into the media center and found it almost empty. It was the middle of the day and most people were out watching matches. If there was anything new on Symanova, there was no sign of it anywhere. He walked over to Kelleher's desk and found no one around. Then he saw the note with his name on it: "Stevie, Mary Carillo took me down to the CBS studio to look around. Come meet me if you're back by 2. Follow the signs in the hallway that say TV studios—Susan Carol."

Stevie looked at his watch. It was one-forty-five. He wondered if the note had been written before or after he'd seen her uncle talking on his cell phone. There was only one way to find out. He was walking back out the door when he saw Bud and Anita Collins walking in. "Stefano!" Collins said, greeting him with a hug. "Where have you been? Björkman pulled up lame in the second set, poor fellow. Probably worn out from the qualifiers. We went to lunch in the corporate village. I'd have liked to have taken you and Susan Carol."

That reminded Stevie that he was hungry again. "Oh, I went to watch Makarova play a little. I'd never seen her."

"Well, judging by the scores, you didn't see much of her,"

Collins said. "But she *is* impressive. So strong. Reminds me of a young Navratilova."

"Has anyone heard anything new on Symanova?" Stevie asked.

"The USTA has announced a press conference at three o'clock," he said. "That gives me seventy-two minutes to write my column and then I'll do a news story after the press conference."

"Can you believe they're making a seventy-five-year-old man work this hard?" Anita said.

"It's no big deal," Collins said.

"Only because you love it," his wife answered.

"Well, I'm going to go find Susan Carol," Stevie said. "I guess she's down in the CBS studio with Mary Carillo."

"Oh, wonderful," Collins said. "They're nice people."

He left the two of them and started down the hall, figuring Kelleher was right when he said there wasn't anyone Collins *didn't* like. It concerned him a little that here he was, not quite fourteen, and already more cynical about people than Bud Collins was at seventy-five.

As instructed, he followed the signs. None of the doors were actually marked, so he ducked his head into two wrong doors before he finally found the right place. "Back here, Stevie," he heard Carillo say as he was starting to explain himself to the woman at the front desk.

He walked back a few steps and found himself in a large office/lounge area. There were two desks in the room and two couches. He immediately recognized two of the people on the couches: Bill Macatee, who he knew had been doing tennis and golf for CBS for years, and Patrick McEnroe, younger brother of John, who was now both the U.S. Davis Cup captain and a tennis analyst for CBS and ESPN. In fact, it seemed as if every time he turned on a TV set to watch tennis, Patrick McEnroe was doing the match. They both nodded hello at him before his attention was diverted by Carillo, coming out of a back room. She was sipping coffee. So was Susan Carol. Stevie decided against a lecture on the evils of caffeine.

"Where have you been?" Susan Carol asked. "You're sweating like you just played a match."

She was right. He hadn't even noticed until just now. "It was hot in the sun in the stadium," he said.

"Really?" Carillo said. "The media seating's in the shade." Whoops.

"Yeah, I know," Stevie said, stalling. "But I . . . decided to sit down close because there were so few people watching the match."

"The ushers didn't stop you?"

"Um, no. I guess they figured it was okay since the seats were empty."

That seemed to satisfy Carillo. The look on Susan Carol's face told Stevie she wasn't buying. He decided to change the subject.

"So what have you guys been reporting about Symanova?" he asked, directing the question at all three CBS people.

Macatee laughed. "They've brought in our news department to handle it," he said. "They don't think we jocks are capable of handling real news. Plus, the sports people are afraid if we do any real reporting, the USTA will get in a snit, and they don't want that."

"I heard they wouldn't let USA Network call it a kidnapping yesterday when everyone else was already calling it that," Stevie said.

"Exactly," Macatee said, shaking his head. "They can't push CBS around like that because we pay them a lot of money. But they can make their position pretty clear. We've all been pulling our hair out about what we can and can't do for the last twenty-four hours."

Macatee had, as far as Stevie could see, the most perfect head of hair on Earth. Carillo read his mind. "Billy is speaking metaphorically, of course," she said.

Stevie turned to Susan Carol. "The USTA press conference is at three," he said, not saying anything they all didn't already know. "I'm hungry. Will you go with me to get a hamburger first?"

"I thought you were getting one before. . . ."

"I got distracted."

"That reminds me," Carillo said. "I gotta get some makeup on. We're going live from the press conference. I hear they're announcing something important but it's very hush-hush. I can't get anyone to tell me anything."

"There you go being a reporter again," McEnroe said. "You should know better."

Susan Carol put down her coffee. "Okay, Ravenous One, let's go feed you. I'm a little bit hungry myself."

"I'll see you guys at the press conference," Carillo said, walking into a room marked MAKEUP.

They shook hands with Macatee and McEnroe and made their way to the door. Once they were in the hallway, Susan Carol stopped, looked around, and said in a quiet voice, "Okay, now tell me what you've really been up to."

"I will," he said. "Let's go for a walk."

✗ ✗ ✗

They walked back outside onto the plaza and through the big midday crowd to the food court.

"You get a table," Stevie said. "I'll get a hamburger. Then I'll fill you in."

"Get me . . ."

"I know, a bottle of water."

"Actually, I think it's time I try one of those hamburgers," she said. "Get me one too." She started to pull money out of her skirt pocket but Stevie waved her off. "It's on me."

He walked up to the counter, thinking, Because it might be the last time you ever eat with me.

She had found a table right on the edge of the food court. He put the food down, then took a swig of the water he had bought and a deep breath. "Okay, I might as well just tell you everything from the beginning," he said. "If you hate me, you hate me."

"I won't hate you," she said. "I might disagree with you, but I won't hate you. Just tell me what the heck's going on."

He started from the beginning, going from accidentally

overhearing her uncle's arrival in the apartment right through their hostile conversation in the Grandstand court. She was pale when he finished. He imagined he was too. She took several bites of her hamburger, causing Stevie to think she might just finish eating, get up, and walk away from him forever. Melodramatic, he thought, but entirely possible.

Finally, she took a sip of her water and shook her head. "Look, Stevie, I don't blame you for being suspicious of my uncle after what you heard," she said, sending a wave of relief through him. "But I can also kind of understand why he lied to me. I'm not saying it was *right* or that I'm not upset about it. But it does make sense that he was worried about the secret getting out before he has a signed contract. He *is* new at this."

"Then why do you think he blew up at me like that?" he asked.

"Well, you *did* call him a liar."

"Because he *lied*," Stevie said, getting a little bit defensive.

"And he tried to explain why. Then, in return, you called him a kidnapper."

She had a point. Maybe he had gone too far. "Okay, maybe I came on a little strong. But let me ask you this: if he wasn't your uncle and you didn't love him, would you feel any differently, given the facts, than I do? Wouldn't it at least cross your mind he might be involved—especially when someone you know to be honest gets caught in a flat-out lie?"

Again, she took a while to answer. "Maybe," she said. "Okay, yes, I would wonder. But I *do* know him. And I know he would never do anything like that. I've known him all my life."

"Have you ever known him to lie before?"

She sighed. "No."

They were both silent for a moment. Then she smiled—something he hadn't seen very often in the last twenty-four hours. "Do me one favor," she said. "Don't be upset with me for defending someone I love."

"On one condition."

"What?"

"That you not be upset with me for asking questions about him when he's left himself open to questions."

"Deal," she said. "Now what do we do next?"

"The first thing we have to do is get back to the media center for that press conference. The second thing we do is check in with Bobby and Tamara. And the third thing we do is figure out where I'm going to sleep tonight."

✗   ✗   ✗

They barely squeezed into the interview room for the press conference. The room was overflowing with camera crews packed into every available inch—and a few that weren't available—and reporters practically sitting on top of one another. Stevie and Susan Carol were almost the last two people let in the door before a USTA official said, "That's it, we can't get anyone else in. You'll have to go listen to the feed in the workroom."

They stood against the wall near the door and scanned the room. Kelleher, Tamara Mearns, and Bud Collins had obviously arrived early—they were in the front row, not far away from where they were standing since the door was near the front of the room. Kelleher looked over and saw them. He stood up. "Meet us at my desk when this is over," he shouted, just as the door behind the podium opened and Arlen Kantarian, the FBI guy from the day before, Hughes Norwood, and Misha Symanov walked in.

"Whoo boy," Stevie said, quickly stepping backward. The last thing he needed was for either Norwood or Symanov to spot him.

He stood just behind a tall guy with a tape recorder and urged Susan Carol to stand behind him. She could see over his head anyway, especially since the room raked up from front to back.

"Keep your head down," he said as everyone settled in.

"No kidding," she said.

Kantarian didn't waste any time with pleasantries. After introducing the other three men on the podium, he quickly turned the microphone over to the FBI guy: Bob Campbell.

"We have been contacted by Nadia Symanova's kidnappers," Campbell began, cutting right to the chase. "Obviously, there is now no doubt there has been a kidnapping. They have made certain demands, which I can tell you aren't financial. We are discussing these demands with Mr. Symanov and his wife right now before deciding exactly how to respond."

"What are the demands?" someone shouted, a simple and logical question.

"For obvious security reasons, we can't share that with you," Campbell said. "We have been told her life is *not* in danger. This has more to do with whether she will be returned in time to participate in this tournament."

"Have the kidnappers identified themselves to you?"

"Not specifically. But we have an idea who they are. Right now is not the time to share our suspicions with you."

"Is it the SVR?" Voices were coming from all over the room.

Campbell smiled. "As I said, I'm not prepared to speculate at this point."

"Can you confirm that it *isn't* the SVR?"

This time he didn't smile. "I can't confirm or deny anything in that area."

Bud Collins broke in. "Misha, can you give us some idea of what the last twenty-four hours have been like for you and Yolanda?"

For the next ten minutes, Misha Symanov talked at great length about what he and his wife and their family and friends had been through. He thanked Hughes Norwood and the USTA for all their help and he said he hoped this ordeal would be over soon. He was far more emotional than he had appeared to be in the SMG lounge just that morning. Perhaps he was more worn out. Perhaps hearing from the kidnappers had made the situation more frightening for him. He concluded by saying he was grateful for all the sympathy and support extended to him and to his family since "this nightmare of our lives began."

He paused for a minute to collect himself. "I know there have been many rumors," he continued. "I want to say this to all of you: the Russian government has been very supportive since yesterday. They have offered to help my family in any way possible. I have lived in this country five years now and I love it, but I am very proud to be Russian by birth. So too is my daughter."

"He's either very good or very upset," Susan Carol said.

Stevie had been thinking almost the same thing. Maybe they were both being a little unfair. He was trying to imagine how his parents would react if he vanished into thin air. And yet Susan Carol was right—something seemed odd about Mr. Symanov. One minute he was as calm as could be, the next he was the brokenhearted father.

Kantarian was breaking up the press conference, saying the media would be kept apprised as more information became available. Before Stevie or Susan Carol could start to leave, a man wearing a USTA shirt walked up and said quietly, "Can I have a word with you two kids?"

Uh-oh, Stevie thought. What could this be? The man walked toward the door and signaled them to follow him. Stevie wondered if they shouldn't go back and grab Kelleher or Tamara or Bud Collins so one of them could vouch for them. The man kept walking toward the door of the media center and didn't stop until they were outside.

"Should we really go out there?" Stevie hissed at Susan Carol as she followed him.

"Beats me," she said.

Once they were in a quiet spot, the man turned around, put out a hand, and said, "Mark Preston."

They shook hands. Preston looked around to make sure no one was listening to him.

"I heard what you guys said in there about the father."

"We didn't mean anything by it," Susan Carol said. "We were just—"

Preston waved a hand to stop her. "Calm down, I'm not here to lecture you. I think you're right. I don't get why any of the so-called pros in there haven't gotten onto this yet."

"Onto what?" Stevie said, because he wasn't sure exactly what they were onto.

"Something is funny with the father. We all know he was blabbing to anyone who would listen yesterday that the SVR did this. Kelleher wrote it; Bud's whole column was on his angst right after the girl disappeared. Now the Russians are his best friends."

"Maybe he has to say that," Susan Carol said. "Maybe that's how they get her released."

"Maybe," Preston said. "But it's all a little too easy, I think. The kid disappears, the father and Norwood are practically chasing the media around yesterday to say the SVR did it. Now it's all hearts and flowers—no more evil Russians."

"Okay, let's say you're right," Stevie said quietly. "What do you think we should do about it?"

Preston looked around. "If I was still a reporter—"

"You were a reporter?" Stevie broke in, causing Susan Carol to give him one of her be-quiet looks.

"For twenty-five years," he said. "My mind still works like a reporter even if doing PR pays my bills. Look, my instincts are telling me something is up with the father, and I think yours are telling you the same thing."

"So where would your reporting instincts lead you right now?" Susan Carol said.

"Easy," Preston said. "The U.S. Open Club. I heard Norwood telling Symanov just before they walked into the press conference that their four o'clock meeting would be there. It's unofficial agent headquarters when they're up to something, because the media's not allowed in."

"Is that the place next to Slew's?" Stevie asked.

"Yeah," Preston said. "Same food, only more expensive."

"*More* expensive—"

Susan Carol cut him off. "If the media can't go in there, how can we?"

"Follow me," Preston said. "I can take care of that."

13: MORE CLUES

THEY FOLLOWED Mark Preston back inside to an office that said USTA COMMUNICATIONS.

"Give me your credentials," he said.

"What! Why?" they said almost together. Stevie didn't feel the least bit comfortable about giving his credential to someone he had just met.

"I'll be back in five minutes," he said. "Stay right here, you'll be fine."

Stevie looked at Susan Carol, who nodded. They slipped their credentials over their heads and handed them to Preston, who—after glancing around *again*—disappeared inside the office.

"Why are we trusting this guy?" Stevie said.

"I'm not sure," Susan Carol said. "Gut instinct? He makes

sense. He has no reason to lie—that we know of, anyway. Right now I don't know *whom* to trust."

He knew she was talking about what was going on with her uncle, but he decided this wasn't the time to pursue it. "Maybe we should ask Kelleher or Bud about him," he said.

"Too late now," she said. "They're nowhere in sight and he's got our credentials. We just have to hope . . ."

The door opened again and Preston reappeared. "See, not even five minutes," he said. He handed them back their credentials. Then he handed Susan Carol an envelope. "Don't open it in here," he said. "Walk outside, and while you're walking around the building, slip your media credential off and replace it with what's in here."

He smiled. "I'm sure you both think I'm nuts, but I'm trying to help and I just have a feeling you guys are onto something. I trust Kelleher and Mearns, but I think you guys might be a little ahead of the curve right now and you might be better able to run this down. Good luck."

He shook their hands and left. "You want to try it?" Susan Carol asked.

"Let's walk outside and see what's in the envelope," he said.

She nodded and they headed out and began circling the stadium. After a few steps, she opened the envelope, pulled out the contents, and smiled. "Take a look," she said, handing a credential to Stevie. "This might work." He looked at it. Like the media credential it had his photo on it. But instead of a giant "M," it had a large "F" in blue lettering. Underneath it said simply: PLAYER FAMILY.

"These will get us into the Open Club, and if we see Norwood or Symanov, we can still stick to our story about being Evelyn's brother and sister," she said. "These don't have names on them, just the player family thing."

"Looks like Mark Preston knows what he's doing."

"So far," she said. "Now it's up to us."

Susan Carol called Kelleher on her cell to let him know they were working on something and might not be back in the media center for a while. Stevie heard her say, "We'll fill you in when we get back" before she hung up. Kelleher was obviously curious.

Their new passes got them inside the door marked U.S. OPEN CLUB—CREDENTIAL HOLDERS ONLY with no problem. Stevie noticed a board on the window that showed who was and was not admitted to the club. There was a very clear X through the "M" badge on the board.

The room was large and open with tinted windows that allowed customers to look out at the plaza but prevented passersby from looking in. There was a very large buffet table in the back. A hostess seated them in a booth that was thankfully tucked away in a corner of the room. Stevie and Susan Carol searched the room for familiar faces. It was four o'clock and only a few tables were occupied. They saw no one they recognized.

"Maybe Preston's not as good as we thought," Stevie said.

"Let's give it some time," she said. "I imagine you're hungry again. It's been almost two hours since you last ate."

She had a point. The waiter encouraged them to try the buffet—"It's a bargain," he said, noting that the cost was only $27.50 for all you could eat. Susan Carol ordered a salad and iced tea. Stevie sighed and settled for the grilled chicken with a side order of french fries.

They were sipping their drinks when Stevie saw Susan Carol's eyes widen. "Don't look," she said.

Stevie looked anyway. Across the room, coming in a back door, were Hughes Norwood, the Symanovs, and another man whom Stevie didn't recognize. They sat at a table in the far corner—good news because they didn't notice Stevie and Susan Carol, bad news because there was no way to hear any of the conversation.

"That man with them looks familiar," Susan Carol said. Then she let out a small gasp. "Oh my God, I know who it is!"

"Who?" he said.

"His name's Glenn O'Donahue. He's a movie director. Does celebrity sensation stuff—really big blockbusters. I think his last big hit was something about Princess Diana's one true love—some guy she dated in high school."

"High-class stuff."

"Yeah, but apparently it sells. Seriously, you've never heard of him?"

Stevie shook his head. "What matters," he said, "is why he would be meeting with the Symanovs and Norwood."

"I'll give you three guesses."

He was about to answer when someone else walked in the back door. His first instinct was to duck under the table, but

Brendan Gibson headed straight for the corner where Norwood, the Symanovs, and O'Donahue were sitting, without glancing in their direction. There were handshakes all around and Gibson sat down. Stevie looked at Susan Carol. Her face was white.

"This is *not* possible," she said, her voice filled with anger. She started to slide out of the booth.

"Hey, wait a second," he said. "Where do you think you're going?"

"Over there to ask my uncle exactly what he's doing with those people."

He half stood up, reached across the table, and hauled her back down. "Are you nuts?" he said, keeping his voice to a whisper because he didn't want to attract any attention. "Calm down. You have to think more clearly than that right now."

She had tears in her eyes. "You hurt my arm," she said.

"I—I'm sorry, I didn't mean to. . . ."

She shook her head. "It's not that bad. But how can my uncle be involved with those people?"

He leaned forward and lowered his voice. "That," he said, "is *exactly* what we have to find out."

✗ ✗ ✗

Their food came a moment later. Susan Carol wiped her tears on a napkin and took a deep breath. They kept an eye on what was going on across the room. Fortunately, Brendan Gibson had his back to them and everyone else was too involved in the conversation to notice them.

Susan Carol picked at her salad and kept glancing at her uncle. "Something's rotten in Denmark," she said.

"And in New York, and Moscow, and Hollywood too," he said, actually causing her to smile.

"Listen," he continued. "You're the smart one here. What should we do next?"

"Don't suck up to me, Stevie," she said. "Obviously we need to find out what they're plotting over there."

"That's the easy part. The question is *how?*"

For a moment she didn't say anything, staring at her uncle's back as if he might somehow not be there if she stared long enough and hard enough.

"Earth to Susan Carol," he said.

"I'm here," she said, snapping her attention back to him.

"Okay, here's what I think," she continued, her eyes refocusing on him. "O'Donahue has no idea who we are. And we have these badges that say 'player family.' What if I bluff him? I'll tell him that I'm Norwood's niece and he told me I could try out for a part in the movie."

"Movie?"

"What do you think O'Donahue's sitting over there for? They're planning a movie. Which means they must know Nadia is safe."

"But if they know she's safe, why haven't they announced it? Why would they keep it secret?"

"Exactly."

"So what do you want me to do?"

She smiled the old Susan Carol smile. "You need to go to Evelyn Rubin's match tomorrow. You have to find out what—if anything—she knows about all this. We need to know if she's somehow involved too."

"How would she be involved?"

"Think about it: Symanova's kidnapped, returns heroically to play in the Open, then loses in the third round to someone younger than her who wasn't even ranked in the top hundred in the world before the summer started and has just recently cracked the top fifty."

"Not a perfect ending for a movie."

"Right. *But* if the beautiful and courageous young star who wants so much to represent her new country makes it to the quarters and takes on the evil, big-hitting, not nearly as attractive Russian . . ."

"Makarova."

"Uh-huh. Good versus evil. That's better."

"So you think your uncle would convince Evelyn to tank the match? Why, though? Symanova should beat her anyway, at least based on ranking."

"You saw Evelyn play. She's a lot better than her ranking. Maybe she makes them nervous. That's what you have to find out."

"But how?"

The smile again. "Stevie, you can be very charming. Charm her."

"Now who's sucking up, Scarlett?" he said, smiling in spite of himself.

The meeting at the other end of the room was breaking up. "Look down and away," Susan Carol hissed.

He did as ordered. They both watched out of the corner

of their eyes as everyone shook hands. They breathed a sigh of relief when the group exited through the back.

"Okay," Susan Carol said. "Now all I've got to do is figure out how to get five minutes alone with Glenn O'Donahue."

✗   ✗   ✗

They split up once they had paid the check. Susan Carol headed off to try to find O'Donahue while Stevie went back to the pressroom to update Kelleher and find out if he could stay with him that night. They had discarded the idea of Susan Carol talking Brendan into forgiving Stevie. Instead, she was going to pretend to be outraged by Stevie's accusations and stay clearly on her uncle's side. At least for the moment.

"Be careful," Stevie said.

"I promise," Susan Carol said.

"I'm serious. These people have a lot at stake. . . ."

"I know, I know. I'll see you back at the media center. If I'm not back in an hour, send a posse out to look for me."

"Keep your cell phone on."

"Yes, Dad."

She said it with a smile—she was glad he cared. He sort of wanted to hug her but held back since he was going to see her in an hour—or less.

Stevie made his way back to the media center. Evelyn Rubin would play the second match on court 4 the next day. Stevie knew from walking around that court 4 was the biggest outside court. It was a long way from where she had played on Monday—court 18 was barely on the grounds.

Kelleher walked up behind him as he was staring at the schedule.

"Where've you been?" Kelleher asked. "And where's Susan Carol?"

"She's working on something," Stevie said. "And I was checking out tomorrow's schedule."

"Well, don't check it too closely," Kelleher said. "It's being changed."

"Huh? Why?"

"Because the SVR has agreed to release Nadia Symanova. Her parents just got a phone call. They left here with a police escort five minutes ago."

"Really?! How do you know all this?" Stevie said.

"Arlen told me. He said the SVR is still denying it was involved. They're going to have a press conference for her tomorrow afternoon and she'll be the first match on Arthur Ashe tomorrow night. CBS is going to cancel its regular prime-time programming to show it. Carillo told me they're making a deal with USA Network right now. Nadia's become too big for cable TV."

He shook his head. "The movie rights can't be far behind."

Stevie almost gagged. "You don't know how right you are about that," he said.

"What do you mean?"

"Sit down," Stevie said. "I have a lot to tell you."

14: TRIUMPHANT RETURN

BOBBY KELLEHER'S jaw kept dropping further and further as Stevie filled him in on all he and Susan Carol had seen and heard. He shook his head when Stevie described the meeting in the U.S. Open Club, and he said, "I feel for Susan Carol. That's got to be a jolt to see her uncle involved in this somehow."

The question, they agreed, was what "this" was. They had no real proof that the Symanovs or Hughes Norwood or Brendan Gibson was involved in anything sinister. "For all we know, O'Donahue approached them and said, 'If everything works out, there might be a movie in all this,'" Kelleher said.

"Do you believe that?" Stevie said.

"No," Kelleher said. "If Hughes Norwood is involved, I always believe the worst. I think you're right. They already knew Nadia was okay when you saw them in the Open Club. They probably knew it earlier today. The question is, why did they hold it back? Supposedly they just now got the word and rushed out of here."

Kelleher's cell phone was chirping. He looked at the number and smiled. "It's Susan Carol," he said as he answered. He listened for a moment, nodding his head.

"No," he said. "I wouldn't push it any further than that. Come on back here and we'll figure out what we want to do tomorrow."

He closed the phone. "Did she find O'Donahue?" Stevie asked.

"Oh yeah," he said. "I guess she gave him a wide-eyed 'I can't believe I'm meeting a famous director' routine."

"I've seen that routine," Stevie said. "It's very good."

"I guess it is," Kelleher said. "O'Donahue told her that he's been here all week because Hughes Norwood invited him to come to the tournament as his guest. He says they've done business before. She gave him a sort of breathless 'Are you gonna do a movie on Nadia Symanova if they find her?' And he said, 'Don't worry, sweetheart, they'll find her.' "

"What did you tell her not to push too far?"

"She was thinking of trying to talk to her uncle, but I told her that wasn't a good idea right now. She needs to cool down first."

Stevie's mind was racing. "What do you think this is all

about?" he said to Kelleher. "Would the Symanovs really try to turn their daughter's kidnapping into something they could make money on?"

Kelleher shrugged. "These are tennis people," he said. "Their number one advisor is Hughes Norwood. I wouldn't put anything past them."

"Okay, but it still seems fast—they barely know she's safe and already they're making movie deals? And I'm still not convinced it was the SVR that did this. They've just been too forthcoming about that."

"A skeptic after my own heart," Kelleher said. "Susan Carol's not the only smart one on the team of Anderson and Thomas."

✗　✗　✗

The good news for Stevie was that the apartment Kelleher and Mearns were staying in had two bedrooms and they were both amenable to his staying with them, given that he was no longer welcome at 52 Riverside Drive.

Susan Carol came back to the pressroom and quickly wrote a very straight story on the day's match results for her paper. The only upset had been Lleyton Hewitt, the one-time Wimbledon and U.S. Open champion who had been beaten by a guy named Paradorn Srichaphan.

"Spell that three times fast," Tamara Mearns said as she sat next to Susan Carol, writing her own story.

Kelleher gave Stevie the day off. "You might have a lot to do tomorrow," he said.

Kelleher had written an early column on the strange press conference, staying away from speculation because it was just too dangerous at this point. "You imply for one second that the Symanovs are anything but victims right now and you not only might have a lawsuit thrown at you, but you will make all your readers very angry," he said. "No sense messing around until we know more."

When he and Susan Carol and Mearns were finished writing, Kelleher drove them all back into Manhattan. Susan Carol called her uncle and was told he wouldn't be home until late. So they swung by his apartment so Stevie could pack his things and then they all went out for dinner. Kelleher asked if pizza was okay with everyone and drove to a place on the East Side called John's Pizza. It was even better than the pizza they'd had on Sunday—which already felt like a lifetime ago to Stevie. He ate six slices.

"You are going to gain ten pounds before you get home," Susan Carol said.

"That's okay, I can afford it," he said.

Kelleher groaned. "Oh, to be thirteen again," he said.

After dinner, Susan Carol insisted she didn't need to be driven back crosstown. "Just put me in a cab," she said.

Stevie walked her to the corner where she could catch a cab headed west while Kelleher and Mearns went to retrieve their car. "We'll swing around and pick you up," Kelleher told Stevie.

As they stood on the corner, Stevie felt a tug of sadness.

"I'm really sorry this is happening," he said.

"I know you are," she said. He could see that her eyes were glistening just a little bit. "Don't worry, it'll be fine in the end."

She whistled and a cab skidded to a halt in front of them. "Promise you'll call my cell as soon as you get inside the apartment," he said.

She patted him on the shoulder. "I'll be fine."

"Promise."

This time she put her arm around him. "I promise. Remember, Stevie, tomorrow is another day."

"Scarlett . . ."

She jumped into the cab before he could say another word. The cab pulled away just as Kelleher pulled up.

Stevie's new room appeared to belong to a child of about four. But it had plenty of room—and lots of toys. He dropped his bag and walked back into the living room to find Kelleher and Mearns watching the opening for *SportsCenter*. The lead story, according to Dan Patrick, was that the USTA had called an eleven a.m. press conference for the next day, "fueling speculation that Nadia Symanova has been found. The question is, what kind of condition is she in? ESPN's Luke Jensen reports that the Symanov family and the SVR have been in negotiations since last Monday when Symanova disappeared."

Kelleher groaned. "This is why I hate ESPN," he said. "Every news outlet in the country has been reporting for two days that Symanova was kidnapped by the SVR and they act as if they have a scoop."

Stevie wanted to stay up and talk, but he was out on his

feet. He set the alarm for eight o'clock and was asleep almost as soon as his head hit the pillow. About five minutes later, or so it seemed, the alarm was going off. He got up, took a shower, and found Kelleher and Mearns sitting in the kitchen drinking coffee. "Want me to make you some eggs?" Kelleher offered.

"No thanks," he said. "Cereal's fine."

"You should think about the eggs," Mearns said. "Bobby's actually a pretty good cook. Sunny-side up is his specialty."

He settled for cereal and had just finished when the apartment buzzer sounded. It was Susan Carol, who was waiting in the lobby. They went downstairs to meet her and walked outside to wait for the car. Stevie was amazed—as always—by how much traffic there was in Manhattan. But it was a beautiful morning, the weather had cooled off considerably, and there was a slight snap of fall in the air.

"How'd it go with your uncle last night?" he asked Susan Carol while they waited.

"Not great," she said. "He wanted to know where you'd come up with the idea that he was some kind of criminal. I told him that you'd really been thrown by the Makarovs being in the apartment. I told him you just overreacted and you were sorry. He went into this long explanation about how dirty the agenting business could be."

"Apparently he's fitting right in," Mearns said as the car pulled up, causing Susan Carol to look a little bit ill.

"You didn't say anything about seeing him in the U.S. Open Club, did you?" Stevie said as they climbed into the backseat.

She gave him a withering look, and he put up a hand to say, "Question withdrawn."

The Midtown Tunnel was surprisingly empty so the trip was short. But by the time they pulled into the parking lot, everyone had an assignment: Susan Carol and Tamara were going to hang out in the U.S. Open Club—Kelleher said he thought he could get Mearns a pass from Kantarian—while Kelleher worked the players' lounge to see who was there and what the talk was, especially if Nadia Symanova made a splashy return at the press conference. Stevie's assignment was to talk to Evelyn Rubin after her match—win or lose.

The pressroom was buzzing when they walked in. Everyone had a different theory on what was going to happen at the press conference. "You heard what they're doing, didn't you?" Bud Collins said as they were putting their computers down. "There's not enough room for all the media in the interview room, so they're setting up a podium and chairs on one of the practice courts."

"Will that mean all the fans get to stand around and watch?" Susan Carol asked. "Won't that be a circus?"

"Exactly, my dear," Collins said. "I'm sure that's exactly what the USTA wants. Can you imagine the TV rating they're going to get when she plays tonight?"

"I'm not sure it's just the USTA that wants a circus," Stevie said quietly to Susan Carol.

"Good point," she said.

They decided to leave early to walk over to practice court 7. That turned out to be a smart decision. A ring of security had been set up to keep people from getting to the walkway behind the practice courts. Their credentials got them through, but they had to wait because the guards were checking people's passes very thoroughly. As usual, Stevie got the double and triple look at his credential. "He's my assistant," Kelleher said. The guard raised an eyebrow but said nothing and let them through without any hassle.

A podium had been set up at one end of the court. There were rows of chairs all the way back to the net, and behind that was an even larger podium that was jam-packed with cameras and their crews. As it got close to eleven o'clock, they could hear the whir of helicopters overhead. "I haven't seen anything like this since the O.J. chase," Mearns said.

By 11:10, a USTA PR guy was demanding that everyone take seats, and even from a distance, they could sense that an entourage of people was moving toward the court. "Reminds me of the posse in *Butch Cassidy and the Sundance Kid*," Kelleher said, bringing up a famous old movie Stevie had watched with his dad. "You can see them coming from miles away."

The posse entered through a side gate near the podium. Stevie tried to count the security people as they poured in—some in suits with earpieces, some in the blue shirts worn by the USTA security people—and gave up when he got to eighteen. In the midst of all of them, Stevie could see Arlen Kantarian, Mr. and Mrs. Symanov, Hughes Norwood, and last but certainly not least, Nadia Symanova. As soon as the fans spotted her, they began to clap and cheer and call out her name: "Nadia! Nadia!" The noise built as they came through the gate and people could see her clearly as she followed her father onto the podium. She was dressed more like a model than a tennis player, in a short blue dress and high-heeled sandals.

"She must be eight feet tall in those shoes," Stevie said to Susan Carol.

"Don't make fun of tall girls," Susan Carol said. "But you're right."

The posse sat in chairs next to the podium and Kantarian walked to the microphone to get things started. There was still a lot of noise from the fans and hundreds of cameras clicking and whirring as Symanova sat down and crossed her legs. She had a broad smile on her face and was waving to people, even blowing kisses at a few particularly amorous fans. *"Marry me, Nadia!"* one of them screamed.

Kantarian, now at the microphone, picked up on that quickly, saying, "No proposals this morning."

Everyone laughed. Kantarian settled into the script that was apparently in front of him. "We're here this morning to celebrate," he said. "As you can all see, Nadia Symanova has been returned safely to her family and to the family that is the world of tennis."

"Oh God, the family of tennis," Mearns said. "Be sure to write that down."

Kantarian went on for several minutes: they could not share details of Nadia's ordeal, he said, because the FBI still considered it an open case. No ransom had been paid. He knew there had been speculation that the Russian SVR had been responsible for her kidnapping but they could not confirm or deny that. What mattered, he said, was that she was safe and "this nightmare is now over and we can go on with this wonderful tournament with Nadia very much a part of it." He announced that her first-round match would be played on Arthur Ashe Stadium court that night at eight o'clock, the start moved back thirty minutes to accommodate CBS.

"What a surprise," Kelleher murmured.

"The winner of the Symanova–Joanne Walsh match will play her second-round match on Friday, and the winner of that match will play Sunday. So the tournament is running right on schedule. When I'm finished, Nadia will make a statement, but please remember she's been through an ordeal and she has to play tonight, so she can't talk long."

Bud Collins stood up in the front row to ask a question and Kantarian waved a hand at him. "Wait till we get a mike to you, Bud," he said as someone rushed in with a handheld for him.

Collins came right to the point. "Arlen, with all due respect, what do you mean, you can't give us details? We're all thankful Nadia is safe, but now that this is over, don't you think the public deserves to have an understanding of who did this and why?"

There was some catcalling from the fans as he sat down, some people yelling, "Yeah, tell us!" and others saying, "Leave her alone, media!"

Kantarian smiled uncomfortably. "I hear you, Bud," he said. "But even though Nadia is safe now, this isn't over.

There are some issues we are still dealing with—like bringing her kidnappers to justice—that make it impossible for us to be as forthcoming as we'd like to be."

Kantarian babbled on for a few more minutes about how cooperative everyone had been, how supportive Symanova's fellow players had been—"I guess he didn't hear Walsh's agent screeching for a default," Susan Carol whispered—and how proud he was of everyone in the sport for "coming together in a crisis." Finally, he brought Symanova to the podium. When he did, Hughes Norwood came up with her.

The crowd went wild when Symanova got to the mike, and she waved and smiled some more.

"This is turning into a damn pep rally," Kelleher said.

"Isn't that the point?" Stevie asked.

"Apparently."

Someone had the mike and was asking a question. "Nadia, McDonald Faircloth from Fox News. Can you describe your ordeal?"

Symanova smiled and looked at Norwood, who nodded. Apparently this question was okay to answer. "It was very awful," she said, her English carrying just the trace of an accent. "Before I knew what was happening, there was something covering my mouth and I was being pulled along. As soon as we were in the car, I was blindfolded. It was all very, very scary. I prayed to God to help me, to save me, and he did. I know many people have prayed for me, and I want to thank them all."

"Did you fear for your life?" the Fox guy said, following up.

She smiled. "Of course I did. If you were shut in a room

with no windows for two days with a blindfold on, I think you would be scared too."

Stevie wondered how she knew the room had no windows if she was blindfolded.

Someone else had the mike. "Nadia, Joseph Frisell from NBC News. Two questions: Were you fed? And do you think you'll be able to play tonight after what you've been through?"

She smiled again. "Yes, they did feed me, though not very much. Last night after I was safe, I had a giant steak. I'm feeling great now." She moved away from the podium so everyone could see her from head to toe and struck a pose. Leaning back into the mike, she said, "How do I look?"

Whistles and catcalls came from all sides. "Boy, she's good," Mearns said.

Symanova was still talking. "I do not know, though, how I will play tonight. As soon as I leave here, I will go for a hit and hope I am okay to play. For now, I am happy to be alive, and I thank everyone for their love and their prayers."

Hughes Norwood now took the microphone. "That's all the time we have for now. Thank you very much."

People were screaming all at once, trying to ask more questions. Bud Collins and a couple of other people in the front row tried to advance on the podium for follow-up questions and were practically knocked down by security guards. Symanova was waving to the crowd as she exited.

"Dog and pony show," Kelleher said, watching the entourage disappear through the gate.

"What's a dog and pony show?" Stevie asked.

"Something sensational with no substance," Susan Carol said. "They're just trying to get publicity without telling us anything."

"Well, they certainly accomplished that," Stevie said. "What do we do now?"

Kelleher shrugged. "I think we proceed just as we had planned."

"Except for one thing," Susan Carol said.

"What's that?"

"I think you should try to call your FBI guy again. He's got to be able to tell you more than we heard here."

Kelleher nodded. "Thirteen-year-olds should not be as smart as you are, Susan Carol," he said.

Mearns said, "You need to get out to court four, Stevie. I can see on the big scoreboard that Evelyn's match has started."

She was right. They hadn't gotten any answers during the dog and pony show, so they would have to go find them on their own. Which is what they should have counted on from the start.

15: MEDIA DARLING

IT TOOK them several minutes to get off the practice court and through the throngs still milling around on the plaza in hopes of getting a glimpse of Symanova, who was now long gone. Stevie walked as quickly as he could to court 4, which was directly behind the practice courts. It had grandstands on both sides with space, Stevie guessed, for about three thousand. He noticed a sign on the far side of the court that said MEDIA ONLY and headed there to find a seat. It wasn't easy. The place was packed. There were at least seventy-five media members watching Evelyn Rubin play Lisa Raymond—which was exactly seventy-three more than had watched her on Monday—and Stevie had to squeeze into a corner seat.

Rubin was up 4–3 in the first set with Raymond serving. Stevie recognized Raymond's name. She was one of the older players on tour. Someone, if his memory was right, who was more of a doubles specialist than a singles player at this point in her career. He looked at the draw sheet in his pocket and discovered he was right: her singles ranking had dropped to number 108 but he knew she had once been a top-twenty player. Rubin was wearing a baseball cap to protect herself from the sun and had her hair tied back, just as she had on Monday. One thing Stevie liked about her was that she didn't grunt or shriek when she hit the ball. If there was one thing Stevie had never liked about Maria Sharapova or Venus Williams, it was all the shrieking. Rubin almost made it look easy. She didn't crush every shot—she'd use topspin some of the time, the occasional drop shot, and a lot of very sharp angles. The trend in tennis had been in the direction of pure power: the Williams sisters, Sharapova, Lindsay Davenport. Rubin had power in her game, but finesse too—unusual for such a young player. She had Raymond running a lot, which, even in the cooler weather, Stevie knew would be to her advantage, just as in the Maleeva match.

He looked around, searching for Brendan Gibson. He wouldn't be so easy to pick out in this crowd, even in his agent's uniform. The place was packed. Stevie saw no sign of him, although it was possible he was sitting on the same side of the court, out of his view.

He was sitting next to a middle-aged man with curly brown hair and a mustache. Stevie glanced down at his credential and saw that his name was Pete Alfano and he worked for the Fort Worth *Star-Telegram*. Stevie turned his attention back to the court just in time to see Rubin surprise Raymond by coming to the net. Raymond had floated a backhand and Rubin closed on it and put it away with a pretty forehand volley. Stevie was reminded of something he had heard Carillo say: that the last female player who could really volley was Martina Navratilova.

"Game Rubin. She leads five games to three, first set."

Pete Alfano wrote something in his notebook and turned to Stevie. "Pete Alfano," he said, extending his hand.

"Steve Thomas," Stevie said, accepting the handshake.

"I know who you are," Alfano said. "You're one of the kids who saved Chip Graber at the Final Four. Nice work."

Stevie was starting to get used to reporters knowing who he and Susan Carol were. But it was still cool.

"Thanks," Stevie answered. "We were very lucky. So why are so many reporters watching *this* match?"

Alfano smiled and started to answer but Raymond was serving. He waited until an interminable backcourt rally ended with Raymond shrieking in anger as her forehand cracked the net tape. "Symanova can beat Joanne Walsh and Annabelle Kim if she plays them left-handed. This Rubin kid can play. She wins today, they'll play in the third round and it will be the most watched third-round match in U.S. Open history. Most of us haven't seen her or have only seen her briefly. So we need to see her today—and talk to her about what she's probably going to walk into on Sunday."

That made sense. It also meant, Stevie realized, that he wasn't going to be able to saunter up to Evelyn Rubin and see if she could talk to him. And judging by the packed stands, the media weren't the only ones who saw Rubin as an emerging story. The rest of the match went fairly quickly. Raymond double-faulted on set point to lose the first set, and just as she had done with Maleeva, Rubin simply wore her out in the second set, running her from side to side with her ground strokes. She was up 5–0 in what seemed like the blink of an eye, then got a little bit nervous and blew four match points to allow Raymond to win a game. She finally ended it on her fifth match point, hitting a perfect drop shot that Raymond simply stood and watched with a smile on her face as if to say, "Kid, you're just a little too good for me." The crowd gave Rubin a standing ovation as the players shook hands at the net. Rubin had won, 6–3, 6–1.

"A star is born," Pete Alfano said, standing up. "Now let's see if the USTA is asleep at the wheel."

"What do you mean?"

"I mean there's close to a hundred of us out here. They ought to take this kid into the interview room. But I'll bet they're so Nadia-obsessed right now, there's no one out here from the PR staff and we're going to have to crowd around her on the court. It will be chaos."

As it turned out, Alfano was right. By the time they worked their way down to courtside, most of the media had formed a semicircle just outside the entrance of the court where Rubin would exit. A few had cornered Raymond as she came out—no doubt to get her to talk about Rubin. Then Evelyn came walking out, head down, still with just one security guard, and seemed shocked when she heard a chorus of voices calling her name. She had probably been expecting to see Stevie and Susan Carol and no one else, just like on Monday. That, Stevie thought, was a long time ago.

Several TV people with cameras and microphones pushed forward, practically knocking Rubin down in the process. Stevie could see the security guy pull his walkie-talkie off his belt. No doubt he was calling for help—which was a good idea. The questions came all at once and, standing near the back with Alfano, Stevie could see that a good deal of pushing and shoving was going on near the front.

"Someone's going to get hurt," Alfano said.

"You called it," Stevie told him.

"I've covered this tournament since the eighties," Alfano sighed. "The USTA hasn't learned very much in that time."

Stevie kept looking around, wondering where Brendan Gibson was. Still no sign of him. He was surprised. This was a big moment for his client. Why wouldn't her agent be here? He wasn't complaining. It would be a lot tougher to talk to Rubin alone if Gibson was around. Perhaps impossible since he might jump in and say no. Stevie continued looking around amid the tumult to see if he was lurking.

Some of the print reporters were yelling at some of the TV guys. Evelyn was standing back, letting the security guy try to create some space for her, looking stunned by what she was seeing. Finally, some sort of accord seemed to be reached and people began asking questions that could actually be heard.

The third question—after a couple about how well she had played against Raymond—got to the point. "Do you realize you will probably play Nadia Symanova next?"

"Well, I know she's the seeded player in my section of the draw," Evelyn said. "I'm just very glad that she's okay. I saw her in the hallway when she was walking to her press conference, but I didn't get a chance to say hello because there must have been a hundred people around her. If I do play her, it will be a thrill to be on court with her."

Stevie was struck by how cool and calm Evelyn was under the circumstances. She patiently answered all the questions: no, she had never played Symanova before (Stevie noticed a TV person asked that, a question that could have been answered by looking at Evelyn's bio); yes, she had been very scared when she had heard about the kidnapping; Nadia was very brave to come back and play; when she'd talked to her on occasion she seemed like a very nice girl. The media crowd began to thin. More security arrived, but by this time things were more or less under control. The TVs, as Stevie heard Kelleher call them all the time, had their sound bites and began to leave, practically taking off the heads of fans—who were being kept back by more security people—as they departed. Finally, just a few reporters with notebooks were left. Stevie moved closer and stood just outside the circle. Evelyn spotted him. "Hi, Stevie," she said as some-one was asking a question.

He was very pleased she had noticed him and said hello. "Great win, Evelyn," Stevie said.

"Is this your boyfriend?" one of the reporters said to Eve-lyn. Stevie certainly didn't mind someone thinking that, but he felt his face flush when the question was asked.

She laughed. "No, no, just a friend. I'm afraid Stevie's taken. He dates my agent's niece."

Whoo boy, now Stevie was turning multiple colors. He started to correct her, then realized it was pointless. Once the reporters were convinced he had no serious connection to Rubin, they lost interest in him. He waited until they fin-ished their questions and finally it was just him and Evelyn and six security guards.

"I'm sorry if I embarrassed you," she said.

"It's Susan Carol who would be embarrassed," he an-swered. "She's out of my league."

"I don't know about that," Evelyn said. "I *do* know she likes you."

"You do? How—"

One of the security guards broke in. "Ms. Rubin, we need to get you out of here. The players for the next match on this court are on their way."

"Oh sure," she said. "Can my friend walk with us?"

The security guard didn't seem thrilled by the idea, but shrugged. "Yeah, I guess so."

The six beefy men in blue formed a gauntlet around them

and one of them began to shout, "Player coming through" as they started walking through the crowd. There were some fans imploring her for autographs.

"I really should sign," Evelyn said.

"Not here," the security man said. "It would completely stop all traffic. We need to get you back inside."

She didn't argue. Amid the shouting as they walked, Stevie said, "I really need to talk to you for a few minutes."

"For a story?"

"Sort of."

She looked at him quizzically, but nodded. "I need to shower. Do you want to meet in the players' lounge?"

That was a bad idea. Too many people around. The same would be true of the pressroom and certainly out on the plaza now that Rubin had suddenly become a star. But where? Why hadn't he thought this through before?

"What were you planning to do this afternoon?" he asked.

"Go back to the hotel and rest."

"How about if I go with you?"

Now she was *really* looking at him with question marks in her eyes. They were approaching the entrance to the stadium. "This must be important," she said.

"It is. I wouldn't ask if it wasn't."

They had reached the doors leading inside. "You're okay from here," the security guard said. He eyed Stevie's credential for a moment. "I guess it's okay for your friend to go with you."

Stevie was getting very tired of security people questioning him. He thought about saying something, then swallowed it.

There were more important things to do. Evelyn stopped once they were inside the doors. "Okay, if it's really important, why don't you meet me at the transportation trailer in an hour." She looked at her watch. "That would be two-thirty. You can ride back into the city with me. We can talk in the car."

He shook his head. "No, we can't. I can't talk about this in front of anyone. But I'll ride with you anyway."

Now the look in her eyes was a bit fearful. "I can't imagine what this is about," she said. "Make it forty-five minutes. Now you have me curious and nervous all at once."

He nodded. Then, trying to sound casual, he said, "So Brendan won't be riding back with you?"

"No," she said, shaking her head. "Makarova's playing tonight. He has to stay out here to watch. He's about to sign her."

Wow, he thought. Gibson had told her about Makarova. He wondered *when* he had fessed up. "Okay. See you at two-fifteen."

She turned and walked down the hall, racquet bag slung over her shoulder. Stevie couldn't decide who was prettier, Evelyn or Susan Carol. It occurred to him that he no longer even thought about Nadia Symanova that way. She was involved in something dirty—or at least her family was—and there was no way for Stevie to see her as attractive anymore. He wondered if that would change when—if—they figured out what had actually happened to her.

He circled the stadium to get back to the pressroom, hoping some of his companions would be back. There was no one in sight. He called Kelleher's cell phone and got voice mail. The same thing happened with Susan Carol. That meant they were probably watching matches. He sat at Kelleher's desk, glancing at his watch every minute or two. He wondered for a moment what it was like for Rubin to be thrust into all of this all by herself. Brendan Gibson had mentioned that her parents both worked but might fly in for the weekend if she was still playing. Well, she would certainly be playing—on a stage none of them could have even dreamed about when the tournament began.

At 2:05, he figured he had better get going so he could find the transportation trailer. He walked out the gate where he had seen players entering and exiting, turned left, and saw it at the end of a row of trailers. Several players were standing outside as cars pulled up. Evelyn walked out of the trailer with a slip of paper in her hands just as he walked up.

She waved at him, put an arm on his shoulder, and whispered in his ear, "Take your credential off. They don't let media in the courtesy cars."

"I have another one that says 'player family,' " he said.

She gave him a funny look. "You do?" she said. "You really are full of surprises. Okay, put it on. Here comes the car."

The driver, a middle-aged woman, popped the trunk as she pulled up, and Evelyn threw her racquet bag in there.

"I'm Evelyn," she said, putting out her hand as the driver got out of the car to help. "And this is my brother Steve."

"I know just who you are," the driver said. "Congratulations on your win." She smiled politely at Stevie. "Are you proud of your big sister?"

"Oh yeah," Stevie said. "She's pretty cool for a sister."

They slid into the backseat and drove away in silence. Stevie hoped the traffic wouldn't be too bad. He had a lot of questions and very little patience.

16: A STAR IS BORN

THE RIDE into the city felt as if it took forever to Stevie. Naturally, traffic was backed up at the tolls going into the tunnel, and the driver was clearly a tennis groupie—why else would you volunteer to drive tennis players back and forth for two weeks?—who seemed to know every match Evelyn had ever played. "When you won fourteen-and-under at Kalamazoo last year, I told people, 'Watch out for that girl, she's going to be a player,'" said the driver, whose name was Molly Weiss. It took nearly an hour to get to the U.N. Plaza. By the time they arrived, Stevie knew most of the details of Molly Weiss's life and he knew that Evelyn had switched from a two-handed backhand to a one-handed backhand a year ago, a decision Molly Weiss fully supported.

"Chrissie"—she was apparently referring to Chris Evert—"perfected the two-hander," she said. "But against these six-footers today like Sharapova and the Williams sisters and Symanova, you have to be able to stand in there and slug and you need to get to the ball with one hand."

Evelyn agreed. Molly then launched into a speech about what had happened to that "sweet girl Nadia," and detailed the three times in the last two years she had driven her. "I wanted to tell her not to wear so much makeup," she said. "But I figured that would be impolite. Now you, Evelyn, you've got that girl-next-door look. Boys like that."

Stevie couldn't resist. "You mean boys are going to like my sister?" he said.

Evelyn gave him a look. "Young man, boys *already* like your sister," Molly said. "Which reminds me, why aren't your parents here?"

"Well, for one thing, they both have to work," Evelyn said. "For another, they're very superstitious. They get nervous watching me."

"Oh, just like Pete Sampras's parents," Molly said. "When he won his first U.S. Open in 1990, his parents were wandering around a shopping mall in California trying to kill time when they saw an awards ceremony on a television in an electronics store. They walked over and saw their son being handed the Open trophy."

"My parents are just like that," Evelyn said. "They check the Internet every thirty minutes to see how I'm doing, but they can't stand to watch."

Stevie was stunned hearing this. He was about to ask if

that meant the Rubins wouldn't even fly in to see their daughter play Symanova when it occurred to him that Evelyn's brother would already know the answer to that question. Fortunately, Molly helped him out.

"So you mean to tell me if you play Nadia on Sunday in the match of the century, your parents won't be here?"

"We already talked about it after the match today," Evelyn said. "They're going to go to a concert. My dad will take his BlackBerry with him."

"Match of the century?" Stevie said, unable to resist.

"Believe it," Molly said. "Young man, you better face up to the fact that your sister is about to become a big star."

Mercifully, they pulled up to the front door of the hotel before Molly could finish telling the story about her first meeting with Mary Carillo. Stevie jumped out and headed for the door. "Steve!" Molly Weiss was shouting at him, standing at the trunk. "Come over here and carry these racquets for your sister."

Whoops. He had flunked Molly Weiss's chivalry class. He started back, but Evelyn waved her off. "It's okay, Molly," she said. "Steve knows I like to carry my own racquets." Molly gave her a motherly hug and climbed back into the car with a wave at both of them.

"Longest hour of my life," Stevie said as they walked through the doors, the doormen offering congratulations to Evelyn.

Evelyn shook her head. "Molly makes that trip six or seven times a day just so she can say she talked to me or

Symanova or Mary Carillo or Andre Agassi," she said. "I keep reading all the time about how tennis has gone down in popularity in the last ten years. If we don't appreciate people like her, who will we have left?"

She was right, of course. Stevie was becoming a hardened cynic—which he hoped at least qualified him to be a reporter. He remembered something Dick Jerardi had said to him once: "Never take anything or anyone at face value. If you do, then why should anyone bother giving you credentials to anything? Always question. *Anyone* can just sit there and listen."

Evelyn was leading him toward the lobby restaurant, which was completely empty. They walked into the room and were greeted by a man in a tuxedo. "We don't reopen until five o'clock," he said.

Evelyn gave him a smile that reminded him of Susan Carol. "I understand completely," she said. "But we aren't old enough to go into the bar. Is it okay if we sit in a corner and just have a Coke or something?"

The man looked at her, looked at Stevie, and then glanced down at the player credential dangling from her neck and up at the racquet bag on her shoulder. "Sure, that's okay," he said. "Did you play today?"

He was now leading them to a booth in the corner of the room. "Yes, I did," she said. "I got lucky and won."

"Good for you. Do you know who you play next?"

"Well," Evelyn said, sliding into the booth, "if she wins two matches, Nadia Symanova."

The man did an actual double take. "Seriously? Look, if you want to order something now, I can take care of it. Wow! What's your name?"

"Evelyn Rubin."

He shook her hand eagerly, clearly dazzled now. "Well, good luck to you, Evelyn. As pretty as you are, I'll bet a lot of people will know your name before that match is over."

"I just hope I play well enough that she doesn't embarrass me," she said. "She's awfully good."

He had taken out an order pad. "What can I get you two?" he asked.

"A Coke would be fine," Evelyn said. "I just ate a little while ago."

Stevie hadn't. He was starving. "Can I get something to eat?" he asked.

"Absolutely," the man said. "Steak, hamburger, chicken, fish? You name it." Stevie decided on a chicken sandwich and a Coke. The man turned to head for the kitchen, where, Stevie suspected, he would make the chicken sandwich himself if that would make Evelyn happy.

"Okay," she said. "Now that you've lived through the car ride, what's so secret?"

He took a deep breath. This would not be easy.

"Something really weird is going on at this tournament," he said. "Still going on—even with Symanova back. I want to know anything you might have seen or heard that seemed suspicious or unusual. And mostly, I need to know when Mr. Gibson told you about signing Makarova, and if he said anything to you at all about Symanova's disappearance."

She knitted her brows for a moment, then shrugged. "Brendan told me about Makarova at dinner last night," she said. "He said she was too good a player to turn down but he would still work very hard for me. I understand. He's trying to build a business."

"What about Symanova?"

She paused. "Stevie, I want to trust you. Why are you asking me about this?"

"Because I want to know what really happened to Symanova."

The guy in the tux came back with their Cokes. "Sandwich will be another couple minutes," he said.

They waited for him to leave. "You don't think the SVR kidnapped her?" Evelyn said when he was out of earshot.

"Do you?"

"No. Well, put it this way, Brendan doesn't think they did."

That surprised Stevie a little. If Brendan Gibson was involved in Symanova's disappearance in some way, it would make sense for him to point the finger at the SVR.

"Who does he think did it?" he asked.

"He doesn't know. But he's convinced Hughes Norwood knew she was safe long before today."

"How long?"

"Don't know. Maybe yesterday. Maybe even Monday night."

"And he thinks this why?"

"All he told me was that Norwood was even more evil than he had thought agents were. He also told me that you accused him of somehow being involved."

"He told you that? Was he angry about it?"

"He said he was at first, but he figured out that you put two and two together and got five. And it helped that Susan Carol stood up for you."

"And do you believe him? That he's not involved somehow?"

"Yes. But I also understand why you thought he was. He told me what happened with the Makarovs. Brendan is a good man, Stevie. I trust him. He's been a lot more than an agent to me—and this was *before* all these people wanted to talk to me."

Clearly, Evelyn trusted him and believed he was innocent. Stevie wasn't so sure. It actually made sense for him to come clean to her about the Makarovs just in case Stevie or Susan Carol said something about them being in the apartment. And he might tell Evelyn he thought Norwood was evil, but he was still meeting with him and the Symanovs and some Hollywood director. . . .

Stevie's chicken sandwich—which appeared to contain a whole chicken—arrived, along with a note. "The front desk found out you were in here, Ms. Rubin," Tux Man said. "They thought you would want this."

She looked at the note. "What is it?" Stevie asked.

"It's from Brendan," she said. "CBS News wants to interview me for a piece they'll air over the weekend if I play Nadia. It also says, 'There will be more of these.' "

"You're a star," Stevie said. "Nadia's kidnapping might be as big a break for you as it's turning out to be for her."

"I'm just the sideshow," she said. "It's all about Nadia."

Unless, he thought, she were to beat Nadia. Then, being a young American, *she* could be the next star.

"What're you thinking?" she asked.

"I'm just picturing you beating Nadia."

She laughed and shook her head. "Did you see Wimbledon? If I lose three and three, I'll feel pretty good."

"This isn't Wimbledon. Her power isn't as important on a hard court as on grass. Look, I've watched you play—I think you can beat her."

She smiled and leaned forward, pushing a wisp of hair off her forehead. "So do I," she said in a whisper. "She needs pace—the harder you hit it, the more she likes it. So I won't give her anything hard to hit. I'll softball her all day, the way Martina Hingis used to do to the Williams sisters." She looked around. "But please don't say anything to anyone. I want her to walk on court thinking I'm just another walk in the park on her way to Makarova."

"What about Serena Williams in the fourth round?"

She shook her head. "Even if Serena gets to the fourth round, she's hurt. She's not admitting it, but you can see it when she tries to run. She won't be a problem for either one of us, I don't think."

Stevie was impressed. This girl had a lot more confidence than he had thought.

"I think you're right about pace—"

He stopped in midsentence. Brendan Gibson was walking into the restaurant. He walked to the table and turned to Evelyn as if Stevie wasn't there. "Did you get my message about CBS News?"

"Yes, and—"

"The Letterman show just called. They want you on tonight. They tape at five-thirty. It's five o'clock now. I have a car waiting outside."

"But . . . I'm not dressed! Letterman? Seriously? Why? I haven't done anything yet."

"I'll tell you why in the car. You can run up to your room, grab a dress, and change there. Hurry, Evelyn, this is huge!"

"Okay. Sorry, Stevie." She stood up to leave. "I'll be down in five minutes," she told Gibson.

As soon as she was gone, Gibson turned on Stevie. "What're you doing chasing my player around?"

Stevie was surprised. Evelyn and Susan Carol had both told him Gibson wasn't angry with him anymore. "I'm not chasing her," he said defensively. "If Letterman wants to talk to her, why shouldn't I?"

"You came all the way in here to talk to her? You couldn't do it after the match like everyone else did? The transportation people told me you posed as her brother to get in the car with her."

"That was her idea," he said, then was instantly sorry—why cause Evelyn problems? "Look, something rotten is going on here and *you* are right in the middle of it. So don't try to make me into the bad guy here. I'm not the one who was hanging out with Hughes Norwood and the Symanovs and some movie guy. Susan Carol knows you're involved in this and you're breaking her heart. And anyone who breaks her heart, *I'm* going after!"

He was shouting and he felt his heart pounding. He had

never in his life spoken to a grown-up this way. Worse, he had just tipped their hand.

But he had also hit a nerve. Brendan Gibson's face was pale. When he answered, it was through gritted teeth. "You know *nothing*, do you hear me?" he said. "And just how the hell did you get into the Open Club? What lie did you tell to get in there, Mr. Knight in Shining Armor? Get out of here right now. Just go. I don't want you here when Evelyn comes back down. God knows what thoughts you're putting in *her* head."

He was tempted to tell Brendan Gibson he couldn't throw him out of a hotel restaurant, but he needed to get going anyway and he'd already said too much. He stood up and walked out without another word. He walked through the lobby and through the revolving doors to the circular driveway. There were two courtesy cars sitting there, but he wasn't going to go that route again. He needed to get back to the tournament and report in to Kelleher, Susan Carol, and Tamara. Then he remembered his cell phone was in his pocket, so he pulled it out and dialed Susan Carol.

"Where have you been?" she screeched as soon as she heard his voice.

"I'm in the city," he said. "I rode back in with Evelyn. Your uncle hasn't called you?"

"No. Why?"

"Long story. I'll tell you when I get back out there. I'm walking to the subway right now. Did you guys find anything out?"

"That movie guy was still hanging around the Open

Club, but no sign of Norwood or the Symanovs. They're putting Nadia on Leno tonight on a satellite feed. Every network—even the majors—broke into their programming to cover her press conference live. Tom Ross told Bobby that Reebok has offered her fifteen million a year when her Nike deal is up and there may be a bidding war."

He was nodding his head as he listened. "Okay. I'll be back in an hour."

"If you want to see the match, you better hurry. The press section will be jammed."

"On my way. I'm walking into the subway right now."

✗   ✗   ✗

Not surprisingly, Grand Central Station was jammed too and it took him a while to make his way down to the platform for the number 7 train. A train was just pulling in when he walked onto the platform, and Stevie had to wedge his way in since the car was packed. After some mild pushing and shoving, he found a place right in front of a seat, close to the door.

They rode in silence, except for the roar of the train, under the East River, to the Jackson Avenue stop in Queens. Stevie could tell some of the people on board were businesspeople on their way home. Others—more casually dressed—were no doubt heading out for the night matches in Flushing. His legs were starting to cramp a little by the time they pulled into the stop marked 61st Street—Woodside. As the doors opened, he relaxed his grip on the pole he'd been holding. Just as he did, he felt someone shove him from behind.

"Hey!" he said, surprised.

Before he could say anything else, he was given another shove—this one much harder—which propelled him through the open door and onto the platform. "What the . . . ?"

The shover, who had followed him outside, was a guy in a suit who had been standing next to him. Someone else, also in a suit, had appeared, standing in front of him.

"Don't say a word," the second man said. He flashed a badge at Stevie. "Police. Come with us, keep quiet, and you won't get hurt."

"But what did I do?" he said. His mind was churning. His gut told him something wasn't right—this wasn't how cops acted on TV.

"One more word and we cuff you," said the guy who had shoved him from the train. They were half pushing him, half pulling him toward a flight of stairs. He wondered if he should shout for help. But the badges would probably convince a bystander to leave well enough alone. For the moment, he decided, he would cooperate. He'd get off the subway platform and maybe make a run for it when the chance came. He was guessing he could run faster than the two men. He told himself to take deep breaths and try to stay calm as they shoved him down the steps.

They walked him through the exit of the station and onto the street, then quickly hustled him into an alley. Stevie's heart began pounding. They walked several yards down the alley, one of them keeping a very firm grip on Stevie's upper arm, the other pushing him from behind so hard that he stumbled several times. He was trapped. He couldn't wrestle free, and now there was no one to shout to for help. The one in back spun his shoulder so that he was standing with his back to a wall and facing the two of them. They weren't all that old, maybe in their thirties. The one who had pushed him out the door, who was about six feet tall with short, dark hair, did the talking.

"You had better listen very carefully right now," he said. "This is the last chance you're going to get."

Stevie had expected a New York accent. It wasn't—in fact, it was very Midwestern. He said "cheance" instead of "chance."

"Chance to do what?" he said. "Get beaten up?"

"Keep talking and you will," the Midwestern guy snarled. "This time you get a warning. Leave the Symanova story alone—got it? It's none of your business. Just watch the tennis and have a good time. Tell your girlfriend the same thing."

"Or what?" Stevie said.

That was a mistake. The second guy suddenly punched him very hard in the stomach, so hard he doubled over and fell to the ground. He had his wits about him just enough to partially break his fall with his hand, but he still bumped his head on the concrete.

"Any more questions?" the guy asked. "Nadia Symanova isn't your concern. Don't test us. If you do, you'll be sorry."

Stevie didn't move or say anything else. He heard them leaving, their footsteps echoing against the concrete in the alley. He waited for the stars he was seeing to clear. Finally, he tried to stand up—slowly—and fell down. The guy had really hit him hard. As he was waiting for the dizziness to pass, he noticed a trickle of blood coming from his mouth. He wondered if someone would find him lying here. Not likely. He finally worked himself into a sitting position and, slowly, his breath started to come back and his heart stopped racing. He sat with his back to the wall and tried to think.

What had just happened? The easy part was that he had been threatened. Someone didn't want him—or Susan Carol—asking questions about Symanova. But why? He didn't know anything and neither did she. He wondered if Brendan Gibson had something to do with this. But that would have been awfully quick, getting someone to follow him from the hotel to the subway after their confrontation. Someone had planned this before he went into the hotel with Evelyn. Had someone been following him all day?

After a few minutes, he tried to stand up again. He managed to get to his feet, but the effort made his head spin. His head hurt almost as much as his stomach. He wiped the blood away from his mouth and slowly—shakily—started out of the alley. For a moment, he wondered if the two men would be waiting for him on the street to go another round. No. He walked slowly back to the subway station, paid the fare again, and walked painfully back up the steps. Another very full train was pulling in. He wondered if he would get sick with the movement of the train, but all he could think about was getting back to Flushing. At least inside the tennis center, he would feel safe.

He caught one break. The train was an express and it flew through most of the stations, stopping only once before it reached the Shea Stadium/Willets Point stop. Stevie noticed he was getting some funny looks as they rode. Someone actually gave him a seat and one woman asked him if he was feeling all right. "I'll be fine," he managed to half gasp in response.

He walked very slowly across the boardwalk, still feeling sick, his head really pounding. He looked at his watch and saw it was a quarter to seven. He walked into the press center and Susan Carol, Kelleher, Mearns, Bud Collins, and Mary Carillo were all standing in a circle just inside the entrance.

"My God, Stevie," Susan Carol said. "What happened to you?"

He looked down at himself and noticed then that some of the blood from his mouth had trickled onto his shirt.

He actually managed a smile—or so he thought. "Turns out tennis is a contact sport," he said.

That was when the room started to spin. He felt his knees buckle and he saw people rushing to catch him. Then everything went black.

17: DOWNTIME

THE NEXT thing Stevie saw was the ceiling of the pressroom. His vision began to clear and he heard someone saying, "Don't try to sit up yet, just take it easy. A doctor is coming."

The voice belonged to Bud Collins, who was kneeling beside him. He could now see that Susan Carol was on the other side of him, and Kelleher, Mearns, and Carillo were hovering. He could hear other voices just behind them.

"Here's Dr. McDevitt now," Kelleher was saying.

A middle-aged man with wire-rimmed glasses and short-cropped brown hair moved into the circle and kneeled down next to him. "How long was he out?" he asked the group.

"No more than a minute or two," Collins said. "Maybe ninety seconds."

Dr. McDevitt looked down at Stevie and smiled. "What happened to you, young man?"

"I got punched," Stevie said. "In the stomach. Very hard. And then I whacked my head falling down."

"Who punched you?" Kelleher asked.

"I don't know exactly. It was on the subway—near the subway, actually—back at Woodside."

He saw Dr. McDevitt's eyes widen. "So you got back on the subway and made it here from Woodside after you took this punch?"

Stevie nodded.

"Well, that would explain why you passed out."

The next few minutes were blurry to Stevie. With Susan Carol, Collins, and Kelleher helping, the doctor sat him up, then slowly helped him stand. They walked him down the hall into a room that had an examining table of some kind. The doctor had Stevie lie down. "He just needs to rest here for a while," he said. "His insides are messed up right now. And he might have a mild concussion. He needs to lie still. I might give him something gentle to let him sleep for a bit."

That sounded good to Stevie.

"Does he need to go to the hospital?" Susan Carol asked.

"Right now, I'd say no," the doctor said. "Let's give him an hour or two and see how he's doing. Why don't you all clear out for a bit and let him rest."

"I want to stay here," Susan Carol said.

"You can stay," Dr. McDevitt said. "But if I have my way, he's going to be asleep in about ten minutes."

"That's okay. I'll stay anyway."

Kelleher, Collins, Mearns, and Carillo all came over and gave Stevie little pats on the shoulder. "We'll see you after the match, Stevie," Kelleher said. "Then we'll try to figure out what the hell happened to you. For right now, get some rest."

Stevie nodded. He wanted to tell them everything but he still felt dizzy and a little bit sick. The doctor brought him a small pill and a cup of water. "This should help," he said. Stevie drank, put his head back, and looked at Susan Carol, who had pulled up the chair next to him and, he now noticed, was holding his hand.

He was about to say something to her but felt too tired to talk. He closed his eyes instead.

✗ ✗ ✗

When he woke up, the room was full again. "I thought you guys were going to watch the match," he said.

Laughter. "Guess that little pill worked, Eddie," Kelleher said. "Stevie, the match is over."

"Who won?"

"Symanova. Closer than you might have thought, though—6–4, 6–4. She looked rusty. Even a little bit slow. Poor Walsh, she's an American playing a Russian in New York and twenty-three thousand people were rooting against her."

He heard Dr. McDevitt's voice. "How are you feeling, Stevie?"

He took stock and realized that the pulsing pain in his

stomach and head was just about gone. "Better," he said. "Hungry."

"That's a very good sign," the doctor said. He turned to the others. "I think you can take him home. He should take it very easy at least for tomorrow. Has anyone called his parents?"

Before anyone could answer, Stevie tried to sit up. He felt a bit dizzy and lay back, but said, "No, *no*. You can't call them. They'll freak and they'll make me come home. *Please*. The doctor says I'm going to be fine. Please don't call."

"Calm down, Stevie," Dr. McDevitt said. "Tell you what. Let's see how you feel in the morning. Is that fair?"

Stevie nodded.

A few minutes later, helped up by the doctor, he walked gingerly down the hall and got into Kelleher's car, which Bobby had been allowed to pull close to the back entrance. Most of the crowd appeared to have gone home as soon as Symanova's match had ended. "Let's see how you do in the car," Kelleher said. "I've got Eddie's cell if you start to feel sick. You might still have to go to the hospital."

"Not going to happen," Stevie said. He knew if he went to the hospital they would *have* to call his parents.

Susan Carol and Mearns were in the backseat. Kelleher gave Stevie an empty bag . . . just in case.

The trip to the city was rocky, but Stevie, sweating profusely, didn't get sick.

Kelleher dropped Stevie and Mearns off in front of the apartment building. "I'll park the car," he said. "Stevie, do you want me to get you something to eat? You up to it?"

"How about John's Pizza?" he said.

"How about some chicken soup?" Mearns said.

"I'll get both," Kelleher said.

Stevie turned to say good night to Susan Carol but she had gotten out of the car on the other side.

"What're you doing?" he asked.

"I'm coming in with you," she said. "I want to be sure you're okay."

"I'm fine," he said. "I'll see you in the morning."

She shook her head. "No, you won't. I'm sleeping on the couch tonight."

"But I'm fine."

"I'm sure you are. Don't argue with me."

He didn't argue. The three of them walked slowly into the lobby and took the elevator upstairs. They let him stretch out on the couch while Mearns went to get him something to drink. Susan Carol sat down in a chair next to the couch. "I guess I should tell you what happened," he said.

"It can wait," she said. "Let your head clear first."

It occurred to Stevie that he had passed out in front of dozens of media people. "What did you all tell everyone in the pressroom?" he asked.

"That you ate something bad and had a mild case of food poisoning. That's what Bud told everyone, anyway. It seemed to work. They were all a lot more concerned with watching Symanova."

"I'm sorry you missed the match."

"I'm not. I wouldn't have been able to concentrate anyway."

She gave him a concerned version of the smile.

Kelleher arrived a few minutes later. As soon as Stevie got a whiff of the pizza, he knew he wasn't eating chicken soup.

"Are you sure you're up to it?" Mearns said. "The soup might be a better choice right now."

"I'm betting he eats the pizza," Susan Carol said.

For the first time since he had stumbled onto the platform at Woodside, Stevie smiled. "You know me all too well," he said.

✗ ✗ ✗

He managed just two slices and some water, which told him he wasn't back to a hundred percent yet. He gave them the bare bones of the story and what he'd learned from Evelyn, but soon felt exhausted. Mearns and Susan Carol mothered him into the bedroom but left him alone to change, which he did—slowly. He was probably asleep an instant after he turned the light out. He didn't set an alarm but woke up at 6:40. When he got out of bed, he felt stiff and there was still a dull pain in his stomach, but it wasn't anything he couldn't deal with. Still in pajamas, he walked into the kitchen, figuring no one would be up yet.

Susan Carol was sitting at the kitchen table drinking a cup of coffee.

"That's starting to become a habit, isn't it?" he said. "Your father won't be happy."

"I know," she said. "But it's been a long week."

"Tell me about it," he said. "You think I can have a cup?"

"Sure."

He sat down while she poured some coffee and mixed in milk and sugar.

"I haven't been able to stop thinking all night," she said. "If my uncle Brendan is really involved with these people, he's completely lost his way."

"We don't know for sure that he was involved in sending those two guys after me," Stevie said, wanting to make her feel better.

She, of course, saw right through him. "Stop it, Stevie. I need to face facts now."

Kelleher came into the kitchen, yawning away sleep.

"Aren't you kids a little young for coffee?" he said. Then, without waiting for an answer, he poured a cup for himself and sat down next to Stevie. "How are you doing?"

"Better," said Stevie.

"I'm going to fix him some breakfast and then he's going back to bed," said Susan Carol.

"You're now my mother?"

"Speaking of which, you need to call them today," Susan Carol said.

"Why?"

"Because they'll have noticed you haven't written anything the last couple days—you know your dad has been going to the *Herald* Web site to read you—and they'll want to know why."

As usual, she was right. The question was, what should he tell them? The truth would have them both in New York within two hours to escort him home. He didn't want that. "Maybe I'll just tell them I ate something and felt sick to my stomach and Bobby gave me a day or two off."

She smiled. "That's good, because it isn't even a lie. You've eaten plenty and you *were* sick to your stomach last night."

"No kidding."

Kelleher was shaking his head. "I'm not hearing any of this. I am blissfully unaware of any parental deceptions. . . ."

They both laughed and Susan Carol started taking things out of the refrigerator. "I'm making eggs," she said. "You like them over easy, right?"

"How do you know that?" Stevie said.

"We ate breakfast in New Orleans. I remember."

They had eaten breakfast together a couple of times—with their fathers—in New Orleans. But if someone offered him a million dollars to remember what Susan Carol had eaten, he wouldn't have a clue. He wondered if that made her a better reporter than he was too.

Mearns joined them and Susan Carol ended up making eggs for everyone. Kelleher offered her advice, as they were his specialty, and Mearns made toast and poured juice all around.

Susan Carol refused to let Stevie have more coffee. "You need to rest," she said. "One more cup and you won't be able to sleep. Drink your juice."

"At what age exactly do girls start to think they're everyone's mother?" he asked.

"Twelve," she answered. "Drink."

They rehashed what they knew as they ate, with Stevie filling in a few more details as he remembered them. Mearns was shaking her head in disgust. "Beating up kids," she said. "These are *really* sick people."

"And one of them might be my uncle," Susan Carol said.

"We'll worry about that later," Kelleher said. "The question is, what do we do next? Do we call the cops?"

"I think we need to play this out a little bit," Stevie said.

"How do you mean?" Mearns asked.

"I don't know how, exactly, but I think Evelyn Rubin is tied into this whole Symanova thing. That would mean their match is the key. Think about it: Labor Day weekend, no football to go up against, the whole world watching on CBS . . ."

"I think Stevie's right," Susan Carol said. "And my uncle has made some kind of deal with the Symanovs and SMG."

"Another fix, like in New Orleans?" Kelleher said.

"That makes no sense," Susan Carol said. "Evelyn is an improving player, but she shouldn't be a serious threat to Symanova."

"What if the deal is for *Symanova* to lose?" Mearns said.

They all looked at each other. "But why?" Stevie asked.

"Who knows?" Mearns said.

"And where does Makarova fit in?" Kelleher said. "Maybe Gibson's deal with the Symanovs involves her and not Rubin."

"Yeah, but somebody beat up Stevie right after he talked to Evelyn," Susan Carol said.

"Could be coincidence," Stevie said. "They could have followed us from the tennis center and had to wait until I left the hotel before they could try anything."

"That still doesn't answer why they would see Stevie as any kind of a threat," Mearns said.

"No, it doesn't," said Kelleher. "But it does tend to point to Rubin as the key. Stevie's gotten close to her, anyway. Maybe too close for someone's comfort."

"So we need to figure out who and why," said Susan Carol.

"And fast," added Stevie.

18: VANISHED

STEVIE KNEW it was pointless to argue with Susan Carol about getting more rest, so he went into the bedroom, figuring he would lie down until everyone left, then get up and take a shower. He wasn't planning on spending the entire day in bed doing nothing. He lay down on top of the covers, closed his eyes, and the next thing he knew the phone rang. He fumbled around till he found his cell.

"Did you call your parents yet?"

"Huh? What time is it?"

Susan Carol laughed. "It's almost three o'clock. There's someone here who wants to talk to you."

Stevie waited until he heard someone come on the line. "Stevie, it's Dr. McDevitt. How are you feeling?"

"Sleepy. I just woke up."

"That's good, you needed some sleep. How does your head feel?"

The cobwebs were slowly clearing now. Actually, Stevie felt fine. "It feels okay," Stevie said. "Maybe I can get dressed and come on out there. I really feel much better."

"Whoa, Stevie, slow down. Susan Carol told me you went back to sleep at about nine. That means you slept for six hours. Your body is still in recovery mode. You need to take it easy for a while longer. How's your appetite?"

Stevie smiled. "It's fine. I slept through lunch, but now that you mention it, I'm kind of hungry."

"That's a very good sign. You take it easy the rest of the day and if you're feeling okay tomorrow, you can come back out here Saturday."

"Saturday?!" Stevie was horrified. "But I'm *fine*. I need to get back out there tomorrow."

"I know you do. But you're not going to. Look, Stevie, I'm not terribly comfortable not calling your parents, so you have to pay me back by doing exactly what I tell you to do. I feel confident you aren't seriously hurt. But you can't rush your recovery. You have to trust me on this. I know more about it than you do."

Stevie sighed. He knew the doctor was right. "Okay," he said.

"You promise?"

"Yes."

"Good. And just in case you forget your promise, we're going to have your credential turned off until Saturday morning. So if you come out here, you won't be able to get in."

Stevie remembered the electronic scan done on his credential each day. He knew when he was beaten.

"I understand. Thanks."

"You're welcome. I'll put Susan Carol back on."

"Kelleher says if you're hungry, there's a menu for a Chinese restaurant that delivers on the refrigerator," she said when she got back on the phone. "Plus, there's chicken soup from last night."

"Maybe I'll go out and get something," he said.

"You do and I'll tell them to turn your credential off for Saturday too."

Stevie groaned. "All right already," he said. "Will you tell me what's going on out there? Or am I too delicate to listen?"

She laughed. "There's not much to tell. None of the major characters in the story are even out here today. Symanova doesn't play, neither does Evelyn. Makarova played her second-round match and won in forty-seven minutes. I haven't seen Uncle Brendan all day. He left me a message on my cell, but I haven't called him back. I'm just not sure what to say to him right now."

Stevie could think of a few things to say—even though he still wasn't sure if Brendan had been involved in his assault. "So you're coming over here later?" he said.

"Try and stop me," she said.

X   X   X

Kelleher and Mearns and Susan Carol gave Stevie the complete update on what he had missed that day over Chinese takeout. There was a rumor going around that SMG was going to announce a movie deal of some kind for Symanova on Monday. Kelleher had tried to confirm it but even Kantarian and Ross didn't know any more than they did.

"I guess you know Andy lost last night," Susan Carol said.

"I saw the highlights this afternoon," he said. "You've had a tough year, haven't you? First Coach K. loses the national championship at the buzzer, and now Andy loses in the first round of the Open."

"And I met you," she shot back. Then she smiled. "For better or worse, I'm glad to see you becoming your old self."

He *was* feeling a lot better. He thought for a second about asking Susan Carol to convince Kelleher to get his badge turned on the next morning, but he knew he had no shot. "We need to find out what's up with Symanova and Evelyn before they play on Sunday," he said.

"I know," she said. "I asked Bobby about confronting Uncle Brendan to find out exactly what he knows. But he talked me out of it. He doesn't think he's likely to tell me anything. I wish I thought he was wrong, but I don't."

She left around nine-thirty to go back to Riverside Drive. She didn't really want to go but didn't have a good excuse not to without making her uncle suspicious.

Stevie went to bed soon after that and didn't wake up until Kelleher came in the next morning to tell him that he and Mearns were leaving. "We'll check in with you during the day," he said.

Stevie didn't argue. He went back to sleep and didn't wake up until eleven. He took a shower, poured himself a bowl of cereal, and turned the tennis on, flopping down in front of the television. Symanova and Annabelle Kim were the second match on the stadium court. Kim was a young American who, Ted Robinson was explaining, was the daughter of Korean immigrants. Robinson was working with John McEnroe and Tracy Austin. Early in the match, Stevie heard a familiar voice—but not one he expected to hear on USA: Mary Carillo.

Kim had just run down a Symanova forehand and whipped it down the line for a winner. Symanova looked stunned. "She needs to wake up," Carillo said. "This isn't a photo shoot or a press conference or a movie set. This is a tennis match, and Annabelle Kim isn't here to follow a script."

Stevie smiled. That comment was *so* Carillo. She never pulled a punch.

"Kim did hit a wonderful shot," Austin said.

"She did," Carillo answered. "But Symanova was flat-footed. She should have been all over that ball."

Stevie sat back and enjoyed the match. Carillo was clearly correct about Symanova. She seemed annoyed by the fact that Kim wasn't just rolling over for her. So was the crowd, which screamed every time Symanova hit a good shot and was near silent when Kim hit a winner. "You don't see this in tennis very often," McEnroe said. "Most of the time when an underdog is playing well, they get behind the underdog. But this crowd wants no part of an upset. They want Symanova all the way."

"That's probably because they're sympathetic to what she's been through," Austin said.

They split sets and went to 4–all in the third, with the crowd—and Symanova—getting jumpier with each passing game. Austin was saying something about the fact that Symanova still appeared to be recovering from the trauma of the past few days when a backhand from Kim, serving at 30–all, appeared to land right on the baseline for a winner.

"*Out!*" Stevie heard the linesman say and heard the crowd roar its approval. Kim approached the chair, asking for an overrule. "Too close to overrule," the umpire said.

"Too close?" Kim said. "I could see it land in from where I was standing!"

TV showed a replay. The ball was clearly in from every angle they showed. "Bad time for a bad call," Robinson said.

"Good time for Symanova," Carillo said. "She needed a break and that was a big one."

Clearly upset, Kim double-faulted on the next point to lose her serve. Symanova then served the match out, mustering her power for two straight aces. As they shook hands at the net, Robinson said, "A narrow escape for Symanova."

"Ted, she will have to play a lot better than this on Sunday," Austin said. "No one knew much about Evelyn Rubin before this tournament, but she has shown herself to be a rising player in her first two matches."

"A rising *star*," Carillo said. "She's got a lot of game and a lot of personality. She was terrific on Letterman the other night."

Stevie had completely forgotten that Evelyn had been on Letterman. He had missed it. Of course, he'd missed a lot in the last two days.

✗ ✗ ✗

Because Symanova had played early and that had been *the* story of the day, Kelleher, Mearns, and Susan Carol turned up at the apartment by seven-thirty and took Stevie to dinner at a steak house called The Palm. Like Stevie, his three companions were surprised by how much Symanova had struggled.

"Evelyn can beat her," Susan Carol said.

"If they play straight up, if there's nothing screwy going on, I think you're right," Kelleher said.

They discussed strategy for the next day. Stevie was to report to Dr. McDevitt in the morning for one last checkup to make sure he was okay. There really weren't any prime matches going on, so they would all have time to check in with the various characters in the plot. Kelleher had talked to his friend at the FBI to see if they had anything new and learned that Symanova had been left by her kidnappers downtown in the Meatpacking District. Her parents had been told where to pick her up. "She told the FBI guys that they kept her blindfolded the whole time," Kelleher said. "They pushed her out of the car—still blindfolded—and told her to walk away. By the time she recovered and got the blindfold off, she had no idea which car she might have been in. Her parents were there a few minutes later."

"I feel like we're very close to figuring this out," Mearns said. "But I'm not exactly sure why I feel that way. We need someone to make a mistake."

✗ ✗ ✗

They were at the tennis center by ten o'clock Saturday morning. Stevie felt as if he was coming home, walking back through the gate he had never seen prior to Monday. Several people in the media center asked him if he was feeling better and, without giving details, he said he was fine. Dr. McDevitt confirmed that, then handed him an envelope. "What's this?" Stevie asked.

"It's a full report on what happened to you," he said. "It describes what I did, what meds you took. Give it to your parents when you get home. I wasn't at all comfortable not calling them, but I was ninety-nine percent sure you had just fainted and nothing more. They should know what went on."

Stevie nodded and thanked him.

The rest of the day was an exercise in frustration. None of the players in the plot seemed to be around. Mearns found Hughes Norwood at one point and asked about the movie rumors. "He gave me that sick smile of his and said, 'When there's something to announce, we'll announce it,' " she said.

"Helpful as ever," Kelleher said.

Bud Collins reported a rumor that Symanova had asked for medical treatment after the match on Friday. If so, Eddie

McDevitt hadn't been the doctor who had treated her. He knew nothing about it. By late afternoon, they found themselves sitting in the pressroom while Mearns and Kelleher attempted to write columns. Stevie felt defeated. On Wednesday, he'd felt that they were on the verge of finding the truth—that there was some momentum behind their investigations. But here it was Saturday and they were no closer. Symanova and Rubin were scheduled to play at three o'clock the next day—technically, they were the second match on the stadium court, but the schedule noted, "not before three p.m." Midafternoon on Labor Day Sunday. CBS had reported that Symanova's first-round match had been the third-highest-rated tennis match *ever*. That was why Carillo had been doing the match on USA on Friday afternoon: CBS had wanted to air that match too, but USA had agreed to pay CBS extra money to hold on to it and to have Carillo work the match. Sunday's match was back on CBS and promised to be *huge*. The USTA had already informed the media that it would issue only one seat per news organization and some—like the *Fayetteville Observer*—would have no seat at all in the media section for Sunday's match.

"This is worse than a final," Ed Fabricius had told Kelleher earlier in the day. "I got a call today from the president of NBC News because I told NBC they could have someone from News *or* someone from Sports but not both."

Something was going to happen in this match. They were all convinced of it.

Susan Carol's cell phone rang—Stevie could tell it was hers because it played the Duke fight song. She answered and then sat up straight. "Hi, Evelyn," she said.

That got Stevie's attention.

She listened for a minute and then said, "But how can you be sure?" More listening. "Have you called the police?"

That *really* got Stevie's attention.

"Okay, okay. I promise. Let me call you right back."

She hung up, stood, and indicated that Stevie should follow her. "We need to talk," she whispered. "Someplace quiet."

Stevie wondered why she hadn't gone over to get Kelleher and Mearns to join them, but he followed her outside. The day matches were just about finished and the plaza was relatively empty.

"That was Evelyn," she said once they were clear of any listeners. "She says my uncle Brendan is missing."

"Oh, come on," Stevie said, incredulous.

"I know," Susan Carol said, putting up her hand to indicate he should let her finish. "She said they were supposed to meet for lunch and he never showed."

"That doesn't mean he's missing."

"Will you let me *finish*?"

"Sorry."

"She waited awhile, then called his apartment and his cell phone. Nothing. She thought he might have had a meeting that he forgot or maybe something came up with the Makarovs. So she went back to the hotel where she *ran into* the Makarovs. Before she could say anything, they asked if she had seen Brendan. She said no, they were supposed to meet for lunch. Then they told her *they* had a dinner appointment with him on Friday and he never showed. No phone call—nothing. They had called and left messages and hadn't heard anything."

"Now *that's* strange. But didn't you see him last night at the apartment?"

"No. To be honest, I thought he was coming in late to avoid having to talk to me. I didn't think that much about it, and I didn't see him this morning either. After she talked to the Makarovs, Evelyn got scared and called me, hoping I had seen him."

"When did Evelyn last see him?"

"Good question. I should have asked her that. I know my dad talked to Uncle Brendan on Thursday, but I haven't seen him since then."

"So what does Evelyn want us to do?"

"Well, first, she made me promise not to tell Bobby and Tamara. She's afraid they'll put something in the newspaper."

"But they won't do that. . . ."

"I know. She's freaked. So am I, to tell you the truth."

"So what should we do?" he said. "Should we call the police?"

"Not yet, I don't think. I'll try calling him again first. And we should check out his apartment. . . . Evelyn wants us to come into town and meet her."

Stevie suddenly smelled a trap.

"I'm not sure that's a great idea," he said. "The last time I spent time with Evelyn, I got beat up. A couple days later, we're still sniffing around and suddenly we get a call from her to come meet her in Manhattan?"

"You're right," she said. "But I can't imagine she'd be involved in this. Then again, I didn't think Uncle Brendan would be involved either. But I still think we need to meet with her. Except we'll do it on our terms."

She took out her cell phone and started dialing.

19: THE SEARCH

SUSAN CAROL'S plan was simple. She called Evelyn back and told her to try to stay calm, that they were going to come back to the city as soon as Kelleher and Mearns finished writing. She asked her to meet them at the apartment at eight-thirty. Kelleher and Mearns had to go to a USTA dinner that night and would be gone by seven-thirty.

"She said okay," Susan Carol said, closing the phone. "All she did was ask again that I not tell Tamara and Bobby."

"So maybe it's not a trap," Stevie said.

"Yeah, but you're right. At this point, we don't need to take any chances."

Kelleher and Mearns finished writing by six o'clock. They asked Stevie and Susan Carol if they were sure they didn't want to go to the dinner.

"We're really tired," Susan Carol said. "I thought Stevie and I would order in Chinese and then I'd go home to bed. Tomorrow is going to be a big day."

Kelleher grimaced. "The problem is, we have no idea what *kind* of big day."

Mearns smiled. "Susan Carol, can I trust you two alone in the apartment?"

They both blushed. Stevie hadn't even thought about being alone in an apartment with Susan Carol. Then he remembered he wouldn't be alone for long. Evelyn would be there soon after they arrived.

The drive into the city took a while because of Saturday-night New York traffic. Kelleher and Mearns were still trying to puzzle out if there was some kind of fix going on. The question was, why would someone fix the match—on either side? "The one who has more to lose is Symanova," Kelleher said. "People are saying that if she plays Makarova in the quarters, it will be the highest-rated tennis match in history. CBS has already cleared the time to put it on."

"But why would they be worried about her losing to a player who started the summer ranked hundred-and-eighth in the world and is still only forty-eighth?" Susan Carol asked.

"For one thing, Evelyn's pretty good," Kelleher said. "For another, Symanova hasn't played well so far."

"But when does the plot date back to? No one knew any of that when Symanova disappeared," Stevie said.

They drove in silence for a while.

"Is it possible," Susan Carol finally asked, "that we're

dealing with two different plots? One to kidnap Symanova, another to fix this match? Could there be two completely different groups at work here?"

"That would almost have to bring the SVR back into play," Mearns said. "Because we've seen everyone else involved meeting together—or at least you and Stevie have."

"Well, maybe there are more people involved still . . . ," offered Stevie.

They went back and forth with theories until they reached Manhattan.

Susan Carol ordered the food while Kelleher and Mearns were quickly changing for dinner. It was almost eight by the time they were ready to go.

"You two stay out of trouble tonight," Kelleher said as they left.

"We'll try," Susan Carol said.

Stevie was glad she made no promises.

✗   ✗   ✗

Evelyn Rubin was right on time, buzzing the apartment at eight-thirty on the dot, just as Susan Carol was paying for the food.

She looked like she had been crying when Stevie opened the door for her, but she accepted some chicken and an egg roll. "I forgot I haven't eaten since lunchtime," she said.

They sat at the kitchen table and ate dinner while debating what to do next.

She told them that she had last seen Gibson on Friday afternoon at a private tennis club in Manhattan where she had gone to practice. "That's when we made the date for lunch," she said. "He told me he was going to wrap up the Makarova contract last night. He was pretty excited about it. I *did* wonder a little if I was going to get shoved into the background once she was on board. But Brendan told me after the Letterman thing that his phone was ringing off the hook. He said he had offers into the millions to sign me for shoe and clothing contracts, plus a camera company, a perfume company, and one of the fast-food hamburger chains all lined up to make offers. I've never had *any* endorsements before."

"Aren't you a little young to endorse perfume?" Stevie asked.

"Jennifer Capriati endorsed a wrinkle cream when she was fourteen," Susan Carol said, again amazing Stevie by knowing something that, to him, seemed unknowable.

"You weren't born when Capriati was fourteen," Evelyn said, apparently just as amazed. "Look, I'm not sure I'm going to sign with any of these people. I'm still in high school and I'm not dropping out. But Brendan says these companies understand that and want to sign me anyway. Staying in school makes me different. Plus, he says all the offers might double if I win tomorrow. That actually scares me a little."

"It should," Susan Carol said. "All of this is scary."

"But Evelyn . . . ," Stevie began hesitantly. "Are you more scared of winning or losing?"

"What?"

"Well, the way this looks to us, we're wondering if someone is trying to fix tomorrow's match. Has anyone approached you at all?"

"What?! Of course not! You think . . . I would *never* . . ."

"We believe you," soothed Susan Carol. "Really. But this whole situation is so . . . out of control. Something big is going on and we're just trying to puzzle it out. So Brendan never suggested to you that you might not win?"

"No! Just the opposite. He's been pumping me up— making me believe I *can* win. How can you, of all people, ask me that?"

"I think we need to go to Brendan's apartment," Stevie broke in, sensing the conversation spinning out of control.

"What? Why there?" Evelyn asked.

"I don't know," Stevie said. "But we might find something."

Susan Carol nodded. "He's right," she said. "Sometimes when you don't know what you're looking for, you just have to start looking *someplace*. Maybe we'll find something. At the very least, we can listen to his phone messages. There might be a clue there."

"Do you guys feel safe running around New York City at night?" Evelyn said.

Stevie grunted. "Good point." She didn't know anything about what had happened to him on the subway and there was no point freaking her out further by telling her. "But I don't think we have any choice."

Susan Carol nodded. "I agree. We can't just sit here and do nothing. I was going to get a cab over there anyway— now you'll both be with me."

They were able to get a cab right outside the door of the apartment building. The cab breezed through the park and deposited them outside 52 Riverside Drive within ten minutes. The street was empty when they got out, causing Stevie to shiver just a little even though the night was warm and comfortable. Susan Carol walked over to the keypad and punched the numbers. They waited for the buzzer to let them know the door was open. Nothing. Susan Carol frowned, hit the clear button, and tried again. Still nothing.

"I've done this a dozen times already this week," she said. She punched the numbers again, this time slowly. There was no response.

"Now what?" Evelyn said, leaning against the side of the building, looking very tired.

"Hang on," Stevie said. "Someone's coming. Susan Carol, get ready to crank up your Scarlett act."

Evelyn looked baffled but Susan Carol didn't flinch.

A well-dressed man with dark hair was approaching. Seeing the three teenagers, he frowned.

"Can I help you kids?" he said, stepping past them to the keypad but making no move to hit any numbers.

"I hope so," Susan Carol said, both the smile and the drawl going full throttle. "I'm stayin' with my uncle this week for the U.S. Open, and for some reason I can't get this keypad to work."

So far, she had told the truth.

"What numbers are you pressing?" the man asked.

"It's 7-5-5-7-0-8-0-6," she said.

The man smiled. "Well, that *was* the right number," he said. "Until today. The code changes the first of every month."

Stevie almost groaned out loud. Today was September 1.

"Who's your uncle, anyway?" the man said.

"Brendan Gibson," Susan Carol said. "He's in apartment 14A."

The man nodded. "I know who he is. I live in 10A. I heard that girl tennis player mention him on Letterman the other night. I didn't even know he was an agent."

"That girl tennis player is me," Evelyn said, appearing reenergized. She was smiling with wattage that matched Susan Carol's.

The man peered at her for a second and did a double take. "My God!" he said. "That *is* you! You're Evelyn . . ."

"Rubin," she said.

He snapped his fingers. "Right!" He started to punch the buttons on the keypad. "So where is Brendan?"

"Got stuck in a meeting out at the tennis center," Susan Carol said, prepared as always. "He said to meet him here."

The door was buzzing. "The September number is easy," the man said. "It's 2-4-6-8-8-6-4-2. I'm Todd May."

They shook hands and Susan Carol introduced Stevie as they walked inside. "And what's your connection here?" Todd May asked.

Before Stevie could answer, both girls said, "He's my boyfriend."

Whoops. Todd May laughed and patted Stevie on the shoulder as they got on the elevator. "That's nice work, Stevie," he said.

Stevie breathed a sigh of relief that Todd May hadn't decided to question the girls' faux pas. He appeared completely dazzled by both of them. He shook hands again when the elevator got to 10. "Good luck tomorrow, Evelyn," he said. "Now that I've met you, maybe I'll root against Symanova. Tough, though, after what she's been through."

"You're right," Evelyn said. "If I wasn't playing her, I'd feel the same way."

He waved again as the door mercifully closed.

"You guys just about blew it by not letting me answer a question he asked *me*," Stevie said to both of them.

"He's right, you know," Evelyn said.

"He is . . . on occasion," Susan Carol said, unable to resist a smile as they reached 14.

As soon as they were inside the dark apartment, they began flicking on lights. "Let's spread out," Susan Carol said. "Stevie, you take the bedroom. Evelyn, you check the kitchen and the dining area. I'll look in the office."

Stevie headed into the master bedroom. The bed had been made, but that told him nothing. The room was very neat, except for the night table next to the bed where the phone was. There were books stacked up on it and what looked like a contract. Stevie picked it up and began to look at its contents. There was a cover letter on top, explaining to Gibson that the enclosed was a proposed contract for Evelyn Rubin. He noticed the swoosh logo on the top of the letterhead. Picking through the pages of mostly unreadable material, he finally came to a paragraph that was in boldface type: "In return, The Company will pay The Player the amount of $2,000,000 the first year; $3,000,000 the second year; $4,000,000 the third year; and $5,000,000 the fourth year." Stevie gasped. Apparently Gibson had been telling Evelyn the truth about the offers he was getting for her. One paragraph was circled: "Player agrees to play at least twelve (12) tournaments each calendar year." Stevie wondered how Evelyn and her parents would feel about that. He was starting to read the paragraph about bonuses for being ranked in the top ten, the top five, or number one, and for winning major championships, when he heard Susan Carol calling.

Clutching the contract, he walked quickly into the room Gibson used as an office. Susan Carol was holding a yellow legal pad in her hands. "Look at this," she said, handing him the legal pad. It was covered with what appeared to be phone numbers and little notes. Stevie noticed one that said "Call Manhattan Café for rez."

"The Manhattan Café—that's where he was supposed to meet you for lunch, right, Evelyn?" Evelyn nodded.

"That's not it," Susan Carol said. "Look at what he circled at the top of the page."

Stevie looked up and saw an address that had been circled: "25 E. 10th—apt. 4B. 5 p.m. DC: 83325A."

"The question," Susan Carol said, "is why did he write this address down and *when* did he write it down."

"And what does 'DC' stand for?" Evelyn asked.

"I'm betting it's a door code to get in the building," Susan Carol said.

"So what now?" Stevie asked.

"Let's check his phone messages," Susan Carol said.

Brendan Gibson had one of those old-fashioned answering machines. It was right there on the desk next to the phone and the notepad. Susan Carol began playing back the messages. There were sixteen and they were in reverse order—the last one to come in playing back first. They went through messages from Evelyn and the Makarovs and a number of people they didn't recognize. The last message—the oldest one on the tape—was the most intriguing.

"Gibson," a voice said. "We can't make it before five o'clock. Take it or leave it. Meet us at twenty-five East Tenth. It's apartment 4B."

Now they knew when Gibson had written down the address and the time. Evelyn looked frightened.

"Should we go there?" Evelyn asked.

Susan Carol shook her head. "It's almost eleven o'clock," she said. "We can't just go charging down there in the middle of the night and kick the door in."

"What're you saying?" Stevie said. "That we *could* go kick the door in tomorrow morning?"

Susan Carol shook her head. "No. I think we need adult help. My uncle may very well be at this apartment. But we don't know for sure."

"How do we find out?"

"I think Kelleher needs to contact his FBI friend as soon as possible. Maybe he can find out who the apartment belongs to or figure out a way to get in there and see if Uncle Brendan's there or not."

Evelyn looked at Stevie, clearly wanting to know what he thought. "She's right," Stevie said. "We have no idea what Brendan has walked into. We don't even know if he's a good guy or a bad guy."

She looked baffled. "Why are you both talking about Brendan like this? What aren't you telling me?"

Stevie told her about what had happened Wednesday after she had gone up to change.

"Stevie, I am *so* sorry," she said. "I know Brendan has been uptight all week. But I can't believe it was him who sent those men."

"Maybe he didn't," Stevie said. "That's why we need help. We don't know what we're dealing with. But we know it's serious."

"Okay," Evelyn said. "Call Kelleher."

Susan Carol picked up the phone on her uncle's desk and dialed Kelleher's cell. "I'm getting voice mail," she said. She left a message asking him to call her cell as soon as possible. "It's *very urgent*," she said.

She hung up and said, "Okay, let's get out of here."

"You aren't staying here tonight?" Stevie said.

"No way. I'm not staying here alone. I'll sleep on the couch with you guys again. It's actually comfortable."

He wasn't going to tell her to stay here, that was for sure. And he figured they should be together when Kelleher called. Before they left the apartment, he handed the contract he had found to Evelyn. "I know you don't care much about this right now, but it looks like Brendan was telling the truth about you getting rich," he said. He showed her the paragraph with the numbers. Then he showed her the one that mentioned the twelve tournaments.

She sighed. "It's an awful lot of money," she said. "This is my eighth tournament this year, so twelve isn't *that* much more traveling. I'm sure Brendan was thinking he could talk my parents into it. Right now, though, I can't even think about it."

They left the apartment and went downstairs. Riverside Drive was deserted. They started walking over to West End Avenue, hoping to find a cab. Every few steps, Stevie found himself turning to look behind to make sure no one was following. There were no cabs in sight on West End either, so they kept walking to Broadway. Stevie's heart was pounding and he breathed a sigh of relief when they reached Broadway and found it brightly lit and crowded with people coming out of nearby restaurants and bars.

Finally, they were able to flag a cab and decided that Evelyn would drop them off at the apartment, then continue on to her hotel.

"You get some sleep," Susan Carol told her as they got out of the cab.

"Easy for you to say," she said, forcing a smile. "I guess they won't come after me as long as they have Brendan."

"They won't," Stevie said. "But call us when you get to your room."

"And we'll call you if we hear anything," Susan Carol added.

The cab pulled away. Kelleher and Mearns weren't back

yet so Stevie and Susan Carol turned on the TV and watched some Open highlights from the day. Andre Agassi had won, which might have been a big story except for the fact that all anyone seemed to care about was the upcoming Symanova-Rubin match. Evelyn called to report she was safely in her room in the middle of a lengthy piece about the match, which included an interview with Brendan Gibson. "I wonder," Susan Carol said, "when they taped that."

Stevie heard the Duke fight song. Susan Carol picked up her cell and looked at it. "It's Bobby," she said.

She hit the button to answer the call and, after a few seconds, said, "There's a lot to tell you, are you in a good place to listen?" A pause. "No, I don't think it can wait for you to get here." Stevie listened as she filled him in. "Okay," she said finally. "We'll see you soon." She snapped the phone shut.

"What'd he say?" Stevie asked.

"He's calling his friend at the FBI," she said. "He says that's the way to go, especially since there may be a kidnapping going on here."

"Two in a week," Stevie said.

She said nothing in response, just stared into space.

"What do we do now?" he asked finally.

She stood up. "We do what we told Evelyn to do," she said. "Try to get some sleep."

"Easy for you to say," he said. Like Evelyn, he wasn't kidding.

20: THE RESCUE

IT TURNED out Stevie was wrong about not being able to sleep. The sun was up and streaming through the windows when he heard a knock on his door.

"Stevie," Susan Carol said. "Wake up. You need to get dressed."

He walked to the door, still in his pajamas, and opened it. "What's up?" he asked.

"The FBI guy just called Bobby. He's going to be here at eight o'clock."

Stevie looked at his watch. It was almost seven-thirty. "Should we call Evelyn?" he said.

"No, not unless we absolutely have to. Let her get ready to play."

He took a quick shower and got dressed. Eggs and an English muffin were waiting for him on the table when he walked into the kitchen. Kelleher was standing at the stove. "My day to make breakfast," he said.

Stevie was finishing his breakfast when the doorbell rang. Mearns opened it and a man Stevie guessed was the FBI agent Kelleher knew walked in. Stevie remembered the FBI people in New Orleans as very stern-looking. This one was different. "Pete Dowling," he said, shaking hands with a smile. Susan Carol offered everyone coffee and they all sat down.

"Bobby briefed me on the phone about what's been going on," Dowling said. "My partner is waking a judge up right now, trying to get a search warrant for that apartment. But honestly, I'm dubious. What you have is hardly definitive."

"Have you been able to find out who the apartment belongs to?" Susan Carol asked.

"Not exactly," Dowling said. "The official listing is a company called TB-Inc. As far as we can figure, it's a bogus name."

"Well, that makes it suspicious, doesn't it?" Susan Carol said. "Can't you find out who's behind the fake name?"

"We're working on it, but it takes a while, especially on Labor Day weekend. These people have insulated themselves pretty well."

Kelleher leaned forward in his chair. "Pete, we don't have time," he said. "We need to know if this guy has been kidnapped, and if so, why."

"Has anyone been contacted?" Dowling asked. "Has Ms. Rubin heard anything leading her to believe this is connected to her match today?"

"Not so far as we know," Kelleher said.

Dowling stood up. "That's the problem," he said. "I can't get a warrant for this apartment based on a phone message and the address being on a notepad. There has to be some tangible evidence that someone is being held against their will in that apartment. If you can get me that, I can make a move. Until then, I can't."

They all looked at one another. "It is a little bit strange that no one has called, isn't it?" Susan Carol said. "If someone wants Evelyn to throw the match, they should have contacted her by now."

Stevie heard the Duke fight song again. Susan Carol answered. She listened for a minute and then said, "Okay, we'll get right back to you."

"That was Evelyn," she said, closing the phone. "The Makarovs just told her that SMG has scheduled a press conference for Symanova after the match today. They're convinced SMG is going to announce the movie deal. They say CBS is going to cover it live—and the other networks are fighting to get onto the grounds to cover it too. CBS is trying to keep it exclusive. Big battle going on."

"They must be pretty confident Symanova's going to win today," Mearns said.

"Exactly," Susan Carol answered. "Now, why would that be?"

It took a while, but they finally came up with a strategy: Kelleher and Mearns would pick up Evelyn and drive her out to the tennis center. She had turned down a ride from the Makarovs and had told Susan Carol she couldn't bear the thought of making small talk in a courtesy car.

Dowling was going to see if he could find a judge to grant some kind of conditional warrant—one that wouldn't allow a search of the apartment but would at least authorize using his FBI badge to get into the apartment. "Long shot," he said. "But it isn't out of the question."

Stevie and Susan Carol would wait for a call from Dowling and then meet him if he found Brendan Gibson. Kelleher wasn't thrilled about leaving them in the city on their own, but Susan Carol was desperate to be close by if her uncle was found. So Kelleher made them promise not to do *anything* until they heard from Dowling, no matter how tempted they might be to try something on their own. Reluctantly, they promised. "This isn't New Orleans," Kelleher said as they were leaving. "I'm not sure those academic types would actually have hurt you guys. But we already know these goons mean business—don't we, Stevie?"

Once they were gone, Susan Carol made more coffee. Stevie tried joking about it stunting her growth, but she could only manage a wan smile.

"I guess I misjudged your uncle," he said finally. "Whatever he was up to, he wasn't involved in this."

"Oh, he was involved," she said. "But obviously not the way we thought. At first, I just couldn't imagine him being crooked. Then I thought I was wrong. Now I just can't imagine him being . . ."

"He won't be," Stevie said. "Mr. Dowling will come through."

The time crept by. They turned on the TV and watched *The Sports Reporters*. Mike Lupica was talking about Symanova versus Rubin. "If you took this plot to a movie studio, they would turn you away because it's just not believable," he said. "This is the Russian supermodel against the girl next door. This is the girl every boy wants to date against the girl they're all going to want to marry someday. The victim of a kidnapping against America's newest sweetheart. This could be the most dramatic tennis match any of us has seen since Bobby Riggs played Billie Jean King in 1973. And the only thing we know for sure? Both these girls are going to be very, very rich no matter who wins this afternoon."

"I guess he's got that right," said Stevie, remembering the contract he had seen the night before.

They flipped around. Tim Russert was interviewing Hughes Norwood on *Meet the Press*. After listening to Norwood talk for thirty seconds, Stevie hit the remote again. George Stephanopoulos was on ABC talking to Arlen Kantarian and Bud Collins. One more click to CBS and, yup, there was Bob Schieffer lobbing questions at Mary Carillo and Billie Jean King. "What happened to Nadia is a nightmare," King said. "But because of all the circumstances, this could be the biggest match in the history of women's tennis—it will certainly be the most watched, based on the ratings so far this week."

"As big as when you played Riggs?" Schieffer asked.

"Bigger."

"I think if the president of the United States resigned today, it would be the second-biggest story going," Susan Carol said.

Her phone rang again. Again, she listened. "Okay, we'll call Mr. Dowling right now," she said. "Don't worry. It's going to be all right. Someone will be there right away. Just sit tight and don't even think about anything except winning the match."

"Evelyn?" Stevie said as she hung up.

She nodded while dialing.

"They called?"

"No. There was a note in her locker. It said something like 'As soon as you lose today, your agent will be released unharmed.' "

"Holy . . ."

"Mr. Dowling," Susan Carol said, "I think we have the tangible evidence you need."

Stevie listened as she filled him in about the note and then saw a frown cross her face. "But that'll be too late," she said. She nodded her head. "Okay, but *please* hurry. The match starts in four hours."

She stood up and started for the door. "Come on," she said. "We need to get going."

"Where?" he asked.

"Mr. Dowling said an agent would go find Evelyn at the tennis center to see the note and make sure she's okay. Then he can get a warrant, but it may still take time," she said. "We can't wait that long."

"But we promised . . ."

"That was before Evelyn got the note. Come on. I'll think of what we're going to do in the cab."

"Cab? Where are we going?"

"Twenty-five East Tenth Street," she said. "Apartment 4B."

✗ ✗ ✗

Neither of them said much in the cab. Even though it was late in the morning, the streets in Greenwich Village were still quiet. They had the cab stop a few yards short of the green awning that said 25 on it and got out there.

"Now what do we do?" Stevie asked when they were standing on the sidewalk.

"I've got a plan," she said.

"I figured you would."

"Mr. Dowling told me that if he knew someone was in imminent danger, he wouldn't need the warrant. The note to Evelyn isn't quite enough."

"So?"

"So I'm going in there. When I do . . ."

"You're doing *what*? What in the world are you talking about? You're just going to walk up there and ring the doorbell?"

"Exactly."

"And what do you expect them to do? Invite you in for coffee?"

"I expect them to hold me against my will."

He looked at her closely to see if she might be joking. She wasn't.

"Why would they even open the door?"

"Because if they won't, I'll yell that I'm going to get the police if they don't let my uncle Brendan go. You can bet they'll open the door then. As soon as I'm in there, you can call Mr. Dowling and say I'm being held and I'm in danger. He'll *have* to come then."

It wasn't a bad idea. Well, it was a terrible idea—but it might work.

"You can't do it," he said. "I won't let you."

She smiled at him. "Yes, you will," she said. "Because you know it's a good idea. And we can't waste any more time."

He thought about it for a minute. "Okay," he said. "We'll try it. But *I'm* going in. *You* call Mr. Dowling."

She shook her head. "Nope, it has to be me," she said. "They'll open up more quickly for a girl." She put her hand on his shoulder. "He's *my* uncle, Stevie. I have to try."

Stevie still didn't like it. But he wasn't exactly full of alternative plans. And he could see there was no talking her out of it. He took a deep breath. "Okay," he said. "But I'm scared."

She smiled. "Me too," she said.

She looked at her watch. "It's eleven-fifteen. If I'm not back down here at eleven-twenty-five, call Mr. Dowling."

"How about eleven-twenty?" he said.

"It'll take me a minute to find the right apartment. And maybe someone unexpected will answer the door, or maybe the apartment will be empty . . . ," she said. "Wait ten. Then call."

"You sure Dowling will come? What if he's mad at us for doing this?"

"Oh, he'll be mad. But he'll come."

She handed him a piece of paper. It was the one on which Brendan had written down the address. "Keep that," she said. "You'll need the door code when they get here."

"I hope you're right about that being what 'DC' stands for," he said.

"Well, let's go see. If I'm wrong, we'll need a plan B," she said.

She squared her shoulders and turned to go. Stevie had an urge to do something before she left—he just wasn't sure what. He caught hold of her arm and pulled her back. "Susan Carol . . . ," he choked out, but he couldn't think of anything to say. Finally, he settled for "Be careful," which was kind of dumb—by walking in there, she was being any-thing but careful.

"Don't worry," she said. "I know you'll come and rescue me." She gave him the smile and walked up to the front door of the building. She punched the code into the keypad next to the door, and in a second she was gone.

Stevie began staring at his watch. And sweating.

✗ ✗ ✗

At 11:24, Stevie decided he had waited long enough. He dialed Dowling, who picked up on the first ring.

"Mr. Dowling, I think you need to get over here right away," Stevie said. "Susan Carol went up to the apartment and she hasn't come back. I think she's being held by the kidnappers."

There was silence for a moment. "She *what*?!" Dowling finally said. "What the hell is she playing at?"

"Can I explain later?" Stevie said. "You said imminent danger. I think she may be in imminent danger right now."

"Dammit," he heard Dowling say. "Where are you?"

"Right outside the building," he said. "Twenty-five East Tenth."

"Don't move. Do *not* go inside. You kids had better have a good explanation for this when we get there. We'll be there in ten minutes."

Stevie wasn't sure who "we" were, but he was glad to hear that Dowling was coming and bringing help. Who knew how many kidnappers there were inside the apartment?

He paced up and down the sidewalk, ignoring the looks from passersby, until he saw a police car and another car, both with sirens going, turning off of Fifth Avenue onto East 10th Street. Dowling got out of the unmarked car with another man in a suit. Two policemen jumped out of the police car.

"No time for introductions," Dowling said. "Let's go."

"Here's the code to the front door," Stevie said, handing it over.

"When we get up there," Dowling said to Stevie, "you stay back away from the door. You got it?"

"Yes, sir."

They rode in silence up the elevator. There were only three apartments on the L-shaped floor. Dowling ordered Stevie to stand at the corner of the hallway, well back from the door to 4B. Stevie peered around and saw Dowling ring the doorbell. There was a pause and then he heard Dowling say, "This is the FBI. Open the door."

Another pause. "You should know that holding a minor against her will is a federal offense that can put you in jail for life."

And then: "We don't need a warrant when you're holding a minor. If you open the door right now, you have my word I will only charge you with holding Mr. Gibson. You've got no chance to get out of there. We know everything. Don't make this any worse for yourselves."

Another pause. "You've got thirty seconds."

Stevie held his breath. This could be very good or very bad. . . . He waited. And waited.

Finally, he saw the door open—a crack. Dowling pushed it open and Stevie saw all four officers pour into the apartment. He ran to the door, then hesitated, hearing a voice shout, "Down on the floor, get down!" He peered in and saw two men lying on their stomachs being handcuffed. Dowling was untying and ungagging Brendan Gibson. Susan Carol, her hands tied in front of her but not gagged, was being released by Dowling's partner.

"Are you okay?" Stevie said, stepping around the two men on the floor to get to her.

"Fine," she said.

"Stevie, go out in the kitchen and get Mr. Gibson some water," Dowling said.

Stevie nodded and turned into the small kitchen. He found a glass in a cabinet and filled it at the sink. He walked back into the living room, just as the cops were standing the two kidnappers up. When he saw their faces, he gasped and dropped the glass of water, which didn't break but clattered loudly on the floor, spilling water everywhere.

"The subway guys!" he shouted. "These are the guys who beat me up!"

The two men said nothing.

Dowling walked up close to them. "You two better be willing to talk," he said. "Or you're going away for a very long time."

One of them shrugged. "Nothing to talk about. We're just the hired help. We get a call, we get paid. We got nothing to tell you."

"We'll see about that," Dowling said.

He turned to his partner. "Bob, you've got their cell phones? Start checking the numbers right away."

Bob nodded. Dowling turned to Brendan Gibson, who was now drinking a new glass of water that Stevie had brought him.

"How do you feel?" he asked.

"Scared—still," Gibson said. "But okay. When does the match start? Someone call Evelyn."

Stevie pulled out his phone and started to dial.

Susan Carol sat next to her uncle on the couch, holding on to him—clearly not wanting to let him go. "Uncle Brendan, I am so sorry for doubting you," she said.

"Me too," Stevie said, then broke off as Evelyn answered.

"Don't worry about it," Gibson said to Susan Carol. "I know why you doubted me. I haven't behaved perfectly this week myself. But you're here now. I can't believe you put yourself in such danger."

"Yes, we'll be discussing that, Ms. Anderson," Dowling said. "Mr. Gibson, I assume you know who had you kidnapped?"

"Oh yeah," Gibson said. "Can I tell you the whole story on the way out to Queens? I really want to see Evelyn and be sure she's okay."

"You think you can walk?" Dowling asked.

Gibson stood up very slowly and wobbled a bit. Susan Carol helped steady him. "I'm okay," he said. "I'm not ready to do any sprinting, but I can walk."

"Mr. Gibson," Stevie broke in. "Evelyn wants to hear your voice." He held out the phone.

"Evelyn, it's me. I'm fine," said Gibson. He listened for a minute and then said, "I'll tell you everything later. You just need to get ready to play. You need to beat the pants off that girl."

21: MATCH POINT

THEY PILED into Pete Dowling's car—Stevie, Susan Carol, and Brendan Gibson in the backseat, and Dowling's partner, who he finally introduced as Bob Ades, up front. The two police officers had taken the two kidnappers away in their squad car, with orders from Dowling to take them to the FBI's Manhattan field office, along with the cell phones and the guns they had found on them.

Before Brendan Gibson could tell his story, Dowling demanded that Stevie and Susan Carol explain how Susan Carol had ended up in the apartment. He kept shaking his head over and over as Susan Carol told him. "Do you understand how stupid that was?" he said. "What if they had decided to turn you into a hostage?"

"But they didn't," Susan Carol said. "They were counting

on not having to hurt anyone. That's what I was counting on too."

"You were *very* lucky," Dowling said. "And I will give you a long lecture when this is over. Okay, Mr. Gibson, tell us what happened."

They were in the Midtown Tunnel, which was now familiar territory to Stevie.

"I'll try to give you the short version in the interest of time," Gibson said. "For me, this started on Monday night— the night you heard me in the apartment with the Makarovs, Stevie.

"Before that, over dinner, they told me they thought that Symanova's kidnapping was a fake—a setup. Mr. Makarov's brother is high up in the SVR. He said there was no way they would pull a move like that—if only because it would ultimately fail. He believed the Symanovs and SMG were trying to pin it on the SVR to make it look real."

"And you believed him right away?" Susan Carol said.

"Not exactly. I knew they were angry at SMG, and I knew how much they hated the Symanovs. But the next day, I saw Norwood walking around with that movie producer."

"O'Donahue," Susan Carol said.

"I cornered Norwood. I told him I knew the kidnapping was a fake—even though I didn't—and I took a flyer and said, 'You're already planning the movie, Hughes. I'm going to blow the whistle on you.'

"He tried the you-have-no-proof speech for a while— which was true, of course. I didn't. But eventually he asked me what I was looking for. Which shook me up a little—I hadn't really thought about it until then. So I told him I would think about it."

"Why, Uncle Brendan?" Susan Carol asked. "Why didn't you just go to the police right *then*?"

Gibson shook his head. "I should have," he said. "But I really *didn't* have proof at that point. I decided to see where the trail would lead. I went back to Norwood and said if I got a cut of the movie deal *and* if he promised not to make any move on Evelyn, I'd keep quiet. He agreed. That's why I was in that meeting at the U.S. Open Club."

"So who actually kidnapped Nadia?" Stevie asked.

"No one kidnapped her," Gibson said. "I'm guessing those two guys you just arrested were in on it and a couple more guys. I think there were four in all. But they were hired by SMG. All they did was hide her out in SMG's offices on the East Side until it was time for her to make her triumphant return."

"By which time the whole world wanted a piece of her incredible story," Susan Carol said.

"Exactly," Gibson said. "This was probably a hundred-million-dollar kidnapping. Symanova will be endorsing everything—for millions—within a month. She's going to be on the cover of *Time* and *Newsweek*, not to mention all the glamour magazines. The bidding for her shoe deal was at eighteen million a year on Thursday—and climbing. Rolex wants to sign her and so does Cartier. Those are massive deals. Some British publishing house is offering ten million for her life story. The movie deal will be worth at least thirty million. Lots more if it does well in the theaters. O'Donahue claims he'll get Britney Spears to play Nadia."

"She's not tall enough," Susan Carol said.

"Yeah, but she's famous enough," Gibson said.

"You realize, Mr. Gibson, you're subject to an accessory charge for not turning them in," Dowling said.

"I understand," Gibson said. "Like I said back in the apartment, I know I screwed up."

"Odds are your helping us now and what just happened to you will be seen as mitigating circumstances."

"I'll help any way I can," Gibson said.

"So where did it fall apart?" Dowling asked. They were passing Shea Stadium now. Getting close.

"After Evelyn's second-round match," Gibson said. "They got a good look at how much she had improved and got scared. Norwood told me the whole deal could fall apart unless Evelyn lost to Nadia today. I told him that was out of my control, that even if I *tried* to get Evelyn to throw the match, she wouldn't do it. He said I needed to get control somehow, because if Evelyn won, the movie deal would go down the tubes. Nadia can't lose so early in the tournament to a nobody. She needs to at least make it to the quarters."

"What about Serena Williams in the fourth round?" Susan Carol asked.

"Serena's hurt. Plus, she's a power player. Power players don't scare them. They think she can beat Serena *and* Makarova, and they're even convinced she would beat

Davenport or Venus Williams or Sharapova. There are only three players in the draw who make them nervous: the two Belgians—Clijsters and Henin-Hardenne, who she can't play before the final—and Evelyn. Because those girls play with finesse; they'd run her around, tire her out.

"If she loses to one of the Belgians in the final, it's okay. But if she loses to Evelyn today, everything could go away. In fact, a lot of the deals might swing to Evelyn."

"But Symanova's a star. She's a beautiful kidnap victim. . . . Are these people that fickle?" Susan Carol asked.

"You bet," Gibson said. "As long as Symanova keeps winning, the stakes go up. But if she loses . . ."

"She could have lost to Kim on Friday," Stevie said.

"Yes, she could have. I think that match is what panicked them. Kim plays finesse tennis but not nearly as well as Evelyn. That's when I got the call saying they needed to meet with me that afternoon. At first I told them there was nothing to meet about, but they upped the ante."

"How?" they all asked.

"They threatened Evelyn. That's why I went to the apartment. As soon as I walked in, expecting Norwood and the Symanovs, the two guys jumped me. You know the rest. Susan Carol, I don't know how to thank you. What you did was unbelievably brave."

"And stupid," Dowling said.

He pulled the car off the Grand Central Parkway and flashed his badge at the guards in front of the entrance to the players' parking lot. The guards looked baffled but waved them through.

They parked and got out of the car. Dowling told Ades to head for the security office and round up several police officers. "It's a crowded place and we've got a bunch of people to arrest," he said. "We'll meet up inside and figure out how best to proceed.

"Now," Dowling said, "let's go find Evelyn."

× × ×

They had just walked inside the gate when Susan Carol's cell phone rang. She opened it, smiled, and said, "It's her."

Stevie could hear Evelyn's excited voice coming through the phone as they walked. "We're walking inside right now," she said. "Where should we meet you? . . . Okay. Be there in about three minutes."

She closed the phone. "She was on a practice court," she reported. "She'll meet us outside the junior women's locker room."

As they headed for the junior locker room, Stevie noticed people lined up to get into the stadium—even though the start of the match was more than an hour away. Dowling noticed too.

"Gonna be a lot of disappointed people," he said.

"Why?" Stevie asked.

"Won't be much of a match with Symanova under arrest," he answered.

Stevie and Susan Carol both stopped in their tracks. Stevie could tell that, like him, Susan Carol hadn't thought through the implications yet. Dowling read their body language.

"You guys understand that Symanova has to be arrested, don't you?" he said. "Clearly, she knew what was going on the whole time."

"I'm afraid he's right," Gibson said. "She knew *exactly* what was happening."

Stevie *had* realized that but hadn't focused on the idea of Symanova not playing the match.

"I'd have liked to see Evelyn beat her," he said.

"Me too," Susan Carol said.

"Me three," said Gibson.

They walked quietly down the halls and found Evelyn waiting for them. As soon as she saw Brendan Gibson, she ran into his arms. "Oh, thank goodness," she said.

"Thank Stevie and Susan Carol," he said. "And Agent Dowling."

Evelyn shook hands with Pete Dowling, hugged Susan Carol, and then kissed Stevie—quite firmly—on the lips. Stevie felt his legs get a little bit weak. He thought—maybe he imagined it—that Susan Carol looked miffed.

"Thank you all for everything," she said. "God, Brendan, you had us scared to death."

"I had me pretty scared too," he said, smiling. "But it's all over now."

Evelyn took a deep breath. "I know. Well, I better pull myself together. I've got a match to play in about an hour."

They all looked at one another. It was Dowling who finally said something.

"Ms. Rubin, you understand that Nadia Symanova was involved in Mr. Gibson's abduction, among other things. . . ."

Evelyn's face clouded. "Oh no! You're not going to arrest her *now?!*"

"We have no choice. We have to arrest everyone involved."

Evelyn looked as if she was going to cry. Bob Ades rounded the corner. "Everyone's waiting at the far end of the hall," he told Dowling in a low voice. "I talked to that Kantarian guy and he said the parents and the agent are in the players' lounge waiting for the match to start. And we believe Symanova is in the locker room here. Kantarian wanted to talk to you before we do anything. He's not very happy."

Brendan Gibson put an arm around Evelyn. "Agent Dowling, let me ask you a question," he said. "As long as you know where everyone is going to be, is there any reason why you can't make the arrests after the match is over?"

Dowling didn't answer. "Agent Dowling, *please*," Evelyn said. "It isn't as if anyone is going to make a run for it. Please let me play this match. I know I can beat her. It won't mean anything if I win by default."

"As long as I stay out of sight, no one will have any idea things aren't going according to plan," Gibson said.

Dowling looked at Ades. "Any thoughts?"

Ades smiled. "It's not exactly our normal procedure," he said. "But they're right. No one is going to bolt, especially with the match going on." He looked at Evelyn. "She hasn't done anything wrong. Why deny her this moment?"

"I forgot you're a tennis fan," Dowling said, smiling. "Okay. Let's go meet with Kantarian. We need a safe place to hide Mr. Gibson, and we need to make sure the agent and the parents are being closely watched throughout."

Evelyn, who was apparently in a hugging mood, threw her arms around Dowling. "Thank you," she said. "Thank you, thank you."

Dowling shook his head. "My life today is being run by teenage girls. *Please* don't tell anyone about this."

✗   ✗   ✗

Evelyn went into the locker room after they all had wished her good luck and cautioned her to stay as far away from Symanova as possible in there. They all went back down the hall, and Ades took Dowling in to see Arlen Kantarian while Stevie, Susan Carol, and Gibson hovered in the hallway. The FBI men weren't gone for long. When they came back, a police officer was with them. "Officer Olmstead is going to take us to Mr. Kantarian's box to watch the match," Dowling explained. "Mr. Gibson, here's a hat for you—try to be inconspicuous. Once it's over, Olmstead will have people where they need to be. Mr. Kantarian's only request was that the arrests be made out of sight of the public. They want as little commotion as possible."

Olmstead took them to a box halfway up in the stands in a corner of the court with a perfect angle to look down at the two players. He gave Dowling the seat locations for the Symanovs and Norwood. Dowling nodded and told him he and Ades would stop Symanova in the tunnel coming off the court. "We'll need a female officer there," he said.

"I understand," Olmstead said.

"This is awful for women's tennis," Gibson said as they sat down. He was in the back corner of the box, hat pulled over his head to ensure that no one in the stands might notice him.

"If Evelyn can win, she might be just what the women's game needs," Susan Carol said.

"I'm not sure she even wants all this attention," Gibson said. "She's still just a kid."

The two players walked on court at exactly three o'clock to thunderous applause. "This feels like a final," Gibson said. "Only bigger."

Both players looked nervous when the match began. But after the first few games, each seemed to find a groove. Rubin was moving Symanova around, trying to extend the points, making her run as much as possible. Symanova was using her power—especially on her serve—to try to end the points quickly. The momentum swung back and forth.

Down six games to five and serving at 30–all, Evelyn tried a drop shot that Symanova got to and crushed into the corner. Set point for Symanova. The huge crowd was silent for one of the first times all afternoon. They had taken turns screaming for Symanova and then for Evelyn. They couldn't seem to make up their collective mind about who they wanted to see win. Evelyn twisted in a serve and Symanova attacked, coming to net behind a forehand. Evelyn lifted a lob and the crowd gasped as Symanova backpedaled, preparing to hit an overhead. But the lob was so deep, she had to turn and chase it down. She sent a backhand across the net, but Evelyn had surprised her, coming to net herself. She picked off the shot and flicked a perfect volley into the corner. Set point saved. Then Evelyn won the next two points in rapid succession to make it 6–all in the set. Tie-break.

Then the *tiebreak* went to 6–all. Evelyn netted a nervous forehand. Set point Symanova. Stevie's heart was in his throat. After all they had done, was Symanova still going to win—and *then* go to jail? The stadium was silent. Evelyn, bouncing on her toes, moved in a half step when a Symanova backhand landed a little short. She took it on the rise and cracked a backhand that Symanova never even moved for. It hit just inside the line. Seven–all.

Now Symanova got nervous and *she* netted a forehand. Set point for Evelyn. The two teenagers stood at the baseline exchanging ground strokes. Finally, Evelyn went for a crosscourt dink. Symanova managed to run it down, but her lunging forehand sailed wide.

"Game and first set Rubin," the umpire said. "She leads one set to love. Second set. Rubin to serve."

Gibson was on his feet screaming along with the rest of the crowd—until Susan Carol reminded him to cool it. Mike Lupica had been right, this match was the gorgeous victim against the girl next door—or so the fans believed— and the crowd loved them both.

Still, the second set was all Symanova and the crowd got fully behind her—clearly wanting the match to go to three sets. Symanova's power seemed to be wearing on Evelyn.

Symanova broke Evelyn's serve at 4–all and then served the set out, winning 6–4. Stevie had thought the noise at the Final Four was as loud as he had ever heard. This felt louder.

The third set was filled with remarkable shots and exchanges but each woman managed to hold serve until Symanova broke to lead 3–2. It looked over for Evelyn. But this time she broke right back, seeming to find an extra reserve of energy. Both players then held serve for 4–all.

The match had now gone on for almost two and a half hours. Symanova was taking more time between points. It seemed like she thought she had the match won when she had broken Evelyn's serve. But Evelyn breaking her back had thrown her and now she was trying desperately to regroup. Evelyn held to reach 5–4 again after hitting a drop shot that Symanova couldn't get to. Suddenly, Evelyn was one game from winning the match.

"In the first set, she gets to that ball," Gibson said. "Symanova's tired. I think she may be done!"

Not quite. Serving at 4–5, Symanova summoned all her strength and held again with an exquisite backhand down the line that was *on* the line. Five games each. Then they each held serve for 6–all.

They would play another tiebreak. The tension was unbearable. The crowd was on its feet now for every point. It sounded more like a football game than a tennis match. People were shrieking *during* points, causing others to shush them, but it was hard to hold back.

As the tiebreak began, Olmstead reappeared. Stevie had almost forgotten about the impending arrests. "We're all in position," he said. "Both players will be interviewed on court when the match is over—loser first—so there's time for you to get down to court level. I've got an elevator standing by for you."

"Thanks," Dowling said.

The third-set tiebreak was like the first-set tiebreak— only more excruciating. Evelyn had a match point at 6–5 but netted an easy forehand. Then Symanova had a match point of her own at 7–6, and just as she had done behind her first-set lob, Evelyn surprised her, coming to net and putting away an easy volley on a forehand that Symanova floated.

"Can you believe she had the guts to do that?" Susan Carol said. "She's amazing."

It went to 10–all and Evelyn attacked again, coming in behind a serve to set up a forehand volley for a winner. It was 11–10—her third match point. They had been playing almost three hours. Stevie remembered the intensity of the final seconds of the national championship game at the Final Four. But this felt *more* tense because it was taking *so* long.

Symanova served. Evelyn had to lunge to return and her backhand came back short. Symanova closed and hit a backhand volley that was just a tad tentative. Evelyn ran it down in the corner and lined up a forehand as Symanova waited at the net. "Crosscourt!" Gibson screamed. "Go crosscourt!"

Symanova seemed to read his mind and moved a step to the right to cut off a possible crosscourt shot just as Evelyn uncorked a bullet straight down the line. Symanova lunged back—too late. The ball flew past her and landed cleanly inside both lines.

"Game, set, match Rubin!" The umpire was shouting to be heard.

The stadium had exploded in sound. Symanova, shoulders slumped, waited for Evelyn at the net. They hugged. On a TV monitor in the box, they could see Symanova was crying. It appeared Evelyn was too.

"Come on," Dowling said, already on his feet. "We need to move."

They hurried out of the box and Olmstead led them to an open elevator. They went straight to the basement and sprinted through the hallways toward the tunnel leading to the court. There were two more cops, both women, waiting for them at the top of the tunnel. They all ran down the tunnel, stopping just short of the entrance to the court. The crowd was still standing and cheering for both players. CBS had Bill Macatee on court for interviews. Macatee was talking to Symanova. The interviews were piped throughout the stadium, so they could hear loud and clear.

"Nadia, I know this is a heartbreaking loss, but after what you've been through this week, to play in a match like this, you deserve cheers—win or lose," Macatee said. The crowd erupted—the applause was staggering.

"This has been a long, long week," Symanova said over the noise. "Evelyn played *so* well." She paused as the crowd cheered again. "I am happy to be part of a match like this, just sad that I lost."

"Well, we know you'll be back," Macatee said as the

crowd cheered lustily again. Symanova waved, blew kisses, and cried some more. Someone had picked up her racquets for her. She headed for the tunnel, the crowd growing even louder as Macatee moved over to Evelyn.

Symanova was surrounded by four security guards as she reached the tunnel. The ones in front of her moved aside when they saw Dowling. "Nadia Symanova?" he said.

Symanova was clearly surprised to see her security people allow someone to get so close to her. "Yes. What is it?" she asked.

"Ms. Symanova, my name is Peter Dowling," he said. "I'm with the FBI." He flashed his badge. "You are under arrest for conspiring to kidnap Brendan Gibson and for conspiring to fake your own kidnapping."

Stevie suddenly noticed that a CBS camera that had been following Symanova as she left the court was recording the scene. But they weren't on live because he could hear Macatee talking to Evelyn Rubin.

"You are now, officially, America's newest sweetheart," Macatee said as cheers broke out again.

Stevie didn't hear Evelyn's answer, because Symanova was screaming at Dowling. "What?!! You are completely crazy! Where are my parents? Where is my agent? They will straighten this out, and then it will be trouble for you."

"You'll see all of them shortly," Dowling said. "I'm sorry, but I'm going to have to put handcuffs on you. You're accused of a federal crime. You will be charged as an adult. It's the law."

Even in sneakers, Symanova was still the tallest person in

the tunnel. For a split second, Stevie thought she might try to bolt past everyone. Instead, she began crying uncontrollably as Dowling gently put the cuffs on her. He turned to the female police officers. "Take her to the holding room with the others," he said. "Then we have to figure out how to get them all out of here."

The cops nodded and led Symanova up the hallway. The cameraman tried to follow, but the security men stopped him.

Rubin was wrapping up with Macatee and taking her star turn around the stadium before exiting. Dowling's cell phone rang and he walked up the hall to answer it. That left Stevie, Susan Carol, and Gibson as the welcoming committee. Evelyn went straight to Gibson. "I'm so proud of you!" he said as they hugged.

She was crying. When she saw Stevie and Susan Carol, she gave them each a very sweaty hug. "I don't know how I can ever repay all of you. Where's Mr. Dowling? I want to thank him too."

"Right here," a voice said behind them. Dowling was walking back down the tunnel with Olmstead.

"Have you got everyone?" Gibson asked.

Dowling shook his head. "No, not everyone," he said. "Ms. Rubin, congratulations." He wasn't smiling. Stevie was baffled.

"Sir, we've got everyone in custody," Olmstead said. "Everyone you told us . . ."

Dowling held his hand up. "I know, officer. Your guys were great. Stay here a minute, will you?

"That phone call was from my office. It took a while, but we finally figured out who owns the apartment where you were being held, Mr. Gibson."

Stevie saw a look of panic come over Brendan Gibson's face.

"You—you did?" he said.

"You want to tell her or should I?" Dowling said, looking at Evelyn. Gibson said nothing.

"The apartment is owned by ISM—Integrity Sports Management," Dowling said.

Evelyn and Susan Carol both shrieked at the same moment. Stevie was too shocked to say anything.

"You staged your kidnapping—just like Symanova did," Dowling said. "We also did a records check on the cell phones of the two men who were holding you. There were two calls from your cell phone number to one of them. One was Wednesday, a couple hours before Stevie was pulled off the subway. They told us they were given cash to beat Stevie up and, later, to hold you. The second call was Friday. Of course, they had no idea that it was *you* who told them to hold you."

Evelyn and Susan Carol both had tears in their eyes. "Uncle Brendan?" Susan Carol asked. "Are you behind this whole thing?"

"No, no," he insisted. "I mean . . ." His shoulders slumped. "What I told you in the car was the truth. I didn't know anything about the original fake kidnapping until the Makarovs brought it up on Monday. Then I *did* get involved with SMG. I was going to get a five-million cut. But when Evelyn started playing so well . . ." He stopped. "Maybe I need to talk to a lawyer."

"You saw a chance to have it all, didn't you?" Susan Carol said, her eyes now flashing with anger. "You knew Evelyn could win the match, but you wanted the Symanovs completely removed from the stage—even if she lost. So you staged your kidnapping to make sure they would go down. They could deny it, but it would all fit. After all, they'd already staged one kidnapping."

"And then you have *both* big stars—Evelyn and Makarova," Stevie picked up. "It was a no-lose situation for you. Five million would be peanuts compared to what you would make if the two of them made the quarters."

"So you really *needed* me to win," Evelyn said, now grasping the whole thing.

"You set it up so we would find you, didn't you?" said Susan Carol.

Gibson hung his head.

"You left the address in your apartment where you knew I'd find it. How about the message on your phone? Who left that?"

Gibson broke. "My assistant, David Salk. He also left the note with a guard to be put in Evelyn's locker today."

"Where is he right now?" Dowling asked.

"I honestly don't know. Probably at our office."

Dowling gave Olmstead instructions to pick Salk up. "You almost pulled it off," he said to Gibson. "I'm going to have one of the police officers read you your rights now."

"I have one more question," Susan Carol said as Dowling was handcuffing Gibson. "What was that apartment for?"

"For clients who want a quiet place to stay and not be hassled. We hid the ownership to make it completely private—not as well as I thought we'd hidden it, apparently."

He looked at Rubin. "I'm sorry, Evelyn," he said. "I just got carried away by the thought of making millions. I let you down."

"You let a lot of people down," Evelyn said.

Brendan Gibson looked at Susan Carol as he was being led away. "Tell your mom and dad not to hate me," he said.

"They won't hate you," Susan Carol said. "But they'll have a hard time forgiving you.

"I know I won't anytime soon."

22: FAREWELLS

EVELYN RUBIN had to go to a press conference once Gibson departed. No one wanted to ask her about the match. Word of the arrests had spread like wildfire. CBS had shown the tape of Nadia Symanova in handcuffs. Suddenly it was as if the match had never happened. Under instructions from Dowling, Rubin said repeatedly that she couldn't answer questions until she had given her statement to the FBI. She was thrilled to win the match, horrified to see her opponent led off in handcuffs.

Stevie and Susan Carol watched the press conference on the TV monitor in Arlen Kantarian's private box. Dowling had them taken there because Stevie had been seen on camera during the Symanova arrest and reporters were clamoring to talk to him. "As soon as Evelyn's ready, I'm going to have all of you taken to our office to give statements," Dowling told them.

"What about Bobby Kelleher and Tamara Mearns?" Susan Carol asked.

"I'm going to have them brought downtown too," he said. "Kelleher is screaming he has to write first, but we have to do it this way. I'll make arrangements for all of you to be able to write from there."

They left in two cars that had been driven underneath the stadium. Stevie's parents had spotted him on TV and had called his cell phone, wanting to know what in the world was going on. Stevie had turned it off during the match but now he called them back from the car to tell them he was all right, but he would not be coming home that night as planned. His mother was not at all happy at the idea that he was going to miss the first day of school. "You're a ninth grader," she said. "Not a celebrity."

"Mom, I didn't do it on purpose," he said, wondering what they would both think when he told them the whole story.

Susan Carol waited until they got to the FBI office before calling her parents. Dowling put her in a private office. She was red-eyed when she came out.

"My dad's going to fly up in the morning," she said. "He's going to see what he can do for Uncle Brendan and then bring me home. He said he's never letting me go to another major sporting event."

"I'm sure my parents are going to say the same thing," Stevie said, tentatively putting an arm around her. "And I'm sure they'll all get over it—in a while."

She threw her arms around him and cried on his shoulder. Stevie didn't say anything. There was nothing for him to say.

They all gave their statements. When they were finished, Kelleher suggested Stevie and Susan Carol do what they did in New Orleans: coauthor a first-person account of what happened. In this case, the stories would run in the *Washington Herald* and the *Fayetteville Observer*. Susan Carol shook her head. "I can't do it," she said. "My uncle is at the heart of the story. It isn't right for me to be involved in writing it and, even if it wasn't wrong, I honestly don't think I could do it."

Kelleher nodded. "You're probably right. You could say at the top of the story that Gibson is your uncle to get around the ethics issue. But the question of your emotions is something you have to decide yourself."

Susan Carol looked at Stevie. "What do you think I should do?" she asked.

"I think you should do whatever is best for you," he said. "Forget the journalism issue, worry about the Susan Carol issue."

She managed a smile. "If you were in my shoes, I think you'd write."

"Why?" he asked. "Do you think I would love my uncle less than you love your uncle?"

She shook her head emphatically. "No, not at all. I just think you're a little bit tougher than I am. Maybe it's because I'm a girl."

Stevie almost laughed out loud. "That may be the silliest

thing I've ever heard you say," he said. "You're the one who walked into that apartment and put herself at risk this morning, not me. You're the one who never loses her cool. So don't even talk to me about toughness. I'm not sure what I would do if it was me. What I *do* know is that you'll do the right thing. You always do."

She didn't say a word in response. Instead, she turned to Kelleher and said, "Stevie will write the story. I'll help him edit it."

Kelleher nodded. "Stevie knows you well. That's the right call—on every level. Tamara and I have to write our columns."

Susan Carol looked at Stevie. "You start writing," she said. "I'll go get you a hamburger somewhere. You must be starved."

Stevie was about to answer when Evelyn and Dowling came into the room. She had been on the phone with her parents. "Now they're upset that they didn't come," she said, smiling. "I reminded them that I *did* win the match, but they said enough is enough. They're going to fly up here in the morning and stay with me for the rest of the tournament."

"You're going to need a new agent," Susan Carol said, a tinge of sadness still in her voice.

"I know," she said. "My dad also said we're going to have to hire a coach who will travel with me when I'm on the road. But I'm not going to worry about any of that until the tournament is over." She smiled wanly. "It isn't as if there won't be people who are interested in me."

One more decision had to be made: where Evelyn would spend the night. She couldn't go back to the hotel; it was overrun, according to Dowling, with media people looking for her.

"You can stay with us," Mearns said. "There are two couches in the living room. No one will have any idea where you are. Susan Carol, I assume you'll be staying with us too?"

Susan Carol nodded. "I'm not going back to my uncle's apartment, that's for sure," she said.

Dowling volunteered to drive Evelyn to the apartment and wait there with her until Kelleher, Mearns, Stevie, and Susan Carol were finished writing and editing. "Call the apartment when you're getting ready to leave," Dowling said. "I'll have food brought in for you. What do you think you guys want to eat?"

"John's Pizza," Susan Carol said before Stevie could open his mouth. She gave him the smile. He was glad to see it.

✗ ✗ ✗

It was nine o'clock by the time they all finished. Susan Carol made a couple of smart suggestions to help with details when Stevie had finished writing, and then Kelleher read the story after she had finished with it. "You write like a pro, Stevie," he said.

"I write okay," he said. "I had a pro for an editor today."

The pizza was waiting for them along with Evelyn and Dowling when they got to the apartment. The TV was on and Evelyn was watching. "They're saying that Brendan has confessed to trying to turn the whole thing on the Symanovs," she said. "They're saying it could have been a hundred-million-dollar deal for Brendan. They're saying I'm going to be the new 'it' girl in tennis."

"You *are* the 'it' girl now," Stevie said.

She smiled. "Just what I never wanted. I never figured I'd make the second week here. I'm supposed to start school on Tuesday, but instead I'm going to play Serena Williams. How do I go back now and act like a normal kid?"

"That was gone the minute you stepped on court today," Kelleher said. "Even without the two kidnappings and all the conspiracy, you were going to be famous after today."

She nodded, picking up a slice of pizza. "I almost wish I'd lost to Maggie Maleeva," she said. "My life would certainly be a lot simpler right now if I had."

No one argued.

✗　✗　✗

Stevie and Susan Carol said their goodbyes the next morning. Susan Carol's parents were coming in on a midmorning flight. Stevie's parents had called back before they all went to bed and asked if there was any reason Stevie couldn't get to an eight a.m. train. He had made his statement and written his story. "We've alerted the teachers you'll be a little late," Bill Thomas told him. "From what I'm hearing, you and Susan Carol were right in the middle of this whole mess."

"I guess so, Dad."

"Well, then I'm proud of you. But we'll have a long talk when you get home. We'll pick you up at the train station."

"Don't you have to go to work?"

"I'll be late."

Mearns made breakfast for everyone and they sat quietly until it was time to go downstairs. "I'll go get the car and bring it around," Kelleher said. "Stevie, I'll meet you outside in about ten minutes."

"I can take a cab, you know," Stevie said.

"It's okay," Kelleher said. "I need to get out to Flushing early anyway. The whole tennis world just crashed. I have a lot of people to talk to. Tamara's going to stay here with Susan Carol until her parents get here."

Stevie wished he could stay to work on the follow-up stories. And to see how Evelyn Rubin did the rest of the tournament.

Susan Carol insisted on going downstairs with him. They stood on the street, waiting for Kelleher.

"I guess I should kiss you goodbye now before Bobby gets here," she said.

"Kiss me goodbye?"

"If you don't want me to, I won't. . . ."

"No, no. I mean, I *do* want you to. . . ."

She leaned down, put her arm around his neck, and kissed him—on the lips—quite firmly and for several seconds. Stevie was fairly convinced he would wake up and find out he was dreaming at any moment.

"Just remember," she said softly, her arm still around him, "Evelyn Rubin is *not* your girlfriend. I am."

He tried to find his voice to respond but couldn't. So he put his arm around her and kissed her back. With feeling.

Kelleher pulled up an instant later. Stevie's heart was pounding. Susan Carol was giving him the smile.

"I'll IM you when I get home," he said.

"Promise?" she said.

"Oh yes, Scarlett," he said. "I promise."